GW00727923

*MODERN
SLAVES*

MODERN SLAVES

A
PROFOUND STUDY OF THE
FORCES OF DESTINY
BY
CLAIRE WILLOWS

WITH TEN FULL PAGE ILLUSTRATIONS

Issued Privately for Collectors

1931

Delectus Books
27 Old Gloucester Street
London WC1N 3XX

ISBN: 1 897767 04 8

Printed by Woolnough Ltd.,
Irthlingborough, Northhamptonshire

TABLE OF CONTENTS

PART ONE
THE CRUCIBLE

PART TWO
THE CONSUMMATION

LIST OF ILLUSTRATIONS

PART ONE
THE CRUCIBLE

I

The Departure

On an unusually warm day in early June, 1925, a young girl sat on a bench in Bryant Park, in the city of New York, gazing pensively at the cloudless sky. One had but to glance at her finely modeled features and her graceful form to estimate her age at about eighteen. She was very well made and her solid flesh fitted easily about a frame happily designed for its lovely responsibility. She was clothed in a modest little dress of pale pink trimmed with ecru lace. It molded her supple form perfectly, while over her head a little white toque emphasized her ravishing complexion. From underneath the hat little wisps of her golden-brown hair revealed the silky quality of its strands. Her eyes were blue, her mouth little, and her nose pointed saucily upward.

The girl's restlessness was apparent in the way she shifted about on the bench she occupied alone. She fumbled with her bag, and time and again folded and unfolded a thick envelope from which she would extract a letter, glance at a few lines and then tuck it back. It was the latest of many letters she had received from her old friend and neighbor, Pauline Davis. She and Pauline were both born in Birmingham, England, had gone to school there together, and from the time she was ten years old—Pauline was her senior by a year—they had played, studied, and fallen into mischief, and out of it

13

again, together. When Laura was fifteen her mother pulled up stakes and emigrated to New York in an effort to collect a small inheritance of several thousand dollars left to her by her godfather. Life had been far from easy for the young widow, and with considerable stinting she put aside enough money to take herself and her only child to the States. Her occupation, after she lost her husband, was that of a cook in a middle-class household, and the fact that she was permitted to keep her daughter with her and send her to school was carefully considered in the remuneration she received. Her tasks were numerous, and the prospect of relief from a life of drudgery filled her with an indescribable elation.

When she arrived in New York she was dismayed to find that the small estate of her deceased godfather was being dissipated by contests which had been started up over the will. Two maiden sisters who had been ignored not only because their brother disliked them, but also because they were possessed of more means than he, set up a vigorous fight for acknowledgement on the ground of testator's incompetency. Mrs. Blake, confronted with this unexpected situation, was obliged to resort to a lawyer, and to take care of his fees and other expenses, she was left with no alternative but to seek work again, this time in foreign surroundings. Her vexation, disappointment, and delay sapped her vitality, which had already been drawn heavily upon through a succession of internal disorders. She contracted a cold which at first seemed inconsequential enough, but after a number of days settled into pneumonia. And at the tender age of sixteen Laura found herself an orphan in a strange land, virtually penniless, and with no one to turn to except a warm-hearted neighbor who made a place for her in the few drab and barely furnished rooms the good woman occupied. The girl was desperate, and without an unnecessary moment's delay proceeded to seek frantically for work. Although young and without any experience whatever her face and her figure stood her in good stead, and she obtained a position as cash girl in a department store. Her wages were very little but she was glad at the opportunity of being able to pay her way with the poor matron who gave her refuge. There she stayed on for nearly a year, living very frugally, working industriously and continually hoping she were already older that she might be able to earn more. Then one fine day an officious and mean-spirited young man who had some authority in the department wherein she worked began to make impertinent advances to the child. These she warmly repulsed, and when the young man saw that his efforts were unavailing he began to goad her until she started to snap back at him in her responses. The young man, without the slightest compunction, seized the first opportunity to recommend her discharge, and at the end of the week she found a slip in her envelope notifying her that she need no longer report for work. After wandering through the streets for several weeks in search of employment again, she procured another position in a biscuit factory where she was set at a mechanical task of stacking wrappers for cartons. This position which paid very little also failed to lessen the difficulty of putting aside any reserve, and six months later she was sent away because of a reorganization and reduction in the number of employees.

Things were coming to a serious pass, the woman with whom she lived was swiftly becoming physically unfit to carry on, and Laura sensed the need of removing herself lest she obstruct the good woman in any plan she might be harboring to ease her latter days. The only ancient contact the lonely girl had was through the letters she exchanged from time to time with Pauline. This girl had gone into service and was now occupying the post of parlor-maid in the home of a Lady Castleton, widow of Sir Philip Castleton who had lost his life in the World War. Pauline wrote cheerful letters, seeming to be completely at peace with the world and thoroughly content with her environment; her mood was always blithe and optimistic, and as she learned of Laura's difficulties in making her way in the world she endeavored to cheer her up with bright predictions that she would soon find herself comfortably settled. But when she saw that one problem had scarcely been resolved before another and greater arose in its place, her heart melted with compassion and eagerness to render some assistance. She began to beseech her mistress' aid, and at the same time wrote long letters to Laura suggesting that she come back to England, and that she was sure to obtain a similar position to her own, wherein she would find the composure which was so essential to a peaceful life. Laura was half-willing and half-unwilling. For one thing, however, she had no funds, nor any place to look for them, and in one of her responses to Pauline she intimated that even if she were willing to come she hadn't the means to make the trip back. To Pauline's unbounded joy the day suddenly came when her mistress expressed the thought that she would soon have to cast around for a chambermaid because her present one was about to be married. Pauline beseeched Lady Castleton to offer the post to Laura, representing her friend as the personification of all the virtues. The good lady consented and Pauline begged her to advance the necessary funds, assuring her that Laura would repay the outlay in good time from her wages. When Lady Castleton consented to do this also Pauline could scarcely contain her excitement, and she dispatched a frantic letter to Laura imploring her to accept, painting a glowing picture of how pleasant life would be for both if only they could find themselves together once more.

It was this letter which our charming young friend was mulling over that warm afternoon in Bryant Park. Her indecision was prompted largely by the uncertainties of the voyage, for the girl was timid by nature, and notwithstanding the fact that she had been thrown on her own resources at so early an age, she was reluctant to make such a long trip by herself. After pondering the matter for a number of days, she decided to go to the office of a steamship company and lay her problems before one of their employees. Luckily she found herself listened to by an attentive and sympathetic elderly man who said he would try to arrange it with one of the officers of the boat to put her in company of some passenger perhaps, who would act as guide and companion for the length of the trip. He suggested that she come to see him again when she was ready. She promptly responded to Pauline stating she was prepared to start whenever Lady Castleton wished her to come. A little more than two weeks had gone by when two letters arrived, one from Pauline expressing her joy at Laura's decision and the other a brief note from Lady Castleton enclosing the necessary funds, and instructions that she take a boat for Southampton, as well as further instructions how to proceed from there to London. Laura hastened to the gentleman at the steamship office and received his promise that he would make an immediate effort to arrange matters satisfactorily. He suggested that she return the next day. When she came this time he announced that he had spoken to a distinguished old couple who were leaving on the next steamer for Havre, and who had expressed their willingness to look after the girl for the duration of the voyage. Because she would have the great benefit of their guardianship and company he urged her to go to that port instead of to Southampton, explaining that at Havre, for the small remainder of the trip, she could take a boat to London via the Thames. To this suggestion the girl readily assented, and three days later found her, properly equipped with passport and information, en route to her homeland.

The details of her voyage need not be described here. Suffice to say that she was made very comfortable on her trip and that when she bade her good friends farewell at Havre, she felt, mingled with the sadness of parting from these good people, the gratification of having made the best part of her journey under such pleasant auspices.

Before leaving the girl, her companions who were departing at once for Paris, directed her to a modest hotel in Havre where she spent the night in perfect comfort. But before retiring she sent off a letter to Pauline, telling her of her safe arrival in Havre, how the kind agent had routed her by way of that port instead of Southampton, putting her under the guardianship of a lovely old couple who had taken excellent care of her during the trip. She was spending the night at the hotel from which she wrote, the next morning she would take the first boat up, and before many more hours had passed, they would be greeting each other joyfully in person.

II

Wherein Laura Loses Her Personality

The next morning, Wednesday, at a very early hour, she went to the office of the steamship company indicated in her instructions, and procured a ticket and stateroom for the "Captain Platt" which was leaving in a few hours.

She proceeded to the quay which she found crowded with travelers, and in order to reach the steward, she had to push her way among the crowds. In the cabin which was assigned to Laura, a lady, an Englishwoman, was already installed. Laura greeted her and the lady returned her salutation.

"Permit me to present myself, Mademoiselle, since we are alone . . . Mrs. Wharton . . . of London. . . ."

"Laura Blake," stammered the young girl. "I am on my way to London, too."

"Splendid!" the lady exclaimed.

She was tall, bore herself proudly, and her whole ensemble conveyed an air of dignity and severity. Her complexion was of a singularly pale tincture, and Laura felt herself quite intimidated before her. She concealed her disquiet, judging it ridiculous, and began to arrange her baggage, but she was disturbed in her occupation by the arrival of another person. The newcomer was a gentleman dressed in black, and wearing a black hat and the formal garb of an ecclesiastic.

"Well, my good friend?" he remarked. "We are installed, finally, eh? Is everything satisfactory?"

19

"Very satisfactory," responded Mrs. Wharton. "And I have a charming companion in my room, permit me! . . ."

She approached the intimidated girl, took her by the hand, and drew her near the clergyman.

"Miss Laura Blake . . . of New York . . . She is returning to London. . . . Mr. Dickenson of Bristol, minister of the Presbyterian church. . . ."

Laura lowered her eyes under the steady scrutiny of the saintly man. Mrs. Wharton tapped her hand gently, and the young girl would greatly have liked to withdraw it, for she found the skin of this woman cold and damp and the contact displeased her, but Mrs. Wharton did not release her hold.

Laura looked up and was surprised to catch the exchange of a rapid glance between her and the minister, but she was too timid to say anything and, besides, too immature to be able to interpret what might possibly have been conveyed.

"Enchanted!" remarked Mr. Dickenson. "You have for a companion, Miss, the best and most worthy woman that I know! You will be certainly charmed by her company."

Laura lowered her head, pink with confusion.

"Now that we are settled," said Mrs. Wharton, "let us chat. That will help us pass the time agreeably, and you might tell us what you plan in London."

A light shadow which passed across Laura's eyes had been noticed by the Rev. Dickenson and he murmured:

"My dear Mrs. Wharton, that is an excellent idea, indeed, but don't you think that the imminent departure of the vessel should be a very interesting spectacle for Miss Blake?"

20

"Indeed, sir, it would be," remarked Laura with a grateful smile.

"Oh! then let us hurry along to the deck!" cried Mrs. Wharton.

They rushed downstairs where the passengers, leaning on their elbows over the rail, were exchanging farewells with their friends or relatives on the dock; and the latter were maneuvering around for better views, shouting across the cries of the officers, sailors and the grinding of the heavy chains. At last the final command resounded. The deafening whistle from the vicinity of the smokestacks proclaimed the departure of the boat.

Mrs. Wharton, the Rev. Dickenson and Laura formed a group at the stern.

"You have left no one behind, Miss?" asked Mrs. Wharton.

"Not here, Madame," said Laura, "except an old lady who was very kind to me in New York. Otherwise I have no one else in the world but an uncle in Chatham."

"Poor child! But you are going to some friends in London, aren't you?"

"Yes, Madame, I am going to meet a girl, an old friend."

"Really?"

At this moment the Rev. Dickenson and Mrs. Wharton exchanged another rapid glance, but this one escaped the young girl's notice.

The boat pulled out slowly and the cries of farewell gradually receded into the distance; the human forms faded out, and one by one, the passengers descended to their cabins or to the dining-rooms. In the latter direction went Laura and her two new friends. Not that our heroine was very hungry but at eighteen, more than at any other age, the appetite makes frequent demands. However, she ate lightly, drank her tea with pleasure and enjoyed the excellent buttered toast.

The minister and Mrs. Wharton, apparently accustomed to ocean travel, literally devoured the meat and everything else that was offered them. Mrs. Wharton appeared greatly interested in Laura whom she called her young friend. She showered her with questions in an endeavor to learn all about her life, her problems and her hopes, and the minister, less talkative, listened with attention, contenting himself with nodding his head.

After lunch he drew Laura back to the deck and, to her considerable annoyance, began to talk to her of religion and to emphasize the moral contentment one could find in the Presbyterian faith. During this time Mrs. Wharton, claiming she was fatigued, made herself comfortable in her cabin.

Soon the English coast appeared and the "Captain Platt," pointing to the north, proceeded to penetrate the mouth of the Thames. It was late in the afternoon when the boat pulled in at Irongate Wharf, which was used for the arrival and departure of all boats for the continent.

Laura, always flanked by Mrs. Wharton and the Rev. Dickenson, went down the gangplank where they proceeded to the office for the examination of passports. For the minister and Mrs. Wharton the examination was brief and permission to land was quickly granted.

"Will you please let me have your passport, Miss," said the officer extending his hand toward Laura.

She gave him several folded papers which were mixed with others in her bag.

"What is your name?" asked the agent.

"Laura Blake, sir."

The officer looked at her and frowned. "I did not ask for your stage name, even if that is your vocation," said he, "but your true name?"

Laura blushed to the whites of her eyes. She on the stage! . . . was this man drunk? He did not appear to be.

"I do not know what you are saying, sir," she said.

The man, thinking he may not have been heard or understood, repeated the question.

"I am asking for your real name, Miss. What is it?"

"I repeat it, sir, Laura Blake."

The officer opened his eyes wide.

"Permit me," said Mr. Dickenson, moving forward, "permit me, sir! This young lady has been travelling with us from Havre. . . . To be sure, we did not know her before that, but she did declare to us from the start that she was Miss Laura Blake."

"How does it happen, then," retorted the officer, brandishing the papers, "that this passport and permit to embark carries the name of Miss Lily Butler, of London, dancer?"

"Lily Butler?" exclaimed Laura, very pale. "Sir, this is a mistake! . . . I am . . . Laura Blake . . . I am going . . . I have letters in my traveling bag . . . look! . . ."

She opened her little bag . . . Mr. Dickenson was very pale, Mrs. Wharton impassable.

In her bag were two letters, only two, and on perceiving this, Laura felt a sudden weakness descending on her.

She was certain that before her departure she had put in her bag a number of letters from Pauline. Now these letters had disappeared!

By this time people were gathering around the group and the girl was scarcely able to repress her tears. The officer was leaning forward, curiously. He was reading the addresses on the envelopes.

Lily Butler, 130, place Saint-André-des-Arts, Paris, France.

"It seems to me, Miss, that there is a little discrepancy in the names!"

Some of the people standing around burst into laughter.

Laura, distraught with shame and anguish, turned in the direction of Mrs. Wharton. She encountered a hard and stern visage.

"Why have you deceived me, Miss?" said she, "and why have you deceived the Rev. Dickenson, here?"

"But . . . But . . . I have not deceived you . . . Madame," answered Laura, bursting into tears. "I do not understand you! Someone has stolen . . . my papers! . . ."

"Oh! shame! . . ." exclaimed Mrs. Wharton with indignation. "Stolen your papers, indeed! Now since it is I who traveled with you, it would appear, then, that I stole them? Dear me! . . . May the Lord help me. I am honest and well-known, and if you do not retract your infamous accusation immediately, you wicked girl, I shall make a charge against you!"

"I have not lied! I accuse no one!" sobbed Laura. "Oh! My God! Where am I? What will become of me! . . . I am Miss Laura Blake!"

"Oh well," interrupted the officer, "I am not going to weary my head with this problem. I shall send for a constable and you can explain everything to him, eh?"

"Oh, sir! . . . I am not a criminal! . . . Officer! Oh, have pity on me! I am alone! . . . and I am traveling for the first time by myself! . . ."

He would not listen to another word. On a sign from

him a boy had crossed the door and, some seconds later, returned with an imposing policeman.

It was not an easy thing, however, to explain matters to this good officer of the law, and at the end of a quarter of an hour, after many repetitions, the policeman turned to Laura, touched her on the shoulder with the end of his stick, and pronounced that the best thing for her was to follow him to the nearest police station and that if she refused she would put herself in a very bad position.

Crushed by this painful turn of events she followed the constable who was accompanied by the Rev. Dickenson and Mrs. Wharton, both of them bursting with indignation at having been so ungratefully treated.

At the station, the inspector made a vain attempt to come to some definite conclusion concerning the matter. But as a result of rather unfavorable information, abundantly supplied by the minister, he decided that the girl might be involved in some nefarious business, and that the case had better be submitted to the judge who would be able to investigate it thoroughly. In consequence of this decision, Laura was, despite her tears and the touching accents of her despair, incarcerated at the police station where she was to await her appearance before Mr. Justice Scott.

III

Which Continues the Foregoing

The courtroom, in which Mr. Justice Scott presided, held its sessions in Great Tower Street, near the station-house where Laura had passed the night. The girl had not closed her eyes. The cell in which they had enclosed her, while large enough, was already occupied by a dirty old woman. It possessed a strong camp bed on which the drunken wretch had been executing a variety of lewd dances in reminiscence of her former days. Laura, horrified by the obscenities of the old woman, and frightened by the groans and coarse oaths of a cabman in a distant corridor, had remained standing up despite her great fatigue. She had cried continually and her eyelids burned as though one had drawn a hot iron across them. She kept asking herself if this was not an ugly dream, and if it were possible the situation could be so desperate that she would be unable to prove her real personality. It was unthinkable that the judge would refuse to believe her!

And these other two, this lady who appeared so amiable during the trip, this pastor, so unctuously sympathetic, both of whom had now turned away from her! Why? Appearances were certainly against her, but couldn't her assertion be verified? They would surely recognize the frightful error which had been committed during her trip, and her nightmare would come to an end.

The light of day was beginning to penetrate in the

obscure chamber, and in the course of some time a woman keeper, whose name was Mrs. Stone, came into her cell.

"Lily Butler!" she called.

Laura did not answer, but the cold of death entered her body.

"Hello! Lily Butler! . . ." repeated the woman, as she approached the young girl. "May the Lord help me! Are you deaf?" Laura made a terrible effort to answer, but her voice was broken.

"I am not this . . . person! . . ." she stammered, trying desperately to retain her tears.

"Really!" laughed Mrs. Stone, scornfully. "I can see you do not want to be Lily Butler . . . but that doesn't make the slightest difference to me, my dear! Follow me. It is nine o'clock, you know, although it appears to be still night in this damned place. Take your bag, your coat. Come! Let's go!"

"Where . . . are you taking me to?" questioned Laura, who felt herself falling.

"You know very well. Come! To the court-house, to be sure. Let's hurry, for Mr. Justice Scott has a fine grouch this morning . . ." she laughed wickedly, and added: "What a grouch!"

"Madame! . . ." sobbed Laura. "Listen to me, I implore you! You are not wicked, I am sure of it. . . . There has been a frightful mistake! . . . I am. . . ."

"Ta! ta! ta!" interrupted Mrs. Stone, tapping the floor with the sole of her shoe. "Come! You can explain all that to the judge! I don't want to hear any of your stories! Oh dear, oh dear! . . . If I were to listen to everything they try to tell me! . . ."

There was nothing to be gained by pleading further

27

with this hardened woman, and Laura followed mechanic-ally. Presently they came to a room where a dozen other women were sitting around under guard of two husky and severe-looking matrons. To one of them Mrs. Stone confided Laura.

"Lily Butler!" she said simply. The woman consulted a list which she held in her hand. "Very well," she answered, and turned to Laura:

"Sit down here and wait your turn."

Laura sank down on a bench and closed her eyes. For perhaps a half hour she remained thus, plunged in a sort of prostration from which she was occasionally pulled up by the call of a name. After some time a little door opened and she heard someone pronounce: "Lily Butler!"

Laura appeared not to have heard.

"Well!" he repeated. "Lily Butler!"

"Lily Butler!" echoed a matron, pinching Laura's arm. "Don't you hear?"

The girl jumped suddenly with pain. She rose hastily and the matron directed her toward a door.

Laura Blake stood opposite Mr. Justice Scott. At his side was an old court clerk who read rapidly and un-intelligibly from a paper he held in his hand. Not one word could be distinguished from another.

We have no intention of describing either an English tribunal or its audience. Let us simply say that to the left of the accused found itself the public and, in the front rank, were the charitable ladies and social-service-workers who were always present to see if they could not redeem some of the girls condemned to Houses of Cor-rection.

In this group Laura failed to perceive either Mrs. Wharton or the Rev. Dickenson, who should have been

*She endeavored to extinguish with cold water appplications the
blazing flames which burned in her buttocks* (page 43)

there to testify. She saw nothing and she heard nothing. She was mad with fear and shame. Everything burned before her eyes. Vaguely she heard, however, at a given moment, a slim young woman with a yellow and sinister complexion, declare that she had known Lily Butler at school where they had occupied the same dormitory, and that she recognized her clearly.

Laura twisted her hands in despair and with a violent sob burst out:

"Sir," she cried. "Write to my uncle at Chatham. . . ."

The judge broke in harshly.

"Please don't forget, young woman, who I am, and that you must refer to me as 'Your Honor'! About six months ago you were up before a judge in Southampton and, because of your youth, he put you in a House of Correction. You ran away from the place and disappeared on the Continent where you have been following your so-called profession of dramatic artiste . . . but your old room-mate recognized you. The people who traveled with you recognized you, likewise . . . they saw you in London some time ago. . . . By the naive process of changing your name you hoped to escape punishment for your offenses."

"Your Honor!" groaned Laura. "I shall go mad! I am not what you say! . . ."

"Nevertheless, Lily Butler, I condemn you to be confined once again in a House of Correction until you have reached your twentieth year. Has anyone any claim on her? . . . Does anyone wish to make application for her? . . ."

He appeared to go into a sudden doze and Laura found herself falling in the arms of a court officer who sustained her.

A slight noise was heard, then Mrs. Wharton appeared before the judge and claimed the young girl in the name of a society for moral elevation, of which she was vice-president, she said; but, strange thing, the papers she exposed before Mr. Justice Scott made no mention of her name. Without a doubt it was not the first time the noble magistrate saw her, for he made no criticism of her documents by which she claimed the right to take charge of Laura, and he endorsed her claim without question.

She bowed herself out respectfully and rejoined the pastor with whom she exchanged a significant look.

"All right?" she asked, laconically.

"Beautifully done!" he answered in a low voice. "And this time the girl is really a great prize!"

Mrs. Wharton went back to the spot where Laura had fainted in the arms of the court officer, and she prayed the latter to help escort the girl out of the building where a cab had been waiting since the beginning of the hearing. The man placed the girl, who still appeared to be in a stupor, on the seat and Mrs. Wharton and the minister sat down on either side of her, after having given the cabman the address of a hotel in Pentonville, close by the Terminal of the Great Northern Railroad. . . .

When Laura recovered her senses, she found herself extended on a wooden bed in one of the rooms in the hotel. Beside the bed stood the pastor, Mrs. Wharton, Mrs. Tilman, the owner of the place, and one of her servants.

"At last! She's awake after all!" exclaimed Mrs. Tilman. "What a time she's had! . . . Generally these girls have more stolid temperaments."

"Where am I?" questioned Laura, as she painfully lifted her charmingly pale head.

"Under arrest!" Mrs. Wharton answered dryly. "Come! make an effort, Lily, and pull yourself together! Accept the fate which has struck you! You are, thank God, in the hands of people who will look after your future life and make it possible for you to resume your place among honest women! . . ."

"My God!" sighed Laura. "I must be dreaming! This can't be true! . . . The judge . . ."

"You have been condemned to the House of Correction!" interrupted Mrs. Wharton. "All that I can tell you is that we have rescued you from this infamous prison and that we are going to take you away, by legal authorization, to a secure and peaceful retreat, where you will have a chance to reform your moral character!"

Laura sat up hastily and with frightened eyes attempted to take in her present surroundings. Little by little the terrible adventure returned in detail to her memory . . . and here she was in the custody of this woman who spoke as though she already possessed all rights over her. What had she fallen into! . . . No! . . . No! . . . It was not possible such a thing could happen in a civilized country! She would cry out, talk, explain, it must be that someone would hear her who could render justice.

She jumped out of bed, without thought that she was showing her ravishing bare legs, for she was vested only in a chemise.

The Rev. Dickenson turned in her direction and sighed. The three women were startled.

"Good Heavens!" Mrs. Wharton exclaimed. "Are you mad, Lily? Have you lost your head? What are you trying to do?"

"I want to get out!" cried Laura, exasperated. "I cannot endure this ridiculous comedy any longer! I want to

33

write to my uncle, to a girl in London who is expecting me, I want to see a judge, other judges! I shall not let myself be confined like this when I am not Lily Butler! Let me get out! Let me get out! . . ."

She was wild, actually, but her beauty seemed only enhanced thereby!

The Rev. Dickenson touched his forehead with his index finger and looked at Mrs. Tilman and the maid. "Insane," he pronounced.

The lady nodded her agreement. Mrs. Wharton clasped her hands.

"Yes, indeed," she said, "this unfortunate girl has lost her mind. Come! Get back into bed, and stay there until we are ready to leave, or by the Lord, I am going to search for a constable and ask him to conduct you to Bridewell where you will have plenty of opportunities to learn what prison is like." For her response Laura threw herself at the door and furiously jerked at the knob.

"Let me get out! I wish to go out! . . . Open this door! . . . Oh, will you open it? . . ."

"What shall we do?" sighed Mrs. Wharton. "I know a good way to calm her, but could we get the necessary things here?"

"In our town, down in Lavenham, in Suffolk," observed the maid, "they subdue the unruly and insane by whipping them. . . it always succeeds very well."

"Yes, indeed! I have seen that method succeed perfectly many times," added Mrs. Tilman, blushing a little and venturing a timid glance in the direction of the minister.

"That is precisely what I should like to do," remarked Mrs. Wharton. "I would willingly assume that task. . ."

34

"Let me go! Oh! Open this door!" shrieked Laura, beside herself, and doubtless hearing nothing that was being said around her.

"I have a good slipper," said Mrs. Tilman.

"Excellent," answered Mrs. Wharton. "Mr. Dickenson, dear friend . . . for propriety sake, will you be good enough to leave us alone, the three of us, with this girl?"

"Indeed, I will," responded the pastor. "And I do fervently hope the whipping will be effective. . . ."

"Let us pull her over on the bed," suggested Mrs. Wharton.

Mr. Dickenson went out, and Laura followed his departure with frightened eyes. Mrs. Wharton, Mrs. Tilman and the servant threw themselves on her and dragged her toward the bed.

In her struggling, she scratched Mrs. Wharton's cheek which made that lady furious.

"Oh! really!" said Mrs. Tilman. "She is possessed, I truly do believe! The very devil is in her. . . ."

"We shall drive him out!" muttered Mrs. Wharton.

The three women had succeeded in depositing Laura on the bed. Mrs. Wharton and Mrs. Tilman kept her helpless by pressing on her with all their weight. The hotel-mistress sent the maid out for cords and the slipper. The girl listened attentively to the order.

"In my room . . . in the bottom of the closet. You know where it is, Mary . . . those which we use when we punish Agnes."

She smiled at Mrs. Wharton.

"Agnes is my daughter, you know," she explained.

The maid hurried off. Laura, during this time, sobbed and implored in pitiful tones, begging the two women to let her go, but Mrs. Wharton leaned forward, put her

35

face close to Laura's while her hot breath burned the girl's cheek:

"No, Lily! No! We shall not let you go! You shall follow me, cost what it may, and I shall master you, you may rest assured! You must get ready to receive IT! You know what I mean, don't you? I am going to give you an excellent whipping, my beauty!"

"Oh! oooh! horrors!..." groaned Laura, struggling with all her strength, but always vainly. "Oh, ooh! is it possible?... Where am I?... I shall cry out! I shall shriek!... I shall report you to the police!..."

She was frantic.

"And you will land in prison with prostitutes like yourself, with drunken women, with all the horrible girls and loose characters of Whitechapel, you know!"

"It is you... who will go... to prison!... Oh!... Leave me!... You terrible creatures!... ah!..."

"It is I? We?... Ah!... We are going to teach you to hold your tongue!"

The maid entered. She approached cautiously, but happy to assist in the subjugation of the rebellious prisoner. She locked the door and approached Mrs. Tilman with her arms extended. In one hand she held the slipper and in the other a dozen pieces of cord, each one four or five feet long. The slipper was of tan-colored leather, but long and frequent usage had darkened it. The stitches were broken here and there, and the old sole glistened as if one had polished it with wax, indicating how often it must have been used and the remarkably energetic thrashing it administered, during its use, on the juvenile rotundities of Miss Agnes Tilman.

"Oh! This is quite good, indeed," exclaimed Mrs. Wharton, with the air of a connoisseur. She examined

36

the slipper from all sides, even putting it to her nostrils to inhale its odor!

"I hope," she said, "that after a vigorous and copious application of our little remedy, Lily will show herself much more submissive and accept her fate with contrition and resignation. . . ."

While inspecting the slipper and expressing her pious wish in a dignified and saddened tone, Mrs. Wharton had not released her hold on the back of Laura's neck which she pressed down with her right hand. She deposited the dreaded instrument on the bed and turned to Mrs. Tilman:

"We shall now stretch this young woman out on her stomach, and your maid shall tie her down according to instructions. Are you ready?"

"Yes!" Mrs. Tilman answered laconically.

"Let us begin!"

It was not very difficult. After two or three movements Laura found herself pulled out flat on her stomach, and her desperate cries were stifled in the pillow.

"Hands first! Attach them with a cord at each wrist," said Mrs. Wharton to the servant, "and then do the same with each of her ankles! The rest will take care of itself."

The young girl executed the orders, notwithstanding the terrible contortions to which Laura delivered herself in her desperate struggling.

It was an old-fashioned wooden bed, made of cherry-wood that had shaded into brown through the years. It had four posts, each one terminating in a little ball. Mrs. Wharton had the four cords attached to the four columns respectively, in such a manner that Laura's arms and legs were stretched out in the form of a cross. An intense terror mixed with shame was visible in her charming face. She threatened no more, insulted no one, she implored humbly, ardently, in accents of deepest despair.

"Oh, oh! Madame! . . . I beg you! . . . Do not treat me like this . . . Madame . . . Please! . . . I shall die of shame! . . . Since I must do as you wish . . . I shall say nothing . . . I shall follow you . . . You will see for yourself . . . Madame . . . that I am not . . . that . . . which you believe. . . ."

Truly, Mrs Wharton must have had a heart of stone not to be touched by such a plea! But she had precisely that heart, for her nostrils throbbed and her lips tightened as she responded:

"We shall see all about that later! For the present nothing in the world will help you escape the excellent whipping I shall give you! . . . And you will confess, yourself, in a little while, that you have amply deserved it! . . ."

Without paying any further attention to Laura's jeremiades, the severe matron proceeded with preparations for the correction. Brusquely, and with an expert hand, Mrs. Wharton pulled back the girl's chemise almost to the shoulders, revealing the most charming posterior in the world, which shivered and contracted in anticipation of the grossly humiliating attention it was about to receive. Laura groaned in the shame and knowledge of exposing this most intimate portion of her chaste body to the cruel and scornful gaze of not only one but three hostile and wicked witnesses.

Mrs. Wharton clasped the slipper in her right hand, firmly by the heel, and with her left she tucked back her sleeve so that it might not interfere with her grim task. She raised her arm and let it descend vigorously on the right hemisphere of her victim. Laura had determined, apparently, not to satisfy her cruel executioners by revealing to them the extent of her suffering, and as Mrs. Wharton warmed to her work, she struggled to control her emotions. Mrs. Wharton whipped on furiously, and the ivory skin which covered the field of the woman's operations became, in turn, pink and red and crimson. Finding the intense heat and smarting almost unbearable, Laura began to groan and twist her head feverishly from side to side. Her eyes were closed in an effort to shut out, at least, the visible picture of her humiliation. Mrs. Wharton, whose strength seemed to increase as she proceeded, was indefatigable in her operations. No part of the girl's posterior regions did she neglect, and from the top of Laura's loins to the base of her thighs the whole area was an angry red, blazing with a fierce heat.

Unable to contain herself any longer, and wild with the thought that her torture was to endure indefinitely, Laura began to plead, for her power of resistance was at an end, and her resolution to retain her pride had been made to vanish by her desperate eagerness to terminate her suffering.

"Mercy!" she cried piteously. "Pity! . . . Oh! have pity! . . . I cannot stand it any more! . . . Oh! . . . oooh! . . . Ah! ah! . . . Please! . . . please . . . I shall do anything you ask . . . obey you in everything . . . Please! . . . stop . . . I am sorry. . . ."

Although Mrs. Wharton would have been glad to continue with her favorite occupation, she recognized that simple prudence dictated putting an end to this initial whipping, and she cheered herself with the thought that before long she would have the girl in the position where she could exercise her will at any moment the fancy might take her. She concluded, then, with a half dozen vigorous blows, delivered with full force, which brought deep groans from the patient. At a sign from her, Mrs. Tilman began to undo the cords with which Laura's extremities had been secured. When her wrists were released, they showed deep red marks produced by her desperate tugging. Her arms folded themselves around her head and she moaned pitifully. Immediately Mrs. Wharton shook her by the shoulder and asked:

"Are you ready to express thanks for the little whipping you have just received for your impertinence? I wish to hear your humble thanks, as well as your hope that it will be a lesson to you for the future. Speak!"

"Oh! . . . oh! . . ." groaned Laura.

"As I thought! You have not had nearly enough! My dear," turning to Mrs. Tilman, "will you help put this stubborn girl back into position again? We shall try once more."

"No! oh no!" shrieked the girl. "Yes! I shall say anything you wish. . . . Please don't hurt me any more. . . ."

"Then speak up, and promptly! I shall not waste another moment with you! Say: 'I am deeply sorry for my conduct, and thank you, dear madame, for the good whipping you have given me."

Bitterly, and dying with mortification and shame, the girl repeated these words, and immediately burst into fresh tears.

A resounding smack from Mrs. Wharton's good right hand, across her inflamed posterior, brought her to a sudden reminder of the danger she was inviting by giving further expression to her wrought-up emotions. Mrs. Wharton reached over on the bed for the slipper, which had served her so effectively, and brought it around to Laura's face.

"Kiss it!" she commanded.

The girl, fearful of stirring up the lady's wrath, drank the final dregs of this supreme humiliation.

"You may get up now and wash your face and comb your hair. Be obedient and submissive, I warn you, or you shall have a supplementary dose at the least provocation. Stay in this room and rest; we shall return to you presently."

Nodding to Mrs. Tilman and the maid to accompany her, the three women left the room, locking the door carefully behind them.

IV

SOME NECESSARY EXPLANATIONS

IN fact, are they necessary? For it is only too obvious that Laura Blake had fallen into this extraordinary adventure which transformed her into Lily Butler, and labelled her with the strumpets, thanks to the machinations of Mrs. Wharton and the Rev. Dickenson. These two persons, members of a powerful band, were engaged in a type of "white slave traffic" which, far from consigning their victims to lives of prostitution, lodged them in certain houses where, under the pretense of moral improvement, they were subjugated so completely in body and soul by an iron and heartless discipline, that they finished by accepting their changed personalities and fulfilling the rôles subsequently assigned them. For some, the future was that of governesses to clergymen, for others, that of chambermaids or rather slaves, frequently, of sadistic ladies who took pleasure in torturing them morally and physically.

Now, it may be remarked that Laura Blake and her future companions, as we shall soon see, were all very pretty, a circumstance which rendered them particularly attractive as so many slaves. After being thoroughly broken in to absolute obedience and submission, prices were put upon them and they were bound out unconditionally. The enormous earnings that Mr. Dickenson, Mrs. Wharton, and some of their associates drew out of this traffic, warranted these people in accepting the risks they did.

From time to time they traveled over the continent, and the object of their expeditions was to seek for rare specimens of feminine pulchritude whose capture might lead to handsome compensation for their pains. En route they stole the baggage of their victims, introducing in them false proofs of identity, arranging matters as we have come to see in the case of Laura. They took precautions to choose the same landing-places or tribunals infrequently and, nine times out of ten, their infernal maneuvers succeeded. The Home for which Mrs. Wharton, or one of the other members, reclaimed the young girls was supposed to exist in the vicinity of London. As a matter of fact it did exist, but it had branches, and it was toward a particular one of them that they directed their prey.

No sooner were their applications granted by the court than preparations were immediately made to discourage the girls from all temptations to resume their old lives, and we shall see how cunning and thorough were the means employed.

For the moment let us return to Laura who, following Mrs. Wharton's orders, had painfully made her toilette, directing most of her feeble efforts to the urgent necessity of endeavoring to extinguish, by applications of cold water, the blazing flames which burned in her buttocks and threatened to consume her virginal seat.

V

Thurso

One hour after the events we have related, Laura was sitting on the edge of the bed which had served for her humiliation. She was attempting to stifle her revolt by compressing her hands over her poor palpitating heart. Suddenly Mrs. Wharton pushed the door open authoritatively, giving not the slightest notice of her arrival.

"Are we ready?" she demanded, and without waiting for any response, "I suppose we are. . . . Yes, take your bag, please, and be careful how you conduct yourself, otherwise I shall punish you, as you know!"

Laura stood up, and without a word, took her traveling bag and her coat and followed the terrible woman. At the hotel-door a cab was waiting, and Mr. Dickenson, Mrs. Wharton and the young girl were driven off. Several minutes later the three travelers entered the vast shed of the Great Northern Railroad Terminal. They traveled first-class, and Mr. Dickenson immediately plunged into the study of a forbidding little, old yellow book, entitled: "Bradshaw's General Railway and Navigation Guide for Great Britain and Ireland," and Mrs. Wharton placing herself favorably near a light began to read a current magazine. Laura, sitting between the two of them, had closed her eyes in an effort to isolate her thoughts. They were the only three in the compartment.

"Lily," said Mrs. Wharton after a few minutes of

silence, "put yourself opposite me so that I may see you better."

Laura obeyed and Mrs. Wharton took her by the hands and tightened the girl's knees between her own. This position was as troubling and confusing as one could imagine, but Laura, however, attempted no complaint. The scene at the hotel had shattered her nerves and abolished her earlier thoughts of resistance against the bad fate which had suddenly descended on her.

"Before the noise of the train prevents us from talking comfortably," began Mrs. Wharton, "I wish to give you, again, some good advice, and to indicate to you a path of life from which you must not attempt to digress. It is absolutely useless, in your own interest, to endeavor to make us believe you are not Lily Butler. You are a girl of very questionable character, and you have great need of accomplishing a long penitence before you can deserve the title of 'honest girl' once again. After many, many lessons, we hope the moment will come when we can place you with an honest lady, or with a minister of religion—we could not say now—where you shall have an opportunity to lead a saintly and pious life in all submission and in all humility. From now on, therefore, think only of penitence and the necessity for expiating your faults. . . ."

Bitter and burning tears ran down Laura's cheeks.

"You will find our discipline very painful, no doubt," continued the lady, "especially after the dissipated existence you've led for so long a time, but you will have to go through with it, depend on that! . . . Especially when you shall be curbed steadily under the government of the whip! . . ."

Laura uttered a profound sigh. . . . She trembled from

her head to her feet, but she forced herself not to give free course to her tears which were ready to burst. It was evident that Mrs. Wharton experienced an intense satisfaction in contemplating this despair and this humiliation. The soul of Laura bled, and in the raw wounds, opened by her, Mrs. Wharton dug around with words which were the equivalent of claws. Mr. Dickenson took a lively interest in his partner's speech, looking at the girl over his glasses. Mrs. Wharton leaned closer to Laura and gripped her hands tighter.

"For you shall be whipped, Lily! . . . Whipped very often! . . . Solidly whipped! . . . Young girls have need of that sort of discipline so their hearts may become softened and return to their original candor."

The lady's lips turned back on her long teeth, in the expression of a grinning cat, as she added:

"And I shall not spare you! You may begin to prepare your bottom!"

Her words whistled like the thongs of a leather whip, and Laura shivered in her flesh. Fortunately, the bell for departure rang, the brakemen closed the doors and the train started off.

For four or five hours the wheels jogged continually over switches, allowing no relief to Laura's flesh, still tender from the beating of Mrs. Tilman's slipper. When the train stopped and they started out, she felt as though she were just coming out of a furnace.

They had reached Aberdeen, which was their destination by train. Although Laura knew of the old and smoky city from hearsay and from reading, her interest in its history and archeology excited in her not the faintest curiosity. She walked along mechanically as though half asleep, her chagrin and the anguish of her despair failing to rouse her from her stupefaction. After a summary but substantial repast her two body-guards conducted her to the dock. It was the hour when the boat for Wick departed. Much merchandise was visible but few passengers. They settled themselves in a cabin where Laura, unaccustomed to the smell of fish and the smoke of coal and tar, felt herself becoming sick. To these discomforts were added the exhortations of Mrs. Wharton and the reading in a high voice by the reverend of passages from the Bible appropriate to the situation. She was so ill that at Wick, Mrs. Wharton and her companion decided to quit the steamer which would have transported them to Thurso. Instead, they took a cab to the latter place, and it followed a straight line over a route offering absolutely nothing noteworthy except, perhaps, the oppressive solitude of the surrounding country.

Thurso, a small town of 2,400 inhabitants, was a calm little place lulled to sleep by the sound of the sea. On the way to the town, at the edge of the bay, between the promontory of Holburn and Scrabster Castle, the ruins of the ancient estate of the Bishops of Caithness clung together in an ensemble of buildings spread quadrilaterally. The principal entrance was on the road running to Wick. The cab stopped before this entrance and, after having deposited the three travelers, continued on to Thurso, about a mile distant. The great iron door, painted in a somber green, opened, and Laura perceived, serving the office of porter, a woman of about thirty-five years, tall, somewhat fat, whose features seemed contracted by a permanent frown.

"Anything new, Anna?" demanded Mrs. Wharton, stopping for a moment.

"Nothing, Madame."

"Anyone sick?"

"No one."

"How many girls are in the disciplinary cells?"

"Three."

"Very well. Get everything ready, I shall go see them presently."

She proceeded through a vestibule wherein was a staircase leading to the upper floors, and she took Laura by the hand.

"Come with me," she said. "See you soon again, dear friend!" she added, addressing Mr. Dickenson.

On the first floor she entered a little office, severely furnished, where a lean woman about forty years old, with hardened features, and dressed all in black, sat writing.

The woman rose and saluted.

"How do you do, Mrs. Reed," said Mrs. Wharton. "Here is a new one for whom I shall give you all necessary instructions. . . . How are you?"

"Very well, madame. . . . Superb creature, on my word!"

"Indeed! Anything special to report?"

"Nothing very much, madame. Everything is all right. The doctor expressed himself as being well satisfied after his inspection."

"I shall see him. Any applications?"

"Two."

"I think we can satisfy them. I shall examine the applications in a little while. Are all the teachers well?"

"Very well. Mrs. Fields and Mrs. Bacon are here, but Mrs. Holliston has gone to London."

"Very good. I shall go into my bedroom with this girl, and I shall turn her over to you in a little while. . . .

Notify Evelyn to get a uniform ready. Come, Lily. . . ."

Once more she took Laura by the hand and led her out of the office. In the corridor she opened a door which led into a bedroom, very luxuriously furnished in yellow. She rang a bell, and pushed Laura toward a large window, one of two which flooded the room with sunlight. Laura saw beneath a vast rectangular court, completely enclosed by a stone wall. This wall was pierced here and there by regularly spaced tiny windows and doors, painted in black. The whole thing had the aspect of a barracks, or rather of a prison, and Laura felt her heart go cold.

"Here is your new home," said Mrs. Wharton. "Ah! It does not compare to the comforts you had in your elegant quarters in London nor to the grand boulevards of Paris, but for your soul this place will be infinitely better!"

Because she talked in a gentle voice and appeared to be no longer angry, Laura suddenly felt completely upset. She fell on her knees, embraced Mrs. Wharton's legs, and shaking with her sobs, she cried:

"Madame! Dear Madame! It is not possible that you can refuse to listen to me! I swear to you by the memory of my dead mother that all this is a frightful error! Allow me to communicate with my uncle at Chatham and you will learn for yourself! You will be amply repaid, immediately . . . I swear to you! I am not Lily Butler. . . ."

Little by little Mrs. Wharton's features hardened into repressed anger!

"Oh!" said she, at last. "You are actually returning to all that? . . . I should never have believed we should find ourselves obliged to deal with so stubborn a girl! . . . Get up! . . . You story-teller! You lost wretch! You insist on recalling to me the episode that took place in London, and the promise I made you and the one you made to me. You shall accompany me in the visit I am going to make through the house, and after that I shall conduct you to a cell where I shall apply the promised correction." As she finished these words a young girl entered.

She had swollen eyes, like someone who had been dragged out of her sleep, and she curtsied, blushing deeply. She was quite tall, slim, of delicate features, very pretty. She had the clear and pink complexion which particularly characterizes the beautiful girls of England, and her golden hair served as a frame to set off her charming but worried face. Her costume was quite simple, but not devoid of elegance. It was composed of a black silk blouse, generously decolletté, the edges of which were festooned in dainty white linen. A soft white leather belt was fitted tightly around her waist and the skirt was of black silk, cut short, permitting full view of her legs and feet, encased in patent leather slippers on which glistened silver buckles. Her stockings were of excellent grade thin black silk, despite the cold and difficult climate in that part of the country at this time of the year.

This toilette Laura was to know very well, for it was the regular uniform of all the pensionnaires at Sloane House—such was the name of this establishment.

Meanwhile, Mrs. Wharton considered the young girl, her face revealed not the least sentiment, and she made the silence harder and more threatening to the anguished heart of Laura, as well as to the unknown girl.

At last Mrs. Wharton loosened her lips and spoke: "Where are you coming from, Eva?" The girl blushed deeper and began to tremble.

"Madame," she stammered, "Mrs. Reed told me you were to arrive today and I was waiting for you . . . in the laundry. . . ."

Mrs. Wharton smiled.

"In the laundry? . . . but why didn't you come when I rang?"

"I did not hear, Madame. . . ."

Eva's voice had broken and the tears were coming to her lashes.

"The bell is out of order, then?"

"No . . . Madame. . . ."

"Come, come!" insisted Mrs. Wharton, "who awakened you? . . . For you were asleep, isn't that so? You were sleeping, that is certain! Why do you try to hide that from me, Eva? You ought to know that no one conceals anything from me. You were asleep? . . ."

Eva fell on her knees and her hands concealed her face.

"Yes, Madame . . ." she sobbed.

Mrs. Wharton hardened her voice, and her nostrils tightened, a sign of anger and threatening severity.

"You lazy thing!" she said. "Is that what I have accustomed you to? . . . You know what that deserves. Get up and fetch me your whip!"

Eva obeyed, and although she glanced supplicatingly at Mrs. Wharton, she did not dare to formulate the least plea. Big tears rolled down her cheeks. She walked toward a little closet, situated near a large four-posted bed, opened it and drew out a black leather strap which she brought over to her mistress. She put one knee on the floor and extended the strap with one hand, while she tried to hide her eyes with her other free hand.

"Quickly! quickly!" said Mrs. Wharton. "Don't start

51

any comedy if you want to sit down in less than a week!
Make yourself ready! Stand up!"

The young girl straightened herself, still crying. She
glanced anxiously at Laura who made a thousand efforts
to supress her emotions, and lowering her head, she
turned her back to Mrs. Wharton and took off her skirt.

Laura who had submitted to a whipping at London had
no doubt of that which was about to happen, but at the
view of this extraordinary proof of submission she experienced a transport of intense shame, absolutely as
though the devastating order to "prepare herself," according to Mrs. Wharton's expression, had been directed
at her own person. And during all that followed she
remained at the foot of the bed, crouching for support against one of the columns, for such weakness did
she experience in her legs.

The skirt removed, Eva displayed a pale-green silk petticoat, very short and extremely tight. In fact it appeared
like a narrow sheath, molding the threatened rotundities,
and Laura, horrified, watched the girl's bare skin gradually reveal itself as Eva pulled the petticoat down: the
girl wore no panties. The black silk stockings extended half way up to her thighs, and they were retained
above the knees by wide red silk bands which served for
garters.

For a moment Mrs. Wharton stood in contemplation
before the nudities the docile and downcast girl offered
up to chastisement, then she rested her cold hand on the
girl's thigh.

"You have been lying down for quite a long time,"
she said, "for the folds of your skirts are still visible, as
are the marks of the creases on your hips. Didn't you
have any work to do?"

And as the response was slow in coming:

"You are still asleep!" she exclaimed. "I shall wake you up!"

Three times her hand slapped rudely across the girl's fleshy buttocks, which vibrated in their entire mass, then she brandished the strap which cut the air with its characteristic noise, and she lashed the lower posterior region crosswise. The shock caused Eva to hollow her loins, while her buttocks contracted, her knees were beginning to give way, when the harsh voice of her mistress resounded again, sharp and imperious.

"Will you straighten up? Or must I tie you down over this armchair? I warned you to be careful! Bend forward! quickly! You know what position you must take when I whip you this way!"

Eva knew. She uttered a groan and took the position required. Her buttocks, not too fat, but perfectly proportioned and splendidly filled out, offered themselves fully to the whip. They were already changing color from the lashes of the strap, the latter having designed fine stripes of a lively red shade. Mrs. Wharton, with her left hand, pulled at the lobe of Eva's ear so that she could maintain the girl's shivering hemispheres in the best position . . . then she whipped.

The first series of lashes were directed at the lower part of her posterior. Those that followed struck higher and higher, so that the warm red color mounted, little by little, until it reached the loins, hollowed with two ravishing dimples. From there Mrs. Wharton continued down toward the thighs. She whipped vigorously, calculating perfectly the direction of her blows, and never visiting the same place twice. Particularly, she seemed to concentrate on the lower parts of the fleshy hemispheres, knowing very well that it is the most sensitive region, and while there is no likelihood of harm, it engenders the most shame and suffering; nevertheless, she neglected neither the haunches nor the greater width of the buttocks, where the lashes presently produced an irregular series of welts. She held her thus bent over, frowning severely all the time, and looking steadily at the chastised flesh. Laura noted the fire in her metallic eyes and the continuous palpitation of her nostrils, as well as the passion she put into her work, for it seemed to her as though it would never cease.

"My God! My God!" groaned Laura to herself. "Is it possible that such things can be! Just for having been asleep . . . to be beaten like this . . . whipped! . . . Lord, how wicked this woman is, for there isn't a doubt in the world that she whips just for her own pleasure! . . ."

Above the noise of the lashes striking on the bare flesh, the cries, the groans, the supplications, choked by the girl's sobs—for although she had been silent at the beginning, Eva could no longer endure her pain—the furious grumbling of her mistress, there came still stranger thoughts to Laura. She asked herself, in her innocence, why Mrs. Wharton did not apply any other punishment than the whip. . . . The whip! That was the only word she had on her lips, and the continuous use of it constantly threatened Laura, as well, doubtless, as it did all the others. Why did she not impose penitence, a cell, deprivation of exercise, extra tasks, or other things like that? And if, governed by her irascible character, she experienced the need of striking, why did she not content herself by slapping or using a ruler on the hand? Certainly it was cruel and humiliating to be struck like a slave, but how much less so than being obliged to submit to the method Mrs. Wharton employed? And if, once again, she did use a whip, as some of the religious do, why couldn't this discipline be imposed on the shoulders! . . . But no, she had to direct it at . . . at . . . this place, the thought of which alone made Laura blush, and the actual sight of which plunged her into an inexpressible troubling, producing emotions she never before experienced.

Meanwhile, Mrs. Wharton continued to whip the unfortunate girl without ceasing for a moment to lecture.

"You miserable girl! You think we are going to feed you, look after your body and soul, exert all our energies and spend all our money recklessly, while you sleep all day? Answer me! Answer me! Answer me! . . . You had no sewing to do? Nothing to prepare? I have bestowed on you the privilege of being my personal maid for the pleasure of finding you asleep, you lazy thing! You idler! you little fool! I shall whip you until your blood runs, if it is too sluggish. You eat too much, that is why you are so dull! Bread and cheese, that will be your menu for the next week! You shall go to bed at eleven o'clock, rise at five, and have a whipping twice each day! After that you will not think of going to sleep, I promise you! Is that understood! Answer! Answer! Answer! Answer! . . ."

"Yes! ah! yes! ye..s! Ma..mad..ame! . . . Ah! aaah! oh! Mad . . . ame! . . . Arrrr! . . . pity! . . . oh! pity! . . ."

An unfeeling smile appeared on Mrs. Wharton's face, but still she continued to whip until the girl's buttocks resembled a big palpitating cushion of flesh, and seemed to have doubled in volume. At the end, Eva could no longer remain on her legs, her knees bent under, and she slumped to the floor.

Then, with the utmost coolness, Mrs. Wharton, who

had remained silent, pushed the girl forward and turned away. She closed her eyes, took a long breath, and sat down in a nearby armchair.

"Get up!" she said. "Dry your tears and ask my pardon!"

The girl straightened herself with difficulty. She appeared utterly broken, and her charming face was as congested as her buttocks, one could say.

"Come! make haste," still grumbled Mrs. Wharton. "Fix your clothes decently. It doesn't seem to matter to you, does it, that you are showing your body like this! Ask my pardon! . . ."

Eva cried bitterly, but she forced herself to repress her groans and sobs. She approached Mrs. Wharton, knelt down, joined her hands and murmured:

"Please pardon me . . . Madame . . . I shall not do it again! . . ."

"Thank me! What are you waiting for?"

"Madame . . . I thank you . . . for having whipped me soundly. . . . It was for my good! . . ."

Laura shivered with shame at the expression of this abjectness. She tried not to think that soon a similar humiliation would be imposed on her, for the good of her soul, as for all the pensionnaires at Sloane House, since that was the rule in this establishment.

Eva, having adjusted her clothes, felt a new discomfort in the contact of them with her inflamed seat. Mrs. Wharton opened her arms.

"Come, you wicked girl!" she said. "Once more I pardon you, but do not ever repeat this again! Give me the kiss of peace and reconciliation."

Eva put her arms around the shoulders of her mistress, leaned her hot, blushing face forward and posed her

"*I am going to give you a good little whipping which will impress these precepts in your memory*" (page 66)

pulpy and burning lips on the pale, thin, cold ones of her disciplinarian. The *kiss of peace,* perhaps still more than the sight of the whip, troubled Laura profoundly. That was something so new and so mortifying! . . . To what degree of servility had Eva fallen, to submit without resistance to so many humiliations!

Laura was far from being a fool. She suddenly thought—and this thought put death in her soul—that to bring Eva to such a frame of mind, she must have been submitted many, many times to similar punishments, for a situation like this could not be created yesterday or a week ago . . . This appalling thought must have been infinitely salutary to Laura. She told herself that the wisest policy must be to submit and accept, as best as one could, the punishments and humiliations imposed, in order not to irritate Mrs. Wharton and the other mistresses, who must have similar characters To do otherwise would only mean to invite additional severity.

That was undoubtedly a wise reflection in the girl's candid brain, but, to tell the truth, it was only a feeble decision, the result of resolutions still but lightly aroused. Indeed, it was soon to be fortified and definitely fixed by a firm conviction that only by submitting absolutely could she hope to increase the intervals and reduce the extent of mental and physical suffering, by the imposition of which these women crushed out the last vestiges of independent will, and molded the girls into the living automatons they were determined to make them. That these ladies were succeeding very well was both evident to them and their subjects. . . .

Mrs. Wharton, whose gravity and dignity never suffered the least diminution, pushed Eva away.

"Now," she said, "let us repair the lost time, and spare

me your tears if you do not want me to start over again. Prepare my bath and get my bathrobe."

Eva walked to the bath which adjoined the bedroom, and Mrs. Wharton made a sign to Laura to approach.

"Help me undress," she said, turning her back to the young girl. Laura's first movement was one of recoil, but the second, much more wise, was one of obedience. Mrs. Wharton revealed strong but somewhat lean white arms, her shoulders were bony and powerful, but her hips, strangely enough, were large and very imposing, and Laura, at the sight of them, became still more visibly confused. Mrs. Wharton sat down in an armchair and posed one foot forward.

"Take off my shoes, Lily."

The girl kneeled, and after having completed this task, she received an order to draw the stockings off and to bring a pair of leather slippers, which brought shivering recollections to Laura of the sound whipping she had received so recently in London. The lady rose and walked to the bath.

Eva hovered around her mistress, and Laura, who dared not budge, heard the light splashing of water and presently the sound of rubbing which gave her to understand that the girl was fulfilling for her severe mistress the full office of lady's maid,

Soon Mrs. Wharton reappeared. She was vested in a white woolen peignoir, gathered at the waist by a black woolen cord, and this attire made her appear still more dominating than ever.

"Go to the laundry, Eva," she said, "and do your task there earnestly and industriously if you do not want to be punished over again. . . . If I do not find sufficient work done when I come in I shall give you a brand new whipping, and in such a manner that you will remember it for a good long time!" Having formulated this kind prospect she took Laura by the hand and walked out with her.

VI

The Regime

They returned to Mrs. Reed's office, where they found her in conversation with a young woman about twenty-five years old, whose hair was of a dark brown color, and whose features were very pretty. She was of medium height, solidly built, and very well proportioned. Laura was surprised at the sight of this young person and wondered what her place was in this establishment. She noted that the young woman's eyes were not unkindly, and her interest therefore grew apace.

"Oh, hello, Evelyn," said Mrs. Wharton. "Here is someone for you. You will dress her carefully, eh! You must certainly have a uniform that will fit her figure?"

"Certainly, Madame," responded Evelyn, with deference. "I shall try my best."

"See that the waist and skirt fit good and tight, Evelyn. Remember, they can't be too tight, you know. In the beginning, particularly, these young people should be closely constrained in their clothes, even until it hurts. Physical and moral annoyance are a pair in the process of correction."

"Indeed they are!" approved Mrs. Reed.

"In a half hour I shall come to inspect this young girl whose name is Lily Butler . . . Mrs. Reed, I shall give you this evening all the necessary information concerning her. See you soon!"

She went out.

"Come, you!" said Evelyn, pulling at Laura's dress. "We'll try and squeeze you into something."

The girl had a great temptation to cry out: "No, it is not true!" when Mrs. Wharton had declared that her name was Lily Butler. But the terror of the whip had stifled her protests in her throat. She followed Evelyn without saying a word. They entered a large room around the walls of which were shelves filled with clothing of various kinds. In the center there was a wide table at which four young girls, dressed like Eva, were occupied at sewing. They did not lift their heads at the entrance of Miss Evelyn and Laura, and the latter realized at once the cause of their diligent application on perceiving at one end of the table a long but narrow leather strap lying carefully posed across it.

Miss Evelyn drew Laura near a window, examined her for a long time from head to foot and said in a brusque tone:

"Undress yourself!"

Laura glanced anxiously at the girls who were sewing. It displeased her deeply to undress before anyone, but what could she do? Miss Evelyn's manner appeared not kindly disposed at all! She blushed a great deal but obediently commenced to undress. When she was in vest and panties, she stopped. It seemed to her that in order to put on the uniform she saw Miss Evelyn selecting, there was no need of taking off any more, but that was evidently not the opinion of Miss Evelyn, who appeared to be in charge of uniforms at the House. The girl planted herself before Laura, her fingers on her round and powerful haunches, and in an aggressive air, said:

"Well? . . ."

Laura's nervousness increased at once, but she mumbled:

"I thought this was sufficient. . . ."

The startling noise of a sharp slap resounded.

"And this," asked Miss Evelyn, "is this sufficient?"

A flood of anger colored Laura's face, while her eyes filled with tears, and her wounded pride impelled her to glance fearfully in the direction of the girls: they had all raised their heads and were looking on. Then she lost all countenance and began to sob desperately, her little hands flatly posed against her face.

"Oh. really! . . . " exclaimed Evelyn. "Here is one that will have to be corrected good and often before we subdue her stubborn traits! Come! Take off your panties and vest."

As she spoke she proceeded herself to unbutton the girl's panties . . . . Not succeeding quickly enough she jerked the buttons off and lowered them, then she pulled off the vest, and without saying another word put her hand on the girl's bare seat. This gesture was so expressive that Laura was unable to repress an exclamation of terror and shame. She knew very well that Miss Evelyn was trying to appraise the quality of the *place,* in the probable event that she was going to whip her. Laura had the distinct impression that she would not emerge from this dressing-room without submitting to that which she feared most. There she stood, naked, before this woman and these young girls, and she commenced to better understand how Eva had so promptly complied with the order to undress and proffer her posterior to Mrs. Wharton's strap.

Once again, Miss Evelyn examined her, first in front

and then behind, and she smacked her tongue in satisfaction. Then she pointed to a wooden bench.

"Sit down!"

She began to search for stockings, turning frequently
in the direction of the girl's feet in order to estimate the
size, then she brought a pair of black silk hose, very
much like those Eva wore, and she tried them on her.
They were a little too large. The second were perfect
and admirably designed the pretty legs, well turned and
properly filled out. She secured them in place with red
silk garters, and then began to select an extremely snug-
fitting shirt of fine glove-silk. The material was of very
good quality and the girl was agreeably impressed by
its contact. After she had put this on, Miss Evelyn
brought over a pale green petticoat. It was necessary
to try three of them on, the first two not being sufficiently
tight to satisfy the young woman. But the last one gave
satisfaction, it clung to the hips and buttocks of Laura
as snugly as though she had been wearing tights, and it
pressed her thighs together so closely that it annoyed her.
Laura had until then submitted quietly, but just because
she had seen Eva without panties, it did not follow that
she must conclude none were worn in this establishment.
She murmured:

"You have forgotten the panties, Madame. . . ."

Miss Evelyn began to laugh. . . . "Really?" she said
. . . "Very good of you to remark that, Lily, but you must
know that our girls wear no panties here, none of them."

"But . . . but . . . that cannot be!" demurred Laura,
overwhelmed.

"And why, I pray?"

"Because," replied the girl with an effort, tears in her
eyes, "because I am not used. . . ."

"Ah! ah! ah!" exclaimed Miss Evelyn. "That is certainly a good reason! an excellent reason! How amusing you are, Lily, with your reflections! . . ."

She laughed, or at least appeared to laugh heartily. Suddenly she put her fingers on her hips and her laugh was replaced by an expression of intense severity.

"Now then!" said she. "Remember this, my girl, that you must never express the least opinion to your mistresses, first of all! And second, remember likewise, that our girls do not wear any bloomers or panties, they are superfluous. They would occasion too great a loss of time in the application of corrections, because, thank God, enough of them are applied here and we have no time to waste."

She sat down on a bench and Laura found herself opposite, their knees touching. Brusquely she threw her arm around the girl's waist and drew her forward; she fell across her thighs before Laura had time to realize it. Miss Evelyn immobilized her at once, gripped her waist under her left arm, and drew the petticoat above the loins; the whole maneuver took scarcely two seconds.

"And to prove it to you, I am going to give you a good little whipping which will impress these precepts in your memory."

Stunned by the suddenness of the attack which had prevented all means of resistance, Laura cried out with fright and anger, and attempted to throw her hands behind in order to protect the menaced region. She succeeded for a second, but Miss Evelyn called out:

"Quickly! One of you! her hands! another at her feet! . . ." There was a rush by the four young girls, who doubtless rejoiced in the opportunity of getting into the good graces of Miss Evelyn by aiding her. Two ran forward and gripped her hands and the others took hold of her feet and held them securely. Miss Evelyn uttered a sigh of triumph.

"Ah! so that is it," she said. "Now I shall whip you until you are unable to stand on your legs!"

Furiously she began to slap the white buttocks which no longer carried any trace of the recent correction. Disdaining the service of any instrument whatever, she slapped with the palm of her wide open hand and each resounding slap left a bright red imprint on the girl's flesh. At first Laura exhausted herself in vain efforts to liberate her hands. She cried with all her strength, but it was especially with rage, although the smarting of the slaps was very painful. Soon, however, an immense lassitude invaded her and she abandoned herself. It was followed, presently, by a sort of insensible dullness which permeated her seat while Miss Evelyn continued to spank without pause, and with no modification whatever. The slaps made the solid mass vibrate, drawing the heated blood up near the surface of the skin and blazing into the flesh, but the sensation traveled to Laura's brain only across an obstacle, one might say. It almost seemed to the girl that it was another who was being whipped. . . .

Little by little her shrieks, then her cries and her groans, became muffled, and she only wept and moaned softly, like a little child who was mildly sick. The girls who held her hands and legs noticed her body abandon itself; and Miss Evelyn still continued to spank.

It was truly an extraordinary spanking. She prided herself on having hands so strong they were immune from pain, and she frequently preferred to punish with slaps on a behind rather than with a martinet having pointed tips such as she had often seen some ladies use.

For ten fiery minutes her arm rose and descended, with a mechanical regularity her hand opened and flattened itself on the violated buttocks, then she stopped all at once and with a shove of her knee made the girl roll to the floor.

"Leave her there, you others," she said. "Return to your work, quickly! . . ."

She rose, stretched her muscles, and gently caressed her hand which had done the whipping, and which, by now, should have been burning. Laura, lying at her feet, felt an extreme weakness in her legs. She shivered, a prey to a crisis of successive sobs, and the smarting returned to her still bare seat.

"Get up! quickly! Get up!" said Miss Evelyn, shaking her. She tried to stand but felt as weak as an infant on her legs.

"Well?" insisted Miss Evelyn. "Why are you so slow to obey?"

Laura made an effort and fell back on her left hip and elbow. . . .

"I . . . cannot! . . ." she sobbed.

Miss Evelyn smiled, disclosing a range of beautiful white teeth.

"Did I not promise you," she said, "that I would whip you until your legs bent under? I shall never deceive you, my girl! Wait! I am going to provide you with some strength." She went toward a drawer from which she extracted a handful of long whalebones taken from some corset, probably, and gathered them together in her hand as one would a bunch of birch-rods, then she leaned once again over Laura and took the girl's waist under her left arm.

"Madame," shrieked the girl. "Madame! pity! oh!

have pity on me! . . . I am going to stand up! . . . I am trying to obey you, Madame . . ."

"Will you keep quiet, fool!" responded Miss Evelyn. "Right now I do not want to punish you, but only to give you back the use of your legs! Be good and let yourself be whipped!"

She began to apply little taps effectively on the buttocks and thighs, here and there. This tapping was benign, and it curiously enervated Laura, causing an acute sense of humiliation rather than pain. But at the same time, and after about fifty of these little taps, she felt life and strength returning, suffusing her whole body. When Miss Evelyn ceased, she rose quickly and lowered her petticoat on her inflamed flesh, then, still shaken by her sobs, she covered her face with her hands.

"Come, come! a truce to your tears!" said Miss Evelyn. "You will receive a good many others! Ask my pardon!"

"But I haven't done anything," thought Laura. She did not say it, however. Wisdom—using an expression that she would come to hear frequently in the course of her existence—wisdom entered her brain from behind. . .

"Pardon . . . Madame!" she mumbled.

"And thank me! You must get used to all these ceremonies quickly, in your own interest. Here it is necessary that after each whipping received you must ask pardon from whomever corrects you and thank her in these words: 'I thank you for the sound whipping you have given me, it is for my good.' Do not forget that and say it now!"

Laura thought she was going to faint, so deep was the shame she experienced, for this additional ordeal appeared insupportable; but she straightened herself, partly closed her eyes, and murmured the consecrated phrase in

69

a dying voice, just exactly as she had already heard Eva's thanksgiving to Mrs. Wharton:

"Thank you, Madame . . . for the sound whipping . . . you have given me . . . it is for my good! . . ."

"Well, we shall see!" remarked Miss Evelyn with satisfaction. "It would seem you are beginning to be more reasonable and that is rare enough for a debutante! You may indeed thank me for this whipping. I know you will not receive more solid ones, nor any more efficacious, in spite of the complicated methods that some of our ladies devise!"

Having thus given expression to her thoughts concerning her superiors, she opened her arms and said: "Now give me the kiss of peace, and we shall not talk any more about it. You are more gentle and charming than I would have believed." These were the first good words Laura had heard since she put her foot on English soil, and she felt profoundly touched. Hence, it was with considerable élan that she put her arms about Miss Evelyn's neck while she embraced her. Warm tears ran down but Miss Evelyn refrained from making any comment about them. Later on the girl was to find in her a measure of kindness conspicuously absent in all the others, and she was to play a decisive rôle in the scenes which were still to be enacted in the strange fulfillment of Laura Blake's destiny.

But let us not anticipate. Miss Evelyn, then, having received the kiss of peace from Laura, and having returned it with a good heart, proceeded to the task of fitting on a waist, skirt and tight belt. That was soon done, and having taken the girl by the hand, she conducted her before a long mirror where she could see herself from head to foot. In spite of her chagrin, Laura—

who was always a woman!—could not suppress a fleeting smile as she contemplated her silhouette. The costume conserved all her natural grace, and the girl was fully conscious of her attributes. Evelyn noticed the smile and smiled back in return.

"Good character, good heart," she said softly. "With these things, my girl, you will be quickly made over. When you feel a great chagrin, come and seek Miss Evelyn!"

Although Laura's seat was still smarting with pain and burning from the severe correction inflicted by the supervisor, she forgot her shame and suffering before these words and, seizing the hand which had whipped her, she lifted it to her lips and kissed it, while her tear-stained face looked up in the direction of the young woman's eyes.

"Come!" said Miss Evelyn, gripping her hand. "We have to rejoin Mrs. Wharton who is no doubt waiting for us in the salon."

She drew Laura along to a room on the ground floor where, surely enough, Mrs. Wharton was standing conversing with two other ladies, one of them medium-sized, a healthy-looking brunette; the second, tall, blonde, haughty and pretty. Both were somewhere between thirty-five and forty years old, and later Laura knew the first as Mrs. Fields and the second as Mrs. Bacon.

"Ah!" said Mrs. Fields, "that's the new one!"

"That is Lily Butler," said Mrs. Wharton.

"The uniform fits her perfectly," remarked Mrs. Bacon, "but it appears she has been crying? . . . Yes, indeed! You have punished her, Evelyn?"

"Yes, Madame," responded the young woman. "Oh! she hasn't offended very greatly, I must say. . . . She merely expressed her astonishment at not being given any panties and said she ought to have something or other under her skirt, therefore I gave her a good little whipping. . . ."

"You did perfectly right!" spoke up Mrs. Wharton. "Lily is still imbued with her ideas of liberty, and she will have to change them quickly. Besides, the little regimen to which she is going to be submitted until to-morrow evening will give her an opportunity to reflect on the change to which she shall have to adjust herself if she wants any peace."

She did not know that Laura had already sufficiently reflected in having taken the resolution never more to make any remark unless she was interrogated.

"Approach, young woman," said Mrs. Fields.

Laura approached, profoundly intimidated, and the lady having taken her chin between her fingers plunged her black eyes in the humid ones of the girl.

"Will you be good?" she demanded.

"Yes, Madame," stammered Laura.

"Are you conscious of the change that we must bring about in your character and in your temperament? Will you encourage our efforts by your application at all times and by a perfect contrition?"

"Ye. . .s . . . Madame."

It cost Laura something to lend herself to this comedy, but it was still further proof of her intelligence that she suppressed any notion to take issue with those who were questioning her.

"I did want," said Mrs. Wharton, "that she accompany me in the visit I am going to make to the girls in punishment cells."

"That would be an excellent lesson," said Mrs. Bacon.

"But . . . I do not see why we should not accompany you ourselves. You are not occupied, Mrs. Fields?"

"Not at all, my dear. . . . We shall all three go and this girl will follow us, then, as Mrs. Wharton suggested, we shall put her in a cell."

Miss Evelyn withdrew.

How Laura would have been anxious to do as much, follow her, thought she, even if she were to receive a new whipping from the young supervisor.

Mrs. Wharton looked at the girl with a certain pride, and then glanced in the direction of her friends and associates.

"Very good!" Mrs. Bacon remarked laconically.

VII

The Regime (Continued)

The "cell" was the name they gave to each of a number of bare, tiny rooms, painted in white calcimine. A narrow window in the ceiling admitted light. No furniture, except a wooden bench screwed to the floor; in a corner were two grey woolen blankets carefully folded, beside them stood a basin and water pitcher, and a rough towel lay nearby. To one of the walls two iron rings were fixed from which hung a number of knotted cords, those were the first things Laura saw. Then her anxious eyes caught the figure of a young girl, dressed like herself, who must previously have been sitting on the bench, for she was in the act of rising upon the entrance of the visitors.

She was a beautiful girl about eighteen years old, tall, healthy, a trifle plump, not too alert, and she had heavy blonde hair which framed a sad and pale face; no color animated it in spite of the anxiety the visit must have caused her. In her hand she held a Bible which she had been actually reading when the ladies entered.

"Florence!" said Mrs. Wharton in a grave voice, wherein severity was mixed with strange tremolos. "They told me on my return from my trip that you have been sentenced to the special regime for a week. How long are you in our Home?"

"Nearly eight months, Madame," answered Florence, lowering her head.

"Eight months! . . ." sighed Mrs. Wharton, "and we are still obliged to chastise you in so exceptional a manner! . . . Oh! truly! my motherly heart aches at this necessity, and I pray the Lord that he will give me the requisite strength to chastise you as you deserve. When did you go on this regime, Florence?"

"This morning, Madame. . . ."

The young girl's voice was broken by sobs and big tears were already mounting at the edge of her lashes, nevertheless, she was still quite pale.

"Have you already been whipped?"

"Yes, Madame. . . ."

"Who administered it?"

"Miss Brenton, Madame. . . ."

"Good. Now I shall whip you this time, Florence. Make yourself ready and stretch out on this bench."

Florence deposited her Bible on the two blankets, took off her waist and skirt, then her green petticoat. She had very large buttocks, extremely white, and thick wide thighs.

Laura sensed herself very much confused and deeply troubled by the view of these nudities so docilely exposed, but she knew already that compliance was the first requisite at Sloane House.

Florence stretched out on the bench, parted her knees and let her arms fall down. Then Mrs. Wharton took from one of the hooks behind the door a big leather strap, a leather sole attached to a wooden handle, and some cords. With the cords she attached Florence who wept silently. First she ran a cord around the girl's waist and under the bench, then the two wrists were attached to its front posts, after which her knees were tied to each other, and the balance of the cord was pulled tight and

75

knotted under the bench. An impressive silence reigned in the cell during these preparations. Mrs. Wharton had locked the door, the walls were thick, the ceiling also, and the other cells were some distance away. When everything was in order, Mrs. Wharton pulled a memorandum from her waist and said:

"Florence, you are being punished for your laziness, your gluttony, and for your indifference at the announcement of a punishment. These are very grave faults, and I am hoping that a week in a cell on bread and water with two whippings each day will be sufficient for punishment. Do you repent?"

"Oh! yes . . . Madame! . . ." sobbed the young girl.

"Are you disposed to receive the present series of whippings humbly and gratefully? And will you make every effort to prove by your attitude, that you will not attempt to deceive me?"

"Yes, Madame," murmured Florence.

Mrs. Wharton took hold of the leather sole, raised her skirts and planted herself astride the shoulders of the patient, who, under this weight, uttered a stifled groan.

"Are you already beginning to complain?" she asked, with a faint smile which made Laura shiver in her marrow. Immediately she raised the leather sole above her head, and with all her strength let it crash down on one of the fleshy hemispheres of the girl, who made every effort not to cry out. The first shot crashed on Laura's brain like a thunderclap; it was followed by a series, slowly applied, alternating from one side to the other, causing the skin to color deeply and the flesh to shiver in its entire mass. To Laura it seemed that it was on her own body that this slow, methodical and severe whipping was being applied, and in which Mrs. Wharton seemed to put all her strength and passion. Around the bench, to the left and right of Laura, stood Mrs. Fields and Mrs. Bacon, their eyes fixed on the girl's palpitating seat. Meanwhile, Mrs. Wharton continued to whip on, with the same slowness and the same regularity. Beneath her, stuffing under her weight, Florence sobbed and groaned in cadence. It seemed to Laura that a whipping of such quality and length must have made the girl insensible to the lashes. She recollected, as one recalls a nightmare, the strange dullness that came over her own posterior while Miss Evelyn was whipping her, with practically the same method, and a new flood of shame shook her once again from her head to her toes.

Mrs. Wharton stopped all at once and took a deep breath. Then she let her instrument slide to the floor, and with both her hands began to rub the vast area she had whipped, and which must have been on fire. . . .

"I guess that is about a hundred!" she remarked, partly to herself. "I hope this will keep you warm for a while, although you don't deserve the consideration of a preliminary heating."

Then, raising her voice as she stepped away from the recumbent figure, she placed herself at the girl's left:

"Florence, what I have done until this is to prepare you for the sound and severe flagellation you have merited. I think your bottom should be ready now for the strap!"

"Oh! Madame ! . . ." sobbed Florence, I have already been soundly punished . . . so well corrected. . . . Have you no pity for me, Madame? . . . I feel so sore! . . ."

"This is for your good, Florence! . . . for your good, be persuaded! Cease your whining, and if you must cry, cry over your deficiencies and your faults! Try to deserve the temporary pardon which may follow after your correction!"

The girl turned her swollen face toward her inexorable directress and her features expressed her great fear of the chastisement yet to come.

"Lower your head!" she cried. "You guilty child! . . . And don't you dare to ask pardon before you have submitted to your full punishment! Just try begging off sometime, and see what a whipping you will get!"

Humbly, and in complete docility, Florence obeyed, her tears rolling down her cheeks, and wetting that part of the bench on which her face lay. Mrs. Wharton took up the long strap, shoved its end against the lips of the girl, who understood that she must kiss it, and then her mistress began to strike her violently across her poor martyred posterior. She applied about fifty lashes pitilessly, with such science that not once did she split the irritated flesh. Only long welts appeared, and here and there, a little blister betokened the severity of the chastisement.

Mrs. Wharton had counted these fifty lashes in a low and steady voice without appearing to occupy herself the least bit with the desperate cries of the fustigated girl; then she doubled the strap in half and handed it to Mrs. Fields who hung it on the door. She leaned forward on the palpitating body and passed her cold hands over the smoldering flesh.

"Florence," she said, "I am going to release you. I hope this punishment will not be forgotten too quickly, and that it will carry its fruits. I also hope it will attune your body, meanwhile, to the regular whippings which you will receive, morning and evening, while you are here. All this is being done in your interest, and in my intense desire to see you return to a life of virtue and goodness."

While she talked she detached the girl from the bench, and then aided her to straighten herself and stand up, but as Laura had known from her own experience, all the vitality of the lower part of her body seemed to have vanished, and for the moment her legs had no strength to maintain her. It is true that, soon the circulation re-established itself, and Florence, released by her implacable mistress, swayed a moment and then leaned against the wall that she might hold herself up. The girl sobbed nervously and her eyes were swimming in tears, while her arms hung helplessly at her side. Mrs. Wharton, stirred by a profound interior emotion, took the girl's face between her hands and looked into her eyes.

"Have you been soundly whipped, Florence?"

Nothing could be so humiliating as a response to such a question, but the girl, although long habituated to these interrogations, was still unable to repress a shiver which Mrs. Wharton immediately perceived.

"Florence!" she exclaimed, "I believe you have not yet attained that degree of humility which we desire to see after a sound correction, despite all the trouble we have gone to. Come here, lie across my lap and present your behind for an additional little spanking!" An expression of intense despair came over the young girl. "And remember, I expect you to accept this additional lesson in discipline with love and gratitude!" added Mrs. Wharton. "Kiss me to show your acceptance!"

Once more Florence burst into tears and began to shake, but she approached, raised her beautiful bare arms, displaying red traces the cords had left on her

lily-white wrists, and she placed them around the neck
of her tormentor; then her soft lips resigned themselves
and pressed on the dry, pale mouth of the directress.
That took but an instant. Mrs. Wharton pushed the
girl's face, bathed in tears, to one side.

"Very good!" she said. "Bend over now and lie
quietly!"

Florence obeyed docilely, and Mrs. Wharton put her
left hand around her waist in order to grip the girl's body
more snugly to her lap. Under her eyes the swollen,
livid posterior, sprinkled with tiny blisters and long welts,
seemed to exhibit a doubly provocative rotundity. Mrs.
Fields picked up the sole and handed it to her friend.

"Thanks," said Mrs. Wharton. "I merely require a
simple proof of submission, my hand will suffice."

She had a large, wide hand, as solid as could be. In
truth, there was little difference to the girl's smarting,
burning posterior whether the spanking was to be applied by that hand or by the leather sole. Mrs. Wharton
slapped the throbbing flesh about a dozen times, always
without haste, in a fashion to vex the patient as much as
possible, then she stood her on her feet and placed the
warm palm which had done the slapping against the girl's
mouth. This hand the latter kissed humbly. Once more
she took Florence's crimson face between her two hands.

"Now," she said, "I reiterate my question; have you
been well whipped?"

This time the girl's shivering was almost imperceptible,
and Mrs. Wharton had scarcely any cause to whip her
anew. She murmured:

"Yes, Madame . . . I have been well whipped! . . ."

"Do you think it will be a warning to you not to fall
back into your habitual faults?"

"Yes, Madame!"

"Very well. Ask my pardon!"

"Madame!" . . . responded the girl, falling to her knees . . . "I humbly beg your pardon . . . and I thank you very much . . . for having given me . . . a good . . . sound . . . whipping. . . . It is for my good! . . ."

"I pardon you, Florence! But on condition that you submit humbly and gratefully to the balance of your punishment for the duration of your confinement here. Stand up and give me the kiss of peace!"

Florence stood up, lowered her eyes, put her palpitating bust against Mrs. Wharton and embraced her. Then this lady, her two friends and Laura left the room.

In the corridor the three women whispered for a moment and then Mrs. Wharton took Laura's hand.

"This should give you an idea of what the regime is like, Lily," she said. "Now you must tell me whether you think rebellion is a sensible thing to attempt at Sloane House, or whether it is wiser to accept everything and submit yourself body and soul?"

"It is better to submit, Madame!"

"Perfect!" exclaimed the ladies in chorus.

VIII

In Which Laura Yields to the Regime

As they stood in the hall they were joined by Miss Brenton who inquired if they intended to visit Alice Devlin first or Mildred Griffith. Mrs. Wharton responded that they would see to Alice's punishment first. As for Mildred, she was to be removed to the *cave* where special punishments were to be imposed upon her because of her attempted flight. The very thought of being obliged to witness these special punishments frightened Laura so that it required all her strength to prevent a scene. So great indeed were her fears, that when they entered the cell in which Alice was confined she scarcely saw or heard what ensued there. All she could remember later was the fact that Alice had been obliged to go through four vigorous spankings over the knees of each of the four women. In turn she had to lie across their laps while each one slapped until her hand could no longer function. Each time, too, she had to go through the usual ritual of begging pardon and kissing the mistress who punished her. Notwithstanding her great distress after these four burning punishments, Mrs. Wharton finished by a vigorous application with a leather martinet on the inflamed posterior of the poor culprit, whose sin appeared to have been that she had made a wry face at some food which had been served her at a recent meal, and denied the offensive act when accused.

When they had ceased their operations on Alice they began to descend a cold, dark and obscure passageway to what was evidently the cave wherein Mildred was now incarcerated. Unable longer to endure these sights and with a great dread of what was still before her, Laura suddenly sank down in a dead faint. When she came to herself, she was lying undressed, except for her shirt, in one of the iron beds in the large dormitory, and close by stood Miss Brenton watching over her. Little by little the recollection of what she had been witnessing returned and the young girl began to tremble. Miss Brenton took her by the hand and shook her roughly.

"You had better not start to complain," she remarked. "It would be well, instead, if you would begin to envy those who are more advanced than you in their ability to endure punishment. How do you feel?"

"Better, Miss Brenton," murmured Laura in a feeble voice.

In reality, she desired to remain like this always, her eyes closed, and to die gently, without agony or suffering. She foresaw such a future that all her being rebelled at the necessity of submitting to it, and death appeared far more preferable to her. For a moment her thoughts returned to Miss Evelyn. The latter, at least, had demonstrated some pity, and since she must submit to the infamous discipline of this House wherein an unforgettable combination of events had landed her, she wished to submit to the authority of Evelyn, even if that authority should show itself tyrannical. But she was not mistress of events, and for the moment she found herself under the government of Miss Brenton. Night began to fall, and she wondered how long she had been in bed. She dared not inquire.

"Since you feel better," remarked Miss Brenton, "you must get up and dress yourself quickly. Mrs. Wharton expected you much before this. She has more important things than to occupy herself with waiting for you!"

Laura sat up on her seat and at once repressed a sigh. That part of her body was still somewhat tender and a sudden blush mounted to her cheeks as she was forcibly reminded of the reason for this discomfort. And this confusion quickly increased, while tears gathered on her lashes because . . . Miss Brenton had told her to hurry . . . Mrs. Wharton awaited her impatiently . . . was it not for the purpose of conveying her to a cell and making her submit to the treatment which would follow? . . . She quit her bed, vexed by the presence of Miss Brenton, because her shirt which was too short revealed so much of her lower body. She pulled on her stockings, tugged at the edges of her shirt, and looked around.

"What are you searching for?" questioned Miss Brenton.

"My panties . . ." stammered Laura, then suddenly frightened as she recalled that such things made no part of the costumes at Sloane House. Miss Brenton's face expressed a queer smile.

"You have a short memory! In a few minutes your panties, even if you had any, would serve you no purpose!"

"Miss Brenton!" groaned Laura, bursting into tears. "Am I going to be maltreated again? . . ."

"Maltreated!" the young lady echoed indignantly. "How dare you say maltreated? . . . I shall report this! No one here is submitted to undeserved bad treatment, you know! Good Lord! When all we have in view is her betterment she dares talk of being maltreated! Come quickly, fool! A little fresh water in your face will do you some good. Come! You will put on your skirt and waist later!"

Laura followed her to the wash-stand, and Miss Brenton copiously soaked a sponge and towel in cold water, applied them to the shivering girl, on her neck, her bare shoulders and along her arms. As a matter of fact this service made the girl feel much better. Vigorously rubbed down, she returned to her bed, or at least what she thought was her bed, and resumed dressing, after which she followed Miss Brenton.

Mrs. Wharton was in her room. She had put on a dressing-gown of black satin, very decolleté, and her arms were half bare. This costume molded her figure with the greatest emphasis, displaying the full amplitude of her breast, as well as her majestic loins and hips, making the lady's figure appear still more imposing.

"At last!" she cried, on perceiving Laura. "Here is Lily Butler! What a weakling, good Lord! If you faint away when you see someone else whipped what are you going to do when we whip you?"

And turning to Miss Brenton:

"Is she all right now?"

"Quite, Madame."

"Good. Lily, you must recall certain promises I made that we would put you in a cell on your arrival, eh? These promises I shall keep. It will give you an excellent chance to meditate in silence for a day or two. You shall stay there until tomorrow night. Come with us, Miss Brenton."

Surrounded by these two women, Laura was led toward a corridor along which were placed some of the small disciplinary cells. Into one of them she was pushed,

85

then they entered behind her and locked the door. The girl trembled in all her limbs; her anxious eyes distinguished as across a haze a leather sole and leather straps of various lengths, a tawse and several martinets.

"Here is your little room!" said Mrs. Wharton. "You will probably find the floor a little hard, but you are young and no doubt tired, you will sleep well. . . ."

She picked up the two woolen blankets and deposited them against a wall.

"Now, Lily Butler, take off your clothes," she said.

"Madame!" spluttered Laura, extending her joined hands supplicatingly. "Is it possible. . . ."

"What?" Mrs. Wharton exclaimed astonished. "You mean to suggest that you do not know you are going to be whipped?"

"Oh, Madame! . . . Madame! . . . I beg you! . . . Do not beat me! . . ."

"You must have it!" returned the directress harshly. "Nothing can prevent you from receiving a whipping! I shall see to that! And I shall see to it well, my dear! . . ."

Her teeth ground in an access of passion and she pressed the arm of the frightened girl with all her might.

"Pardon! Pity!" sobbed Laura, overwhelmed by the expression of cruelty which had appeared on Mrs. Wharton's face.

"Undress yourself quickly!" was all the response.

Scarcely able to stand on her legs, Laura undressed. She shivered as if she were being exposed naked in the dead of winter.

"Take off your shirt and skirt. You can keep your shoes and stockings on . . . they are of no importance."

Presently she found herself in the prescribed state of

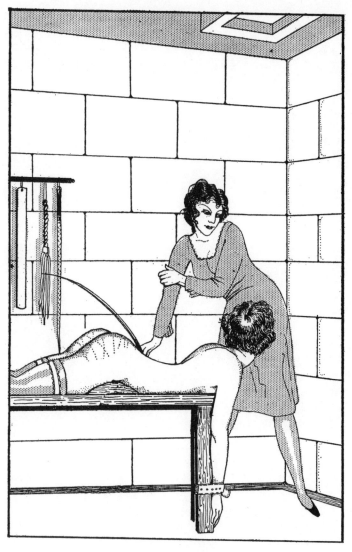

"Have you been soundly whipped, Florence?" (page 79)

nudity, and before she could attempt a gesture of defense, her hands had been seized, one by Miss Brenton, the other by Mrs. Wharton, each one having provided herself first with a strap, and both commenced to fustigate the girl as they held her arms extended,——Miss Brenton lashing one hemisphere and thigh and Mrs. Wharton the other. . . .

Ah! the atrocious humiliation! She tried to tear herself out of their grip, and the contact of their arms against hers revolted her flesh like an immodest exploration! She twisted under the biting of the straps until she fell to her knees. With a vigorous effort the two women pulled her up. She cried lamentably. . . . Cruel strokes accompanied their efforts which seemed inexhaustible. Soon Laura presented a skin which looked as though it were infected with measles. From her waist to the edge of her stockings, her entire body was covered with an eruption of ardent little blisters pressing one against the other. This enraged fustigation was prolonged for some minutes. One might have thought a peculiar drunkenness had taken possession of these women, transforming them into demons. But after awhile they stopped and Mrs. Wharton gripped Laura in her arms and shook her furiously.

"Madame . . . oh . . . Madame! . . ." sobbed the overwhelmed girl.

Mrs. Wharton became calmer. She put her hands on Laura's shoulders and fixed her gleaming eyes on hers.

"You are going to remember your debut at Sloane, eh?" she said. "Come on my knees now so that I can proceed with your whipping!"

"Pity! oh! I am going . . . to die! . . ." cried Laura in a heart-gripping tone.

89

"Bend over!" snapped Mrs. Wharton.

Laura bent over.

The directress gripped her waist with her left arm and commenced to whip the girl who writhed in her pain.

When she released her, Laura fell back to the wall where, overwhelmed, her hands to her seat, her chin lifted, her mouth twisted in suffering, she cried bitterly like a desperately sick child.

Mrs. Wharton regarded her coldly, her arms crossed, while she recovered her breath.

"Get dressed!" she commanded in an unfeeling voice.

Laura assembled what strength she had and proceeded to obey. Soon she was enclosed under her narrow skirts which irritated her flesh wherever they touched, but particularly in the rear. It seemed to her that millions of mosquitoes were sucking at her skin with their sharp needles. . . .

"We are going to leave you, Lily," said Mrs. Wharton. "Dinner will be served to you here, and I want you to eat every bit of it. If you don't you shall receive a good supplementary whipping . . . precisely like this."

A discreet knock was heard at the door and Miss Brenton opened it. A maid entered carrying a plate on which was a large piece of bread, a big slice of cheese, and a tall glass filled with water. She deposited them all on the bench and withdrew at once.

"You see, Lily," resumed Mrs. Wharton, "you must eat this bread and cheese and you must drink this water before you go to bed. Come and put yourself on your knees and ask my pardon! You have seen sufficiently what our girls must do and say after they are whipped for you to know how to go about it!"

Laura had for a moment hoped to evade this supreme

humiliation. Despite the dull sense of revolt which
rumbled in her, despite the dictates of her pride and self-
respect, she kneeled, joined her fingers, that she could
have broken one against the other to relieve her power-
less rage in some way, and murmured:

"If you please . . . Madame . . . pardon! . . ."

"What else?" Mrs. Wharton asked coldly.

"I . . . I thank you humbly . . . oh! . . . for the . . .
the whipping. . . ."

"Say: 'for the sound whipping'. . . ."

"For the sound whipping . . . that you have given
me. . . ."

"What else?"

"Oh! Madame. . . ."

"Miss Brenton, will you get me the strap?"

"Madame! . . . oh! . . . pity! . . . it is for my good . . .
Madame . . . it is for . . . my good . . . oh! . . . ooooh! . . ."

"It is for your good, precisely . . . this also! . . ."

She threw herself on Laura, extended her on the floor,
pressed down on her with her knees, pulled her skirts
back brutally, and put her swollen and congested posterior bare again. Again the long, thin, wicked strap in
her hand, she lashed her vigorously. Crack! slash!
crack! slash! . . . with the widest swings of her powerful
arm. At least a dozen times it snapped like a pistol shot
as it cracked against the girl's puffed flesh, fanning the
smoldering flames into a white heat again, which licked
remorselessly at the seething area. Then she rose, breathless, leaving Laura to twist like a worm on the floor.

"Isn't it for your good? You are ready to admit it
now, I suppose? . . . Isn't it for your good? . . ."

She tightened her jaws, ready to begin again. Laura,
making a superhuman effort, cleared the disorder of her

brain, raised herself on her knees and joined her hands.

"It is for my good," she articulated in a dying voice.

Mrs. Wharton exhibited a triumphant smile. She leaned forward, took Laura by the armpits, and pulled her up.

"Each time you dispute with the whip," she said, "it is always the whip which will have the last say! Never does it fail to persuade, remember; and the sooner you show respect for its power the better off you will be. Get that settled in your head, let a deep sense of humility penetrate it, abandon yourself body and soul to the will of your superiors, and just to prove to me that you are trying, come here and kiss me!"

A sob of shame shook the girl, but she rose wearily and put her arms around the neck of her disciplinarian; her sweet lips offered their adorable pout, and Mrs. Wharton, suppressing a very comprehensible emotion, went out after having exchanged kisses with her subject, followed by Miss Brenton who closed the cell with a double lock.

IX

In Which Laura Begins Her New Existence

LEFT alone, Laura experienced a veritable access of despair.

A sense of horror invaded her at the thought of having to endure such humiliations; she pounded wildly at the wall with her little fists and would perhaps have done the same with her head if the pain it brought to her hands had not dissuaded her.

Despite her chagrin, she was famished, and to her horror of every cheese in the world was added the knowledge that this food made part of a penitence, causing her to struggle against it all evening in an effort to impose silence on her stomach; and these problems were greatly enhanced by her fear that she would receive a supplementary whipping the next morning if she did not eat what had been put before her.

Her stomach and her fear triumphed, because at her age, Laura could scarcely resist these two things. With an expression of disgust she masticated her bread and cheese, then drank about half of the glass of water. She reserved the other half for her toilette, under the impression that no more would be accessible to her. Then she sank wearily on the floor in all her clothes, extended herself painfully on the woolen blankets and began to make vain efforts to fall asleep. Throughout the night she was agitated, a prey to many troubles she could not explain. Try as she would to drive out the remembrance of punishments she was submitted to and the dregs of shame she had to drink, she could not dismiss the least details of the scenes, and they ranged over her thoughts ceaselessly. Most of all she endeavored to dismiss a vague complacence, as well as an indistinct urge to submit unreservedly, and their persistent bobbing-up irritated her so that her efforts to revolt against them made it still more difficult to compose her mind. . . . But at last sleep overtook her.

The next morning, at about nine o'clock, her door opened and Miss Brenton entered, alone, this time. She locked the door behind her and explained to Laura that as Mrs. Wharton was occupied with other corrections, she had been charged with the task of herself inflicting the routine morning whipping. But as heretofore, it was necessary for the girl first to make her ablutions. She drew her toward a bath, made her wash herself and then put a robe around her body, after which she drew her back to the cell for her whipping. A faint thought of resistance was promptly dispelled by the girl herself because of a firm resolution she had made to obey immediately any order her mistresses might issue.

At Miss Brenton's command, she stretched out on the bench and quietly permitted herself to be prepared. The whipping smarted terrifically, but Laura gripped the bench and clung desperately to it, with the result that she succeeded fairly well in supporting the chastisement until it ceased, without wriggling away.

Her only remaining meal which she took in her cell was similar to that of the night before, and a long sad afternoon rolled by.

In the evening Miss Brenton came for her and she

dined in the refrectory frugally, but much better, nevertheless, than in her cell. That night she slept like a log.

Beginning with the next day she became part of the
household brigade, so to speak, and she had the special
good fortune of being assigned to the laundry, under
Miss Evelyn who, in order to conceal the content she
experienced, took a most belligerent air toward the girl
in the presence of Mrs. Wharton.

"My child," Miss Evelyn said, when the directress
had gone out, "I am glad I have been chosen as your
surveillant. You may thank your stars you were not
put under the direction of Miss Williams, or any of the
others that I know very well. However, do not imagine
that your training under my charge is going to be a para-
dise for you. You must already have learned how
strictly any leniency or indulgence is forbidden here,
and if I should punish you infrequently or lightly, they
should not be long in finding it out and I would be
accused of partiality. . . . I shall whip you, consequently, as often as your companions, but . . . I shall
know how to measure the degrees of severity! . . ."

So it was that Laura found herself, without knowing
it, in the situation of Heloise in her relation to Abelard
before Canon Fulbert. For Abelard, in order to dissimulate the ardent love he bore, whipped his tender pupil
with severity and sternness when her uncle, the Canon,
was present, and the latter was always enchanted by
the young man's sincerity.

And, in fact, Miss Evelyn never neglected her *duty*,
Scarcely a day would go by but that, for one motive or
another, the supervisor would make some real or fancied
show of annoyance at Laura's conduct, call her over to
a corner, tuck up the girl's skirts, and apply a burning

correction on her pupil's behind. Laura suffered and wept but she understood that Miss Evelyn was merely performing her duty in the interest of both of them, and it was with a good heart and a total absence of resentment that she exchanged the kiss of peace with her disciplinarian.

———————

Some days after her arrival at Sloane House Mrs. Wharton sent for Laura and showed her a newspaper. The paper was entitled the *Chatham Gazette*. Mrs. Wharton questioned the girl on the gentleman that she pretended to know at Chatham and whom she called her uncle. Then she showed her a column in which it was related that a Mr. Blake had perished in a fire which consumed his cottage. Near the body was found the remains of a young girl, about eighteen years old, who appeared to resemble a photograph left untouched by the fire. Subsequent investigations disclosed that the old man had a niece named Laura Blake and the authorities, convinced the body was that of the girl in question, officially recorded that name in the town records as one of the deceased.

Laura listened to this reading and fell to the floor in a dead faint.

When she had recovered her senses, Mrs. Wharton said:

"Now, do you see the young girl whose name you tried to take, Lily Butler? Once and for all that should prove to you how impossible it would be for you to assume her name, since her decease is officially recorded, and if you attempted anything in that direction you would be condemned to a long term of imprisonment at hard labor."

Let us say at once, that this so-called sheet from the *Chatham Gazette* had been composed and printed in its entirety in one of the basements of this establishment. Mrs. Wharton was the author of the article which she felt must cause Laura to abandon all hope of resuming some day her real personality.

If this be true, thought Laura, it would appear that destiny had decreed that a fire should burst out and destroy her only remaining relative in the whole world. There was no one to turn to now except her friend, Pauline, whom she couldn't possibly reach.

For some days Mrs. Wharton was really worried about Laura, but youth triumphed and vanquished the melancholy and despair which had struck her down. The girl resumed her place at the sewing-table in the laundry where Miss Evelyn reigned, and little by little, the monotony of her existence settled on her, animated only by the incessant spectacle of chastisements which never ceased to rain on the fleshly buttocks of the pensionnaires.

Six months passed thus. Laura Blake had indeed been completely submerged into Lily Butler. Then, one beautiful day, a grand lady from the vicinity of Thurso came to visit the establishment. In the laundry she stopped suddenly before Laura, and in a low voice expressed her admiration of the girl to Mrs. Wharton. That lady saw at once the possibility of an excellent piece of business. She boasted and spoke at great length of Laura's gentleness and docility—as well as of her undeniable physical charms, and proposed to the visitor that she would be glad to consider binding her out.

The deal was promptly concluded, and the second day following Laura, now and henceforth Lily, left Sloane House, to the sincere regret of Miss Evelyn, in the custody of her new mistress.

PART TWO

THE CONSUMMATION

X

The Carriage

It was a biting cold morning in March when an old carriage, its wheels grinding on its axles, left Thurso; it proceeded along a snow-covered road which wound its way almost constantly along the northern coast of Scotland. For the tourist the road is among the most picturesque in that country, permitting one to admire the Cape of Duncansby, the ancient *Berubium* of Ptolemy, the Pentland Firth, against which break the waves of the North Sea where it flanks the Atlantic, and still further north the Orkney Islands come to make their appearance.

On the driver's seat a surly-looking old coachman sat, his brushwood beard frosted with the cold. He appeared to be half asleep as he let the horses follow their noses in reliance on their good-will to keep to the road. He was enfolded in a cloak of multiple capes, and the upper part of his face was buried to his ears and eyebrows in an enormous furry headgear.

In the carriage, the windows tightly closed, sat two travelers.

One was a young girl, little more than eighteen years old. The other was a lady of possibly forty, tall, stout and matronly, and possessed of a square and forbidding-looking chin arrogantly projected forward. Her cheeks were colored by an abundance of blood, her nose was authoritative, her eyes narrow and cruel, her lips quite thin. She was enveloped in a huge fur wrap and from the corner of the carriage where she sat, she stared fixedly at the young girl sitting opposite her on the seat facing backward. On the girl's face was an expression of infinite sadness, her features were pale with cold and perhaps anguish, and she offered a startling contrast to the face and figure of her traveling companion.

The horses had ceased laboring up a steep grade, and the infernal squeeking of the axles, the groans of the ancient coach and the rattling of the glass windows had subsided somewhat; when the big woman, judging that her voice would now be more apt to reach the girl's ears, leaned forward and spoke:

"Lily! Come over here beside me! You don't suppose I am going to wear myself out shouting at you!"

The poor child sighed and obeyed, greatly confused and fearful of irritating the lady.

"Now then, please do not forget that you have become my maid. You do not know me, but I know you very well. More than six months ago, when you became an inmate of Mrs. Wharton's Training School for Girls, your directress had dragged you, after considerable trouble, out of a mess which made you virtually a fugitive from justice."

The lady's voice was hard and severe. She talked, this important personage, in the tone of a schoolmistress scolding a pupil before administering a flogging. She resumed:

"You tried to make yourself pass for another and gave yourself the name of Laura Blake, but your imposture, thank heaven, was discovered. Now I know that your mistress has trained you to be docile and submissive, but it is one thing to submit yourself to the rules of a girls' training school and quite another to submit to my own. You know my name?"

"They told me, Madame. . . ."

"Madame! Milady to you, hereafter, do you understand? What is my name, or have you forgotten? Who am I?"

Tears gathered on the girl's lashes. She swallowed a sob and stammered:

"Lady Manville, Milady. . . ."

"Yes, Lady Manville. I am a widow. I have two other maids, a page-boy, a groom, and a governess who is authorized by me to look strictly after my personnel. I am rich, yes, indeed! And I could live luxuriously in London, or anywhere on the Continent, Lily, all year round, if I liked, but I prefer Duncaster House. Did you ever hear of Duncaster House?"

"No, Milady. . . ."

"You shall very soon come to know it. Its history is a strange one, but what does it matter? I shall tell you only this: The old place, which is close to the celebrated Houna Inn, was built in the 16th Century by the Hollander, Peter van Weem. It is of octagonal shape and has an entrance door on each side. Peter van Weem had eight children and when they and their families came to visit, to keep them from quarreling, he made each family enter through the door which was designated for them. Thus his children and their families were able to remain under the paternal roof without coming into conflict."

Lady Manville paused for a moment and then resumed:

"At my house you shall have much work to do, and

you will find me very severe. . . . Does that frighten
you?"

"No, Mad . . . Milady," murmured Lily.

A faint smile came over Lady Manville's face.

"So much the better!" she said. "I do not like frightened faces around me. I like youth, cheerfulness, even
when I punish. . . . I shall teach you a little song I
shall require you to sing sometimes while I am whipping
you. I like to hear that much better than I do cries
and grinding of teeth!"

A great sigh filled the breast of the charming young
girl. What, indeed, was likely to be her fate around a
woman of this sort! To spend her life as her lady's
maid! Was it possible! For she had never, even in her
most trying moments, despite the appearance of absolute
submission she exhibited toward her former mistresses,
abandoned hope of deliverance, of a resumption of her
true personality. Even the dubious affection, if one may
call it affection, that Miss Evelyn had for her, had been
meaningless when it came to binding her out arbitrarily
to a hostile mistress—sale is the proper word—and which
delivered her into the hands of this strange woman whose
manner and appearance was as far from engaging as
possible. Broken morally by the severe discipline of the
Training School, she had not dared to deliver herself
of even the sign of a protest, and meekly she had assembled her trifling belongings and taken her place in
the old coach which was now leading her toward the
unknown. . . . The words of Lady Manville plunged
her into a bitter despair which she was forcing herself
to dissimulate.

Meanwhile a new grade was reached, the carriage
had begun to roll from side to side again, and the horses

seemed to be fired with a sudden zeal for work. The jolting shook the travelers terribly, and each moment threw Lily against Lady Manville and vice-versa.

The lady regarded the young girl at her leisure and seemed to take pleasure in her embarrassment.

"Lord! but you are an encumbrance, Lily!" she exclaimed finally. "How I regret not having made you sit with the coachman. But you are so badly dressed and so scantily that you might have taken ill before our arrival, and I must guard against anything like that, for I paid much more for you than you are worth!"

There was silence, then Lady Manville spoke again:

"We cannot continue like this: Get on your knees here before me. In that way I shall be able to watch you, and when I talk to you I shall know that you hear me."

Lily took the position indicated, but there was very little room and she found herself quite firmly against her mistress who pulled her still closer.

"There! Now you are like a little girl in penitence! I like to see you that way. . . ."

She pinched the girl's chin and pulled her head upward.

"Why are your eyes full of tears? You are sensitive, I can see that. So much the better! I prefer it; at least when I shall scold or chastise you, I shall have the pleasure of seeing that it does not leave you disrespectfully indifferent! . . ."

She leaned forward and her hot breath swept across Lily's face.

"For I shall chastise you, you know! You have been whipped frequently, haven't you?"

Lily, strangled by her anguish, gulped hard and could not pronounce a word. She was scarlet.

"Well? Didn't you understand me? I asked if you have been whipped often?"

"Mad . . . ame . . . I . . . yes, Milady. . . ."

"You are stupid, truly, Lily! Your tongue is para-lyzed, I think! I am going to punish your little tongue, Lily! . . . Stick it out!

"Oh! . . . oooh!" groaned Lily, overcome. "I beg you, Milady, if you please. . . ."

"It pleases me, you stubborn child, to have you thrust your stupid little tongue out of your mouth! At once!"

Lily half-opened her lips and the extremity of her pink tongue, like that of a kitten, appeared between her pearly teeth.

"Oh! you wicked girl! Is this the way you obey? . . . Will you stick it out entirely? Here! Here!"

Before the child had a chance to protect herself, she received two sonorous slaps, one on each cheek. She burst into tears and covered her face with her chubby little hands which the extreme cold had reddened.

"Put your hands behind your back at once, you disobedient girl!" ordered Lady Manville, frowning severely. "I forbid you to conceal your face! Did one ever see such rebellion!"

Lily obeyed this time. The slaps had left definite red imprints on her velvety cheeks.

"And your tongue? . . . must I go search it in your mouth with a pair of tweezers when we arrive? Stick it out, immediately!"

The tongue was stuck out. It was pink for its entire length, a sign of perfect health, and its darting point trembled!

Lady Manville extended her hand, and with her thumb and index finger pulled it down and pinched it.

"That will loosen your speech, I hope! Will you answer me properly now?"

Lily emitted a yell of pain, and her eyes bulged with fright. She had brought her hands around in front, but did not dare, however, lift them toward her torturer. The latter released her hold at last and the girl was able to withdraw the wounded tongue. She wept bitterly.

"Oh! yes, you are sensitive!" remarked the lady with a visible satisfaction. "I see that you like to cry! Will you answer me now, my beauty? I reiterate my question. Have you been whipped often?"

"Y . . . es . . . Milady! . . ." sobbed Lily.

"Before coming to the Training School or only there?"

"At the Training School . . . Milady!"

"Never before?"

"Nev . . . er . . . Milady!"

"Poor education!" sighed the big woman, lifting her eyes to heaven, which for the moment was represented by the roof of the carriage. "Fortunately, Mrs. Wharton and her assistants have remedied that a little! . . . And as for myself, I shall do even better than they. . . . Doesn't it make you feel content to know that you will be whipped even more frequently and more soundly than you were before?"

Sobs alone responded to the strange question, but once more Lady Manville's hand slapped the still reddened cheeks. Lily cried out in surprise and pain.

"That seems odd to you to be slapped like this, eh? . . . But I must never be kept waiting an instant for an answer! Oh! you shall soon become better acquainted with Lady Manville, my girl! Answer! Won't you feel grateful for being soundly whipped?"

"Milady! I . . . do not know. . . ."

107

"You must know! You have been sufficiently disciplined to know that if you are whipped it is for your good, and that, consequently, you should consider yourself very well satisfied! Will you be?"

"Yes . . . Milady. . . ."

"Oh! cease this weeping and this senseless whining! Reserve your great chagrin for more serious occasions! You shall not find them lacking!"

She pulled from the interior of her fur wrap a little perfumed handkerchief and dried the girl's tears. Outside, a fresh thick snowstorm had started suddenly. The wind whistled into the interior of the coach, and the sound of the nearby sea could be heard dashing furiously against the rocky coast, adding to the infernal howling of the storm. Lady Manville experienced a voluptuous pleasure in finding herself sheltered from the unchained forces of nature. She tightened the girl more firmly against her knees, in a grip almost maternal, and this grip, coming after the slaps and threats, did not go astray in the profoundly troubled soul of Lily.

"How much better it is to be in the carriage now!" murmured the lady, as though talking to herself. "At the rate we are going, it should be fully two hours before we arrive at the manor."

Her eyes fell once again on Lily.

"You regret leaving the Training School, do you not?" she demanded, softening her voice a trifle. "Come! acknowledge it! I understand that very well! No doubt you left some close friend behind whom you think of affectionately, notwithstanding the very good discipline under which you were trained?"

Disturbed by this question, Lily could not retain her tears which fell anew.

"Yes, Milady!" she murmured.

"You regret leaving! And yet you told me they whipped you frequently there, is that not true?"

"Yes . . . Milady . . . but in spite of everything . . . I had a good friend. . . ."

Lady Manville's voice softened once more, became quite unctuous, indeed.

"One of the girls, no doubt? One of your companions?"

"Oh, no! Milady! . . . A governess . . . the one in charge of the laundry. . . . She liked me very much. . . ."

"The one called Miss Evelyn, I believe?"

"Yes, Milady."

"It seems to me I heard them say that she was a disciplinarian of exemplary severity? That she was, in fact, one of the most capable chastisers in the school, which numbers quite a few, I am sure."

"Miss Evelyn was severe . . . even with me, Milady . . . but she loved me just the same."

"Then, my poor little thing, I understand your sorrow, for at my house you will have no one to love you!"

Lily raised her eyes on her new mistress, her big eyes, made more beautiful and touching by her tears, and her look had the air of saying: "And you, Milady? . . . Will you not love me a little bit?"

But she found nothing in the hard and sensual face except eyes sparkling with irony and cruelty.

"No, indeed," repeated Lady Manville," you will have no one. . . . For in my home I do not tolerate any affection. . . . In my house everything is as rigid as can be. You are, all you who serve and wait upon me, nothing but my slaves! I have paid for you and for them, you are merely living objects that I own outright, obedient things, that I discipline and punish according to my fancy. Everything moves to the sound of the whip! No recompense! Why should there be any when I can obtain everything by fear? For the least fault, the whip! In my house, Lily, your bottom will never have a chance to catch cold!"

The voice had recovered all its dryness, all its harshness, and Lily had the sensation that this woman played with her as a cat does with a mouse before devouring it. . . . She sensed herself horribly abandoned, the unhappiest of beings, and convulsive sobs shook her from head to foot.

"Ah! ah! you cry! you regret leaving the Training School, eh? You will regret it still more when we arrive home! Stupid child! to think that I am going to waste any affection on her! Your affections! . . . I shall give you affections of a different sort! . . . Keep quiet! I forbid you to cry stupidly like that! Enough, I told you! Are you going to obey me? . . . Stop your crying, at once!"

She had taken the girl by the ears, as one would grasp a vase by its handles, and she pulled her head up, shaking it meanwhile and wresting cries of pain from the dear lost child whose tears redoubled.

"Oh! will you stop that crying? . . . You are as stubborn as a mule, but I can promise you shall become the humblest thing imaginable, and quickly too, you miserable girl!"

She was intoxicated with fury and the desire to cause pain to her victim and to humiliate her in every conceivable way. She returned once more to the girl, pulling her again by the ears.

"Come! come! So much the worse for you! Right

110

here in this carriage you are going to receive a whipping!
. . . If it were not snowing, I should take you out on the
road and flog you at the nearest curb, on your knees
and with your skirt up to your neck! . . . Ah! are you
trying to resist me?"

"No! oh! . . . oooh! . . . No . . . Milady! . . . pity!
. . . I am obeying . . . I am obeying . . . I . . . am not
resisting . . . Milady! . . . oh! . . . pity! . . . please don't
harm me . . . Milady!"

"Oh, stop your supplications. Come! . . . Bend over
my knees! I wish to see your bottom. . . . I wish to see
it immediately so that I can spank it as it deserves . . .
if it's worth bothering with at all! . . . ah! . . . Why
didn't I provide myself with a good whip before we
left, Lily! How well I could use it now!"

She was a prey to a veritable hysterical crisis and
had apparently lost all control of her passions. She
abandoned herself to the savage joy of wounding this
tender little heart that she divined was of unusual de-
licacy and exquisite sensitiveness—to lacerate the virgin
flesh which was palpitating in its outraged modesty.
Although pulled violently, Lily let herself be taken, with
shame and, already, with suffering. She found herself
suddenly couched across Lady Manville's knees, her
head brushed the side of the coach and her feet were
tucked under the seat because her legs could stretch no
further than the inner wall of the opposite side of the
carriage. Her hand gripped Lady Manville's cloak which
fell over her powerful haunches.

The latter's lips, drawn back to the gums, seemed to
leer like a panther crouching before the prey it is about
to pull apart. With her two hands she tucked back the
girl's mantle and skirt. And all at once, she discovered

111

the flesh of her thighs, pink with the cold, and the snowy mass of the croupe whose satiny skin could not conceal the quivering of the muscles beneath. For an instant she remained transfixed before this spectacle. The customary color in her cheeks heightened and her nostrils throbbed with excitement.

"Oh! . . ." she exclaimed at last, "you are not wearing any drawers, you impudent, shameless girl! How did you dare leave your drawers off, eh?"

To hurry the response, she pinched the left buttock of the recumbent girl, who uttered a cry and burst into fresh tears:

"Oh! Milady! . . . I haven't any! . . . Forgive me, please, Milady . . . pardon me!"

"You haven't any? . . . They dressed you without drawers at the Training School?"

"Yes . . . Milady."

"Oh! . . . Indeed, that is an idea, and now I see why. They wanted you to be in a state of readiness, always, for whipping. . . . But I shall dress you quite differently, do you know that, Lily? You shall have bloomers, and very tight ones, very, very tight ones. They make the ceremony of undressing and preparing for a whipping much more humiliating, as you shall very soon see. For when I order you to come and be whipped, it is you, you alone, who shall have to unfasten and take down your bloomers so that you can properly offer your bottom to the whip! Do you understand?"

"Yes, Milady! Please have pity on me."

"Oh! pity! You ask me to have pity! . . . You shall see before many days have passed that sentiment is totally absent from my discipline. I know just what has to be done to obtain perfect obedience, perfect ser-

*"You are going to remember your debut at Sloane, eh?"
she said (page 89)*

vice! I have no pity for my slaves, indeed not! . . . Ah!
. . . why was I not born in Nero's time! What pleasures I should have had from my slaves! They should
have danced to the crack of the whip, all day long! I
should have had some of them whipped to death, my
love!"

"Milady! Pity! Mercy! . . . Oh, I shall go mad! . . ."

"I shall cure you! . . . Don't you know that not so
long ago they used to cure insanity that way . . . why
have they changed the method? The whip is a universal
remedy! Why have they begun to abandon this good
old custom? . . . You shiver, you wretched child, don't
you? This discourse annoys you, doesn't it, while your
bare bottom remains exposed awaiting the beautiful
warming it is going to receive? That's very humiliating
to you, isn't it? . . . Yes, no doubt, and it is just because
I am aware of it that I wish to prolong your anguish!
. . . I have a good mind to make you remain like this
until we reach our destination! A little spanking every
few minutes will insure your bottom remaining warm
and it will not be in danger of catching cold itself. Besides, my own knees have been really cold, and this way
you can keep them warm. Excellent idea, indeed . . .
I think I shall begin whipping you now, Lily! Are you
ready for your whipping? Come, my still inexperienced
little slave, prepare to submit your bottom to the most
humiliating and infamous chastisement that exists!"

In the matter of chastisement, at least, Lily was far
from inexperienced. She was not, as we already know,
at the beginning of her studies in the way these things
were arranged for her, but before this flood of words,
before this indisputably refined fashion of beginning a
whipping, she felt herself burning up with shame. Not

even her first whipping had shocked her modesty, produced such terrors, released such strange emotions, as this discourse and her present position stirred up. No, this was infinitely worse than the first time, when Miss Evelyn and Mrs. Wharton had drawn her across their knees and flagellated her behind. . . .

She gasped. Her posterior muscles contracted in the expectation of the baking they were about to undergo, and then, wearily, they abandoned themselves only to retighten anew:

"I am going to show you that I know how to whip a wicked and stupid girl, Lily!" resumed Lady Manville, "and you are going to tell me when I have finished whether I whip better than Mrs. Wharton! I shall look for your interesting opinion on that subject, remember!"

She grazed with a light tap the suddenly bulging rotundities and uttered a little grumble of satisfaction, then, suddenly, she raised her arm and applied the first slap with all her strength. The entire mass of the fleshy region shivered and at once a deep red mark appeared where the first blow had landed. Others followed, hurried, burning, numerous, and Lily quivered wildly, emitting groans, sobs and pleas, while she tried from time to time to bring one of her little hands around to her smarting buttocks in a forlorn effort to protect them, but the gesture only succeeded in redoubling the severity of the noble lady.

"Will you keep your hands in front of you where they belong? Is this the sort of docility you have been trained to?" she complained. "Is it? Is it? So you were trying to revolt! That is revolt, my dear! And signs of revolt are vigorously punished! . . . Here! Here! Here! Oh! how I wish I had a good whip handy or an

116

excellent tawse such as we have at home! Ah! . . . I should make you squirm beautifully for that! Here! Here! Here! And here's another and still a better one! Cry! cry! cry! you wicked child! Your tears are an encouragement to me—and a satisfaction! . . ."

She whipped on furiously during some minutes, seeming certainly to have forgotten where he was, and the circumstances of the correction so hypnotized her that the sight of the movements made by the croupe she was spanking and the words she was expressing, as she proceeded, absolutely intoxicated her.

And then she stopped and took a long breath. . . .

She passed her hand across her forehead and wiped off the perspiration. It was burning from the furious contacts it had made, and at last she appeared to take cognizance of herself. She looked down on the reddened posterior, now shading to violet, so thoroughly had she beaten it, then she turned the girl's congested face half way around and looked at her exhausted victim.

"Well now, my dear," she said, "how did you find the whipping I just gave you? Better than Mrs. Wharton's or less severe?"

Lily was certainly incapable of responding, even if she had been willing, for her sobbing was choking her. She made a gesture of supplication accompanied by an expression of intense despair, but a fresh slap warned her of the importance of responding promptly when her mistress interrogated her.

"Whose whipping would you say is more thorough, mine or Mrs. Wharton's? Answer promptly, or I shall let you have some more!"

"Yours . . . Milady," stuttered Lily.

117

"Answer in more precise fashion! Are you afraid of committing yourself, perhaps?"

"Yes, Milady . . . I think . . . you whipped me more thoroughly . . . than Mrs. Wharton. . . ."

"More effectively, don't you think?"

"Yes, Milady. . . ."

"Does it bake more, smart more?"

"Yes . . . Milady."

"And whose whippings do you think will do the most good in training you properly, mine or hers?"

"Yours . . . Milady."

"Yours what? I told you to be more precise. Listen to me carefully, Lily. When I whip my slaves I frequently ask many questions during and after each whiping and I require full, prompt, detailed answers. If you have any regard for your bottom you had better listen to my warning. For if you answer haltingly, one word at a time, I shall understand it as a request from you for two whippings instead of the one intended originally, and you may rely on me to grant your request immediately. Now, do you wish to answer the last question?"

"Yes, Milady . . . I do. Please forgive me . . . I think when you whip me . . . My training will be better than what I received from Mrs. Wharton, Milady."

Her sobbing still interrupted her responses and this interrogation was a torture more painful, perhaps than the spanking itself.

"At last!" exclaimed Lady Manville. "I am enchanted to find you share my opinion. And you will show your eagerness to be punished, as my other maids do, whenever you make a mistake?"

"Yes, Milady, I shall. . . ."

She made Lily continue to lie across her lap, but with

her skirt still turned back. The girl was shivering in all her extremities, and her mistress did not withdraw her hands from those fleshy parts which were burning as the result of the smacking.

"You are going to remain in this position for a while, and after that you shall rest on your knees before me," she said. "It is very humiliating, of course, but humiliation is extremely profitable to those in your station. I shall see to it you do not catch cold down below."

The carriage continued to roll on. Lily, breathless, remained bent across the lap of her mistress, the upper part of her body slumped forward, bowed down by the weight of her misery. Her mind was blank, it was impossible for her to think. The conflict of despair, shame, fear, suffering, physical and moral revolt, annihilated all possibility of ordered thinking. She was as one unconscious. From time to time only a great sob would shake her whole body, then Lady Manville would maternally slap her behind once or twice to remind her, as it were, to be patient and submissive.

"Be good, Lily. You are not cold, are you?"

"No, Milady . . ." murmured Lily in a dying voice.

A new silence established itself. Thus a half-hour passed. A half-hour! Let one imagine if one can what such a lapse of time must have meant for a person in Lily's position! . . .

There were certainly good reasons for her going mad. And perhaps that would have been exactly the result were it not for the fact that she had gone through relatively similar experiences and punishments at the Training School.

At the end of the half-hour Lady Manville placed her hand on Lily's bare flesh and frowned. Instead of the

119

glowing heat she had felt there previously there was now but a faint warmth, scarcely perceptible, and even the purplish color visible awhile ago, on each buttock, had little by little faded into a pale pink.

"Lily," said Lady Manville, "you are commencing to get cold, aren't you?"

"No, Milady . . . please pardon me, Milady. Oh, please! I am not cold," demurred Lily, shivering.

"Are you a liar, too, by any chance?" the lady inquired severely. "I say that you are getting cold!"

"Milady!" implored Lily pitifully, suspecting a fresh chastisement suspending itself over her posterior.

"Oh! you do not want to admit it, you miserable thing! And they gave me to understand you were as docile and submissive as one could wish! I can see that either they have deceived me or they have deceived themselves. But I shall take it on myself to complete your education! I am going to give you a good whipping, Lily!"

"Milady! Oh! . . . Have pity!" . . .

Lady Manville had already raised her hand to spank Lily when suddenly the carriage stopped. She pulled the girl's skirt down quickly and straightened herself at once. Lily moved over painfully on the right of her mistress, completely broken.

The door was being opened and the coachman, transformed into a Santa Claus by the snow which covered his mantle and his fur cap, presented himself.

"What is it, Joe?" inquired Lady Manville.

"We are at the half-way inn, Milady," he answered. "We can feed the horses and give them some rest. Would Milady care to enter and take something warm?"

"Thanks, Joe. That's that. We shall come in, I and my maid. Order two cups of hot tea and toast."

XI

The Inn

SHE pulled the shade aside and dried Lily's tears. The girl's breast was still heaving with sobs, more from emotion than from chagrin, for the first sentiment had vanquished the other when the shade was pulled away. Lily felt herself dying at the thought that one second later the coachman would have seen her receiving a spanking!

"Lily," said Lady Manville, "we are going in. I do not need to recommend to you an humble and deeply respectful attitude, I trust. Pass before me and open my umbrella."

Lily stepped out and her little feet, still shod in the light uniform slippers of the Training School, sank into deep snow. She opened the umbrella and Lady Manville stepped out in her turn, but in the distinguished manner which belongs to a lady of importance, that is to say, head thrown back, the rustling of silk as she arranged her fluffy skirt, and uttering tiny cries scarcely to be expected of the implacably stern and authoritative lady she had demonstrated herself to be. At the entrance of the inn a tall, angular woman awaited them. She exclaimed on the inclemency of the weather and the misfortune which required so charming a lady to expose herself to it.

In the spacious dining-room the coachman was already

occupying an inconspicuous corner, near two healthy-looking maid-servants with literally pink complexions, and by the side of one of the girls stood a small boy. No other patron. Although she was not particularly thinking of anything, Lily experienced a tremendous relief upon noting the fact that there were no travelers present.

Lady Manville approached the fire and turned around.

"Well, fool!" she cried. "Aren't you going to take my cloak off?"

It was as though two resounding slaps had fallen across Lily's cheeks. She turned scarlet and came forward as quickly as her heavy lower limbs and smarting posterior would permit, and she withdrew the cloak which she deposited on a chair.

"Stupid girl!" exclaimed Lady Manville. "Don't you know that a cloak isn't put down like this? You hang it up!"

And turning toward the inn-keeper who regarded her open-mouthed, she said:

"My good Katherine, take it from her hands; she is an idiot, upon my word! I don't know what detains me from correcting her right now, before everyone here!"

Lily trembled in all her limbs. She had the intuition that she would not leave the inn before receiving the whipping she had been spared in the carriage but a few moments ago. The thought of it made her knees weak.

"Bring me a bench, here, before the fire! What are you waiting for? Oh, how stupid she is! Shall I ever succeed in breaking her into instantaneous obedience?"

"She is young," remarked Katherine, "they don't know. . . . If milady wishes. . . ."

"No, no, Katherine! Thanks, my dear. Lily is my maid. It is necessary that she learn her duties, if she doesn't know them yet. And I have charged myself with teaching them to her, even if I have to whip her every morning and night!"

Big tears rolled down Lily's cheeks. Her confusion was so great that the blood burned in her temples and she could see only things and people as through a haze. The little boy stared at her stupidly; the two maids tried their best to stifle their tittering, so much pleasure and amusement did they find in the humiliation of a girl that they divined was out of their class, and who was being treated like the meanest slave. The coachman seemed exclusively absorbed in his eating and drinking. For him this was no unusual scene.

Meanwhile, Lily had brought a bench and Lady Manville sat down. Katherine brought over a tea-table on which she deposited two cups, sugar and a tea-pot. On the stove the bread was toasting and the water was boiling in the kettle.

"For whom is this second cup, Katherine?" Lady Manville asked coldly.

"I thought," the confused inn-keeper responded, blushing, "that miss . . . that your maid. . . ."

"You think badly, my good Katherine," the lady interrupted dryly. "I do not eat with my domestics. Lily will take hers down below, with the coachman. Well, Lily? You look half-asleep! Come here to me!"

"Milady," quaked the poor bewildered girl, beginning to cry.

"Well, what? Milady what? Why are you so stupid? You look half-asleep, I said, and here is something to wake you up a bit!"

Clic! Clac! . . . two sonorous slaps burst across the ominous silence. Lily began to cry softly.

"Would you like a whipping instead?" demanded Lady Manville in a loud tone. "That would revive you, I am sure. Take this cup quickly. You will serve my tea, then you will sit with the coachman and take yours."

Lily obeyed. The two servants were not laughing any more. The lady's manner had imposed itself on all present, even on Katherine, who knew her for a long time, although she had nothing to fear from her. Katherine busied herself preparing the tea and toast, put them all on a serving-tray and confided it to Lily who still continued to tremble. The girl approached her mistress and deposited the tray on the little table, then she started to pour the tea. It was not the first time, to be sure, that she rendered this service, for her former mistresses at the School taught all the girls how to serve and wait on table; nevertheless, she trembled so much that her actions were awkward, and she spilled some drops of the burning water on the napkin and on the toast.

Lady Manville had been watching her steadily. Her eyes were cold, troubled and humid—to the young girl she appeared like a serpent fascinating a little bird with its staring. Then Lady Manville gathered a drop on her finger, showed it to the girl and spread her knees.

The cold of death invaded Lily, and she was obliged to lean against the chimney to keep from falling.

"Milady! . . ." she implored, in so feeble a voice it was more like a breath.

The lady repeated the same gesture, as eloquent as though it had been expressed in a loud voice. A deadly silence reigned in the room. The coachman himself, so indifferent up to the present, looked up, the servant girls shivered, the little boy pressed himself against his mother's skirts, and the latter was red with emotion.

Lily's legs would not support her and, suddenly, she fell on her knees.

"Milady, please I beg of you!" she exclaimed in a voice low and ardent, the words wrenched out of her blackest despair, "I implore you, Milady! Not here! . . . Oh! not here! . . ."

"Take care!" warned Lady Manville.

And as she pronounced these words, for the third time her rigid index finger pointed to her lap.

Then, in a frightful anguish which gripped her whole being, Lily abandoned herself. She was like a person hypnotized. A strange force emanated from Lady Manville and invaded her, annihilating all her will, delivering her, so to speak, hand and foot to this woman who was about to inflict on her the most terrible humiliation possible to imagine. She stretched herself out, face down over the knees of her mistress with a sob that made all the witnesses shiver.

On Lady Manville's face was a smile of triumph and, slowly, very much at her ease, as if she were at home, she hugged Lily's body close under her left arm, enlaced the girl's feet with her right leg and commenced to turn back her skirt which she carefully disposed in neat folds on the girl's loins, in a fashion to prevent them from falling in her way. At the same time her voice became strangely soft, as though she had arrived at the paroxysm of her severity.

"You see now, you wicked child," she was speaking gently, "that you must always yield to me! I am going to whip you, Lily, in front of all these witnesses! . . .

125

Don't you feel yourself dying of humiliation? . . . Now submit quietly, my girl, demonstrate by your conduct here on my lap that you are co-operating with me in your punishment, otherwise I shall attach you to a ladder when we get home and whip you there again! Be good!"

Then she turned toward Katherine and asked:

"My dear, don't you have a tawse to lend me? Where is the good Scotch mother who doesn't keep one hanging conveniently in her home?"

The entrance door had opened and two people, white with snow, stamped their way in with a gust of wind before them.

"Who is that?" a masculine voice inquired. "Who is asking for a tawse?"

Lady Manville turned around on her bench, without in the least releasing Lily, and looked in the direction of the new arrivals. Her expression was arrogant, denuded of all friendliness, but, suddenly, her features relaxed in a hearty welcome.

"Well, well! Herbert Clawson! and charming Marjorie too, as sure as can be! My word! You out in this weather? . . ."

"Lady Manville!" they exclaimed in unison. "By George! Who expected to find you here?"

They divested themselves of their cloaks, their fur headgear, and revealed their young faces, he tall, brown, energetic, clear complexion, thirty years old; she twenty-five, blonde and pink and nearly perfect features, except for michievous eyes that had no playfulness in them, only wickedness. They approached quickly.

"But . . . my word! . . . Who is this, my dear friend, you are holding over your knees?"

A groan, coming from an agonized throat, demonstrated that it was a living thing, and a tortured one, too.

"My new maid," responded Lady Manville. "She suffers from an inconceivable clumsiness and I am about to punish her for her latest exhibition of it."

"By Saint Hubert! Marjorie! Come, my dear! Come here and take a lesson in energy and administration!" he said with a laugh.

That young lady did not wait to be invited twice. She approached, curious, a blush in her cheeks, and her eyes sparkled as she leaned down and examined Lily's congested face.

"Quite young!" she pronounced.

"Yes, about eighteen. I have just taken her over for my service. She comes from Mrs. Wharton's Training School."

"And I see you are wasting no time breaking her in to her new obligations," smiled Herbert.

Lady Manville shrugged her shoulders.

"I must begin promptly. These girls require turning over and whipping twelve times a day if one wishes to keep them properly in place. It is true that they know how to do some things at the Training School in that direction, because, look, they do not supply them with any drawers down there, so they can get at their bottoms more easily."

She drew the folded skirt down once more to prove her statement to the visitors, in spite of the heavy rearing and terrible efforts of Lily who was just beside herself.

"She is far from docile, it seems," remarked Marjorie. "Did you have much trouble making her take this position?"

"No, she took it by herself, submissively enough! But I think this is the first time she is being punished in a public place and her humiliation is so great that she is quite outside of her ordinary character. But she will have to get used to that, also."

She raised the girl's chemise and Herbert could not retain an "oh" of admiration, which was responded to by an inexpressible groan from Lily who managed to utter an only word.

"Pity!"

"Would you pity her, Marjorie dear?" asked Lady Manville ironically.

"Oh, no! Whatever she has merited she ought to receive in full measure!" responded the young woman with a decided expression of wickedness.

"And you, Herbert?"

"Hum!... How can I fail to be of your mind, ladies? I admit that one can't help being moved by an intense expectation before thinking of pardoning her, the present spectacle and what is to follow is much too provoking, upon my word!"

"Oh, yes!" agreed Marjorie, "provoking is just the word!"

Lady Manville smiled and looked toward Katherine.

The inn-keeper tendered her a band of leather, more than a foot long, thick as the sole of a bedroom slipper, the width of three fingers, and one end of which was cut about the length of a hand into five separate slices of equal size. It was the famous Scotch tawse, the renowned instrument thanks to which the mothers of Scotland maintained in religious rectitude generations of sons and daughters. The little heir to the house must have known it well, undoubtedly, for fearing to make unnecessarily too close acquaintance with it, he had disappeared, unannounced, into some unknown corner of the world where neither he nor his buttocks would share in the latest distribution.

"Thanks, Katherine," said Lady Manville, as she took hold of the instrument. "I knew very well you had need of one here. Don't you use it on Charlie?" That was the name of the little boy. Katherine smiled and looked in the direction of the two servant girls who blushed deeply and lowered their heads.

"It is not I who uses it," she said, "it is my husband. He thinks I would tire myself out too much, with them. . . ." Her finger designated the two maids who suddenly began to fidget and appeared unable to find a place for themselves.

Lady Manville and Lord and Lady Clawson burst into laughter.

"I understand your husband, Katherine," said Herbert.

"But what does it matter after all," added Lady Manville, "as long as these good principles are safeguarded?"

She swung the leather belt, caressing it as if it were a thing endowed with life. Lord Clawson pointed his finger in the direction of Lily's exposed seat which continued to shiver without respite.

"I can see that she has already received a whipping today."

"A whipping? Certainly, my dear friend! In the carriage! I took her across my knees and I spanked her thoroughly. . . . Oh, yes, with all my heart! But frankly, and in all sincerity, I prefer this!"

She raised the tawse. Everyone remained quiet, awaiting the execution of the punishment, and for some seconds, not a sound could be heard except the whistling of the wind outdoors and the raucous gasping of the girl. Suddenly the lash snapped like the crack of a circus-rider's whip and Lily shrieked. A large purple band designed itself on the fleshy hemispheres, then almost at once, another appeared beside it leaving its similar stigmata. So powerful was the swing of Lady Manville that no comparison was possible between the spanking Lily had received in the carriage and this whipping which her terrible mistress was now inflicting on her. At each blow the skin puffed up, and soon her entire seat appeared to be double its normal size, so much had it swollen and reddened.

Lily twisted like a serpent in the grip of her mistress. She cried lamentably, uttering acute shrieks and groans, and agitating her arms in all directions—her arms only, for her legs were tightly enlaced by the powerful right leg of Lady Manville. She received thus about twenty-five terrific lashes, then Lady Manville ceased, almost out of breath herself, so much energy had she put into the correction.

For a moment she allowed Lily to squirm, permitting herself and her friends, as well as Katherine, the luxury of watching the supple movements of the patient, overwhelmed by her infinite pain; then as these movements became slower, she pulled down the girl's shirt, lowered her skirt and put her down. Lily sank to her knees and concealed her face in her folded arms. In spite of her efforts to control herself, she continued to twist about. She felt the fires of hell under her skirt.

"Well, Lily?" demanded Lady Manville, "do you think you will still be as clumsy as you have been?"

"No . . . Milady . . . no . . . no!" sobbed Lily whose tears were scalding her cheeks.

"I hope this lesson will not be lost on you, eh! Come! Stop making these grimaces if you do not want me to start over again! Put your arms behind you and lift your head up!"

Lily obeyed, terrorized. She scarcely had the strength to hold it up. Hot tears ran down her face and her sobbing shook her whole body.

"Kiss the tawse!" commanded Lady Manville.

Lily lowered her eyes and posed her lips with an indescribable pout of disgust and shame on the horrible black leather strap.

"Well? Aren't you going to thank me? Didn't they teach you what to say after a whipping at the Training School?"

Lily, without lifting her eyes, made a terrible effort and spoke.

"Milady . . . I humbly beg your pardon . . . for the trouble I have put you to . . . in my behalf . . . and I thank you . . . with all my heart for . . . the good whipping . . . you have just given me . . . I hope it will teach me how to serve you better."

"Oh!" murmured Marjorie, enervated. "The formula is charming!"

"You really ought to go to the Training School, Marjorie, when you wish to select new maids," counselled Lady Manville.

"I was just going to say that," remarked Herbert, dreamily.

"Now, Lily," said Lady Manville, "go and rest yourself. You have been the cause of my tea becoming cold, stupid girl! I should really give you another whipping for that! But you will lose nothing by waiting! Go!"

Lily arose, staggering, and managed to make her way to the table where the coachman sat, impassably, sipping his Scotch whiskey.

"She is charming, that girl, really," said Herbert in a low voice, "and she will be still more charming after you have finished with her training."

"I hope so, indeed!" smiled the lady of Duncaster House.

Lord and Lady Clawson lived in an old dwelling not far from Lady Manville, who knew them for a number of years, and the latter had been in the habit of communicating to Lady Clawson her ideas on the good direction of a home and how to manage servants.

"We must go, dear," remarked Lady Marjorie, when they had finished their own tea. "How are you getting along now with your two other maids, Myra and Ellen?"

"Pretty well, thanks. Myra, at present, is just about what I desire, but Ellen doesn't quite satisfy me yet, and I am frequently obliged to treat her vigorously. But she is coming along slowly and showing a better disposition to learn, so I am being especially careful not to relax, particularly now that she is doing satisfactorily. And your Annie, how are you progressing with her?"

"Oh! she is far from being properly broken in and I have whipped her on several occasions recently."

"I should have broken her in a long time ago, but my wife insists on handling her in her own way, for some stubborn reason," remarked Lord Herbert.

Marjorie frowned. Lady Manville considered them both carefully and turned her magnetic eyes on Herbert who flushed lightly.

"Perhaps we can arrange all that. We shall speak of it again."

They shook hands and she directed herself majestically toward Lily after having bid good-bye to her friends. At her approach Lily stood up.

"But you have scarcely touched your tea!" exclaimed her mistress. "And your toast! Not even broken it! Why? Did I not command you to eat? What sort of stubborness is this, I ask?"

"If you please, Milady," . . . stuttered Lily, whose sobs were strangling her voice. . . . "I cannot eat . . . and scarcely drink. . . ."

"Oh, that is nothing but comedy!" affirmed Lady Manville. "You are going to drink and eat at once, understand, otherwise you can prepare your bottom again!"

Lily sat down and forced herself to drink the tea and eat the toast. During this time her mistress paid her bill to Katherine. When she returned to her maid, the latter had swallowed the last drop of her tea.

"It is a good thing for you that you have finished!" remarked the lady, tapping the girl lightly on the cheek. "If you had not I would be watching you turning up your skirt now, and I should have given you a fresh whipping before everybody here!"

Having pronounced these words in a high and clear tone, she directed herself toward the door and stopped.

"Well?" she said. "Why are you waiting? And the umbrella? . . . Pass before me!"

Katherine opened the door to let them proceed. Lily opened the umbrella and went out, then she held it over her mistress' head, while the latter carefully adjusted her skirts, revealing her beautiful legs severely encased in fine black silk stockings.

The lady made herself comfortable in the carriage, arranged her skirts and made a sign to Lily to sit op-

posite her. She waved a final good-bye to the inn-
keeper and closed the carriage-door. The horses started
off at once.

The snow had not ceased. During their stop, Katherine had put fresh hot water into the hot-water bottle
which Joe had carefully placed for his mistress' feet.
Lily was commanded to put her own feet between her
mistress' legs.

"You have made me frightfully ashamed of you,"
began Lady Manville. "To oblige me to whip you in
public! In a public inn! . . . Have you any conception
of how ridiculous that made you appear? Now all these
people will be able to furnish the full details of a whipping you should have endeavored to conceal at all costs,
if you had the least bit of modesty! I shall recall this
humiliation to you often, my girl, I promise you! You
stupid and clumsy thing! . . ."

She ceased for a moment, playing with Lily's confusion and tears, then she resumed:

"I am very angry with you, and you may expect a
good solid whipping when we reach home! You miserable slave! . . . I do not know what should retain me
from whipping your right here, at my ease, now that
we two are back in the carriage! Eh? What do you
think of the idea? Wouldn't it be just as well to begin
this minute? . . . Silence is consent, my girl! Turn up
your skirt!"

Lily remained stunned for a moment, then an enormous sob rose in her breast and she burst into fresh
tears.

Already her suffering seemed to have increased, especially because of the bumping of the carriage over all
the ditches and stones in the road, so badly had the

wicked tawse inflamed her seat. What would it be like
when Lady Manville would begin whipping it again?
And what an existence she foresaw for herself in those
moments when the succession of rapid and brutal emotions permitted her to reflect on it! Scarcely two hours
that she was with her new mistress, and here she was,
already, about to receive her third whipping! She felt
horribly broken, her spirits crushed in body and soul.

"Milady! Please have pity on me!" she groaned. "I
have suffered so much already! Please permit me to
rest a little while. I shall obey you in everything,
Milady! I shall be so submissive! oh! so submissive!"

"And to prove that you are, you argue with your
mistress," snapped Lady Manville. "Come! Quickly!
Raise your skirt and extend yourself over my knees to
receive your next dose."

Lily closed her eyes. It was the only way she could
isolate herself, relatively, and she profited by it. Tight-
ening her teeth, suppressing her sobs, she reached for the
ends of her skirt and pulled it above her loins, then
she rose and stretched herself across her lady's knees.

"Now beg a good whipping, girl!" she demanded.

"Please, Milady, I beg you . . . to give me a . . . good
. . . whipping."

"You shall have it! But I want you to promise before
I begin that you will remain in proper position so that
I can get at you without trouble. Do you promise?"

"Yes . . . Milady . . . I promise. . . ."

Once again she felt on her loins the grip of Lady
Manville's left arm, and on her calves the humiliating
warmth of her mistress' right leg; she heard the preliminary sighs that preceded the energetic action to come,
and all her flesh trembled suddenly under the pride-

crushing hail of slaps applied with all her lady's strength. Like in the previous corrections, she twisted like a worm, hoping vainly to escape the infernal smarting, but Lady Manville held her firmly. She counted on a short whipping, one that wouldn't last longer than that she received with the tawse, but her mistress did not stop. It was frightfully long, and when Lady Manville ceased, Lily felt as though her skin was in tatters and she could barely breathe. Her tormentor waited a moment and then pulled her up.

"Come!" she said. "Cease this whining and embrace me! I have no doubt you haven't sense enough to understand how much good I am doing you!"

She rested her mouth on the girl's cheeks down which tears were trickling, and waited for her kiss which Lily tried to make gentle, but which revolted her as though it were an indecent contact. Then her mistress pointed to the opposite bench.

"Sit down over there and do not budge!" she ordered. ... "What are you doing? Are you trying to pull down your skirt? No, no, Lily! I do not permit that! You must sit on your bare skin, girl, and on nothing else!"

XII

Duncaster House

ONE hour and a half passed thus while Lily ate herself up with chagrin. Sitting as she was, her pain gave her no respite, while the carriage bumped along, adding to the irritation she would normally have had anyway from the tenderness of her seat. Besides, the humiliation of sitting like this and her mistress staring at her, was burning into her heart.

After a while, Lady Manville reached toward the window and wiped away some of the frost. Lily noticed great black rocks against which a furious sea was beating, with waves rising to formidable heights. At this spot the road turned toward the south and at a little distance there appeared a spacious, sprawling mansion, and presently the carriage stopped before it. At the entrance before which they stopped, she noticed a great iron grilled door which the heavy mists had rusted.

The door opened and a boy of about fifteen stood before it, under a great umbrella that he had all he could do to control. Joe opened the door and the boy advanced.

"Come nearer, boy," said Lady Manville in a stern voice.

The lad obeyed. He had a piteous air which he tried to conceal behind a forced smile. He trembled all over and Lily thought it must be as much from fear as from the cold.

Lady Manville walked swiftly into the vast room, followed by Lily whose feet were covered with snow. An exceedingly tall man wearing a multi-colored Scotch kilt which came only to his bare knees, made a deep bow before his lady.

"Anything new, Collins?" asked the mistress.

"Nothing, my Lady, everything is all right."

Lily followed her mistress through a large hall, in the center of which was a wide staircase leading to many large rooms and to Lady Manville's boudoir which offered a splendid view of the sea. It was her favorite room.

In the hall a tall, dark woman of dour aspect and hard, austere features received her mistress with a display of eagerness.

"What terrible weather, Milady! Oh! I hope you haven't caught cold? This snow. . . ."

"Thanks, Larkins, I am very well, quite well. This is my new maid. . . ."

Mrs. Larkins, the housekeeper, fixed her glasses, which hung from her neck on a black silk band, to her nose and carefully inspected the girl for some time without saying a word. Then she looked up at Lady Manville.

"Good impression, Larkins? . . ."

The housekeeper shrugged her shoulders. She did not know yet. She put her finger to her jaw.

"Stubborn!" she remarked, now running a finger over her forehead. She was a physiognomist. In fact, Lily did possess characteristics of willfulness, but of a gentle willfulness, however.

"I know it," said Lady Manville. "She has already given me proof of it, and I have given her proof, also, of a sample of my severity!"

"Really!" replied Mrs. Larkins. "You chastised her in the carriage?"

"Both in the carriage and at Katherine's inn . . . Lily, take off your cloak. Lift up your skirt and show Mrs. Larkins how I corrected you!"

Lily once again felt she was about to die. That was how her torture was going to continue. It would continue all the time she remained at Duncaster House, all her life, perhaps! All her life! . . . But that wouldn't be long. She would have to die soon under such a regime. She was certain of it! . . . These reflections crossed her brain with the speed of lightning, but she could not make up her mind so quickly about accepting this fresh humiliation. She joined her hands in supplication, waiting, hoping, against all reason, for Lady Manville to rescind the order she had given her. But her mistress never went back on an order. Surprised at the girl's hesitation, a hesitation she was far from expecting, Lady Manville frowned and moved toward the girl, seized her firmly by the left wrist and began twisting it in her hand.

"Don't you understand me, Lily?" she asked in a voice trembling with repressed fury.

"Yes . . . Oh! Milady . . . Please don't harm me! . . ."

The girl was deathly pale and quaking with fear.

"You heard me and you understood me, yet you do not obey?" insisted Lady Manville.

"Please forgive me!"

Lady Manville, without saying another word, turned the girl's left palm up, and dug the nails of her thumb and index finger into Lily's flesh. The girl uttered a horrified cry and tried to disengage herself, but Lady Manville held her wrist in such a way that the wrist bone would have been easily broken had she struggled more. Lily fell to her knees, weeping.

"Oh!" she groaned. "This is too much! I am suffering too much! Kill me, I want to die! . . ."

"What insolence!" the lady exclaimed. "I am going to teach you to talk to me in that manner! Larkins! Get me my riding-whip, down there near the fireplace!"

The housekeeper hurried to obey and Lady Manville took the whip and lashed her a half-dozen times on the shoulders and arms. The unfortunate girl started to roll away, in order to evade as much as possible the contact of this biting whip. Lady Manville pursued her, forced her flat on her stomach and rested her knee in the hollow of Lily's back. The girl's beautifully turned calves excited the lady's attention and she proceeded to crack her across her legs with another five or six well-directed blows. . . . Soon, Lily was at the end of her breath and strength. Her arms folded themselves around her head and she yielded, allowing her mistress to do as she liked. The latter continued to strike wildly in all directions, and with each lash came a raucous groan which sounded like that of a soul in agony.

Despite her customary impassable nature and the complacency with which she witnessed similar spectacles, Mrs. Larkins began to feel frightened. Was Lady Manville really going to kill the girl? The noble lady seemed to have actually gone mad. . . .

Lady Manville calmed herself, however, as though a gleam of reason had suddenly traversed her brain, until then suffused by her temper.

"Get up!"

Lily dared to look around and seeing her mistress calmer, took breath again. She suffered horribly in all

"I can see that she has already received a whipping today" (page 129)

her body, lacerated, broken. Brief sobs shook her and she was as feeble as an infant. She straightened herself, however, with the greatest pain, leaning against a chair for support, and she looked up at her mistress.

"Well?" said Lady Manville. "Why are you waiting to execute the order I gave you?"

Lily heaved an enormous sigh and obeyed. She lifted up her skirt and held it to her waist. The absence of drawers or bloomers facilitated the task. Mrs. Larkins was soon able to contemplate the colors and welts on this flesh which seemed to have been created expressly for caresses and which, in the last six months, had subsisted on nothing but injuries and suffering.

Next to Lady Manville, Mrs. Larkins was from a good school; she also understood the girl's confusion which she took pleasure in prolonging, making her examination of the object presented to her as detailed as possible. At last she raised her head, readjusted her glasses, and spoke her simple mind.

"She has been very well whipped," she declared.

"I think so," agreed Lady Manville with becoming modesty, "but she will be frequently repeating these experiences if she does not modify her ways!"

As she spoke she looked so threateningly at Lily that the girl felt new shivers running up and down her spine.

"Now," added the lady, "cover it up, Lily, and be carefully on your guard against defying me again, for if you do you will smart for it. Follow me to my room."

She started and Lily followed. Her chamber was on the first floor. She motioned Lily in and the girl found herself in a spacious and richly furnished boudoir. Lady Manville walked directly behind her and sank into a deep armchair.

"Here we are at last, Lily," said Lady Manville, uttering a sigh of satisfaction. Her anger appeared to have vanished completely and she spoke quietly, as if the events of the day had never happened. After resting a few minutes, while the girl stood anxiously by, wondering what would happen next, she rose and walked into an adjoining room. Presently she returned, divested of her former outer garments and clothed instead in a toilette of sombre gray which molded her powerful form with detailed precision. She sat down once more and crossed her legs. She shook her loose leg in the direction of the girl.

"Here! Begin your service. Take off my shoes, and be especially careful!"

Lily kneeled and pulled very gently on the slipper which came off with difficulty but without too much effort. Lady Manville presented the other foot and Lily began the same task, but this time her mistress made a grimace.

"I must warn you, Lily, that on this side I have a corn which gives me a great deal of trouble. Pull it off very cautiously, mind."

Lily was seized with a new anguish. She tried to pull the slipper off but she could not and Lady Manville uttered a little cry and pulled her foot sharply away.

"Oh! you clumsy girl!" she said. "You did that purposely! I warned you, however! Put your head forward!"

"Oh! Milady!" Lily wailed, her face turning livid.

"Come here to me! Otherwise!"

Lily obeyed. Lady Manville seized a lock of the girl's hair and pulled it slowly, more and more forward.

"You cry!" she said. "You find that insupportable!

144

Nevertheless you cause me unnecessary pain, don't you? Are you going to take greater precautions? Answer me! Answer me!"

"Oh, yes . . . oh! Milady! . . . oh! yes! . . . pity!"

"Fool! I ought to tear every hair out of your head, one by one, and I do not know what keeps me from doing it. . . . Since you are going to be my personal maid from now on, I shall train you to perform satisfactory service, my dear! And when you show the first sign of clumsiness, you shall smart for it, I tell you! . . ."

Lily did not dare make a move and supported her pain with eyes closed, face pale and big tears rolling down her cheeks. Lady Manville released her at last, and once more extended her foot, with which the girl took infinite precautions.

"Much better, you see! . . . Now kiss my foot as humbly as you know how! Show me that it is beginning to penetrate into your dull head that you are only my slave! For you know you are nothing but a slave, don't you?"

"Yes . . . Milady."

"Yes what?" and she leaned forward angrily. "What did I tell you about being more precise in your answers? Am I to understand that you are begging for another whipping?"

"Oh! no! Milady! . . . Yes, Milady! I am your . . . slave!"

"Well, I am not yet sure that you believe it in your heart, and until I do feel every doubt removed, your days and nights are not going to be very pleasant for you, my girl! But we shall take that subject up frequently again, remember!"

The troublesome shoe off and the kiss humbly im-

145

printed, Lily began to breathe easier. She then shod her mistress' feet in bedroom slippers, and on her order, started to unclasp a gold choker that ornamented the lady's well-molded neck. Some stray hairs were hanging loosely at the nape, and while the girl was struggling with the tight clasp, Lady Manville turned furiously, pulled her around and slapped her face.

"You are pulling my hair!" she exclaimed.

"It wasn't my fault, Milady," moaned the girl. "They were caught. . . ."

"A fine excuse! It wasn't your fault!" mocked the lady. "Clumsy thing! Give me your hand!"

"Milady! . . ."

"Are you hesitating still?"

"No . . . Milady. . . ."

"We shall see about that later. . . . There now. Here is your nice, soft little hand, your clumsy little hand. . . . It needs chastising too!"

On her dressing-table near which she was sitting, lay a little whalebone, about a foot long, out of some corset, no doubt. Lady Manville grasped it and rudely struck the little shrinking hand about a dozen times, holding it up in the air and gripping the girl's wrist tightly.

"Give me the other one, now!"

Lily paused but only for a second. She extended the hand and on the cushions at the base of her fingers her cruel mistress applied an equal amount of blows.

"There now," she said, replacing the whalebone on the dresser, "that is one way of training clumsy little hands to become more experienced. . . . Finish what you are doing."

Lily returned to her task. Her hands were very red and trembled a great deal.

She was able, however, to unhook the choker without any further trouble, then she handed her mistress a commodious velvet peignoir.

"Remain here," said Lady Manville. "Put all these things away and remember where you put them. I shall see if everything is in order when I come back."

She was away about twenty minutes and when she returned, she found Lily standing by the window, looking upon the raging sea and the hillside covered with snow. The girl had been crying.

"What are you thinking about and what are you doing there?" demanded Lady Manville. "You have been crying? Why?"

Her tone was hard, aggressive. And Lily had such poignant chagrin! Fresh tears welled in her eyes, but she held them back and remained still.

"Will you answer me?" reiterated the lady, raising her hand. "When, oh when, will you come to understand that you must instantly obey every one of my injunctions, and that I must not be kept waiting, even for a second, when I question you?"

Lily, frightened, yielded under the menace and stammered:

"I . . . I had no reason . . . Milady. . . ."

"Really! Then you were doing that just to displease me? I like cheerful faces in my house, I told you that earlier. Why don't you sing when you are alone? Myra and Ellen, to whom I shall introduce you soon, sing all the time, and I shall expect the same from you. Come now, don't stand around with the air of a beaten dog!"

At this moment, through the corridor, could be heard the voice of a young girl.

"Listen!" said her mistress. "That is Myra, to be sure.

You see how they sing when they are not in my presence?
Do you understand how happy they are? That is precisely the mood you will always be in when, like them, you
come to understand how much good we are doing you."

She walked to the door, opened it and called the maid.

XIII

Myra and Ellen

A young girl, about twenty-two years old, came hurrying in. She was tall, solidly built, blonde, and had large, gentle blue eyes which immediately attracted Lily's notice. A smile on the girl's face disclosed ivory teeth, perfectly set. She advanced quickly toward Lady Manville who had seated herself in a chair near the center of the room. The girl took no notice of Lily, although she could not help seeing her.

She knelt promptly before her mistress whose hand she took, then she put it to her lips and appeared to kiss it with marked devotion.

"Oh! Milady! I was so glad to hear you have returned to us!"

Lady Manville remained impassable, smiling no recognition, and looking somewhat coldly at the kneeling girl.

"Well, I haven't been away very long, only since yesterday."

"Yes, Milady, but I missed you just the same," replied the girl softly.

"Indeed! But Larkins gave you and Ellen your five o'clock whippings yesterday afternoon, didn't she, and I whipped you both myself in the morning before I left?"

"Yes, thank you, Milady."

"She didn't whip you this morning, did she?"

"No, Milady. We reported to Mrs. Larkins for the

149

eleven o'clock whippings, but she said she expected you back soon, Milady, and that you might prefer that our whippings wait for you."

"Yes, that was the proper thing to do. Occasionally Larkins shows some intelligence. Did she whip both of you well yesterday?"

"Yes, thank you, Milady."

"Has the tenderness subsided with you as yet?"

"Not entirely, Milady."

"Then if you still feel it, why did you miss me, unless you wanted a supplementary whipping last night from me, did you crave for that?"

"Not exactly, please Milady, but. . . ."

"But what, slave, speak up!" Lady Manville was becoming impatient.

"Please, Milady, we prefer to be whipped by you . . . or, at least, in your presence, Milady."

"Oh! that is silly! What difference can it make who is present, as long as the routine of discipline isn't neglected? Besides, my girl, are you aware that you have just expressed a preference, that you said you *prefer* this to that?"

"Oh! . . . I have blundered, Milady! . . . I know that word is forbidden, and I have no right to use it. . . . I deserve to be punished. . . . If you would be good enough to whip me for it, Milady, you might permit me to beg your pardon afterward for my offense."

"I should think you ought to be whipped! Seems to me you have had a few lessons before on the choice of your language."

"Yes, thank you, Milady. . . . May I receive it now, Milady?"

"Yes, now!"

"Thank you, Milady. What instrument does it please Milady to use?"

"Get me that whalebone on my dresser," commanded her mistress.

Myra rose quickly, brought it back, knelt again, put her lips to the formidable instrument, kissed it distinctly, and handed it up to her lady.

"Please, Milady, what position do you wish me to take for my whipping?"

"Bend over this armchair," directed her mistress.

"Thank you, Milady," responded the girl. She bowed very low, backed away, and immediately began to unhook her skirt which she folded carefully and deposited on a nearby chair. Lily noticed that she wore bloomers which fitted her lower body like a pair of fine silk tights, and that they molded and set off in high relief the generous contours of her buttocks and thighs. Myra stooped over and carefully removed these bloomers, which were made of glistening white satin, clinging so tightly that they had to be removed with the utmost precautions. One can well imagine what the consequences might have been had the bloomers been damaged in the process of taking off. Not a tear did the girl shed, on the contrary, a fresh although forced smile reappeared on her lips. She then raised her shirt above her loins and held both sides to her body with her hands. Lily could see the marvelous and elegantly designed slope of her loins and the rest of her lower body down to her knees. Old marks of a whip were still plainly visible, disclosing stripes here and there. Myra extended herself face down over the low armchair, and in the expectation of what was to come, her flesh began to quiver.

Lily was stupefied with amazement. She thought of

151

the amount of punishment that must have been inflicted
on Myra to have brought her to such an unparalleled
state of subjection, to such absolute groveling, one might
say, and she experienced an insurmountable horror at
the thought that the day might come when as a result of
similar physical and moral discipline as that to which
Myra must have been subjected, she, in her turn would
also be smiling her gratitude at the imposition of these
frightful humiliations; and that she would lick gratefully
the hand which would whip and curb her to this iron
discipline.

"Oh!" she groaned to herself, "I prefer to die!"

Meanwhile Lady Manville advanced with a calculating
slowness and took up her position at Myra's left. As
though by accident, she grazed the nudities of the young
girl with the end of her whalebone, and she noted the
great shivering which, at this contact, animated her *subject*. Then she turned to Lily and called her attention to
the denuded girl.

"You see, Lily," she said at last, "how we obtain perfect submission here? Myra knows she has made an
error and it is with joy and gratitude that she values the
opportunity I am giving her of expiating it. Isn't that
true, Myra?"

"Yes, Milady," the girl promptly answered.

Without another word, Lady Manville began to inflict
the whipping. It was brief and severe. Impartially applied on each of the exposed cheeks, the lashes soon
began to transform lilies into roses, as our forefathers
would say in their ornate manner.

Myra did not remain insensible to what was taking
place. She squirmed and fidgeted, but except for an inch
or two, did not move away from the position designated,

and even that little ground she hastily recovered each time. When the lashes became more brutal she uttered little groans, but never raised her voice.

Lady Manville ceased finally and walked around to where the girl's face lay to take note of the expression appearing on her chastised slave. Her mistress perceived that although hot tears ran down the girl's cheeks, her lips were opened in a brave smile, disclosing again her beautiful ivory teeth. Lady Manville addressed the whipped girl:

"I am glad to see, Myra, that the whipping you have just received makes you happy, and that you realize how good it is for you!"

The fustigated young girl, suppressing a sob, responded:

"Oh, yes, thank you, Milady!"

"On second thought, perhaps I ought to give you a little more! You will not be whipped again until tonight and I ought to make sure the lesson carries over. That will make it more effective, don't you think?"

"Yes, Milady, thank you. It is very good of you to take so much trouble with me."

The lady resumed whipping the prostrate girl and continued for a long time. In reality it was not terribly severe and the girl took it with an experienced stoicism, but the humiliating conversations, preparations, ceremonies, and the act itself all served to make a particular picture which suited Lady Manville's object. For indeed, it was principally intended to convey to Lily the type of submission that would be demanded of her, too. In good time, she stopped whipping Myra and ordered her to get up and resume her clothes. This Myra did, after which she knelt before her mistress, kissed her hand in what

153

seemed a transport of appreciation, smiled as much as she could under the circumstances, and murmured:

"Dear Mistress, I am deeply grateful for the correction you were good enough to bestow on me. I have thoroughly deserved the whipping you have just given me and I pray you will not become indifferent to the need for correcting me whenever I offend, and to whip me soundly each time in the hope that the day will come when I will serve you perfectly, Milady."

These words stumbled slightly in the utterance because the girl could not refrain from twitching as she knelt, but Lady Manville had not dictated a single word of it, and for Lily it was quite clear that Myra was truly *well-broken in!*

The chastised girl stood up and awaited her mistress' next word.

"What is Ellen doing now, Myra?" suddenly asked Lady Manville, while Lily was still trying to put a little order in her thoughts.

Myra started slightly but quickly recovered and responded:

"She must be in her room, Milady . . . she had some sewing to do. . . . If you please, I shall go look for her. . . ."

"You are going to stay right here!" said Lady Manville. "I shall take care of that myself. Doesn't she know I have returned?"

"I . . . I was going to tell her, Milady, when you called me."

"Oh, very well. But you remain here. Lily, you will tell me when I return if Myra has been good and has not chattered."

"Yes, Milady," spluttered Lily.

Their mistress went out and Lily found herself greatly embarrassed before Myra.

"You have been here a long time, miss?" asked Lily in a low voice, after an oppressive silence which she endeavored to break. She called her "miss," persuaded that Myra was a young girl of good stock who had been reduced to this abject servility as a result of an adventure resembling her own, perhaps.

Myra stared through the window, not even turning her eyes in response. For a moment Lily was annoyed, but on second thought she understood the docility and perfect obedience which was part of Myra's character and how disobedience on the latter's part was unthinkable. Lily, therefore, desisted, and the ugly silence resumed. But it did not last long.

In the corridor angry words could be heard, then the door opened violently and a young girl of about eighteen was precipitated into the room. Immediately behind her was Lady Manville. This girl was undoubtedly Ellen. She was of medium height, firmly filled out in the proper places, quite pretty, and particularly attractive because of a shock of gloriously red hair. She appeared more flurried than frightened and she rubbed her eyes energetically, although there appeared no sign of tears in them.

"Ah! this is too much!" exclaimed the lady, folding and unfolding her hands. "What! You dare to lie down and sleep during the day with all the work you have to do? You were sleeping, weren't you?"

Ellen looked up terrorized, incapable of uttering a word. Her angry mistress turned toward Myra.

"And you, you deceitful thing! You are her accomplice! You knew she was asleep, and having learned of

155

my return you were on your way to warn her when I called you! You shall both smart for this, both of you! Myra, you will come to me before dinner and remind me to give you another whipping for this, and if I am too tired later in the evening, Mrs. Larkins will give you your usual whipping before bedtime instead."

"Very well, thank you, Milady," Myra answered, bowing low.

"Ellen," she turned to the other, "bring me the riding-whip!"

The young girl paled at the order, but uttered not a sound.

Lady Manville extended her arm and indicated a corner near a window. There, hanging from a hook near a tapestry was a ladies riding-whip with a gold handle. It was a flexible switch covered with fine twisted cord, with a knotted silk tip, and its cutting effect appeared to be quite terrible. Lily remarked that the thin end of the whip was colored here and there with a somber red, but for the moment gave no thought to the significance of this color. Meanwhile Ellen walked toward the instrument, took it off its hook and brought it to her mistress.

The girl was dressed in a white peignoir of silk and wool, held together at the waist by a cord of the same material. Lady Manville ordered her to remove it at once. Ellen obeyed, laid the gown carefully over a chair and stood revealed in shirt and exceedingly tight bloomers which accentuated the solidity and curves of her lower body. She proceeded to remove the bloomers carefully, and at a sign from her mistress she extended herself full length on the carpet, face down, and tucked her shirt around her breast. Ellen was unable to smile as Myra did, and one could see she was obeying each order from her mistress out of pure fear and under the menace of the threatening whip.

As soon as she had stretched out, Lady Manville pulled the girl's arms around on her back and tied them together with a handkerchief. Then she put her foot on Ellen's neck, obliging her to kiss the carpet, and she commenced to fustigate her with violence, preventing her from moving away by the pressure of her foot, striking her at every point, so that the lashes fell irregularly from the beginning of her haunches, over her buttocks and down to the lower part of her thighs. Lady Manville slashed away heartlessly, and the tip of the lash flicked steadily with resounding snaps at the girl's flesh. From time to time one of her hips would turn upward—a movement she was unable to control—and the point of the whip would snap against her abdomen, her navel, or her inner thighs, causing her to shoot her legs frantically forward and extend her body flat against the carpet once more. . . .

When the skin became swollen and livid welts crossed and recrossed in all directions, her mistress finally ceased. The groans of the girl had subsided and it seemed as though she were about to faint.

"Ah!" exclaimed Lady Manville when she had recovered her breath, "I shall teach you to sleep during the day because you think I am absent. This ought to keep you awake for awhile now, you ungrateful slave. Get up! Report to the kitchen and put on the clothes of a kitchen scullion. Until tomorrow evening you will work under the cook's orders. and I shall order her to whip you again tonight and give you your regular two whippings tomorrow."

Ellen, who had already arisen, threw herself at her

mistress's feet, kissing them feverishly in her anguish, imploring her permission to remain at her side, begging piteously not to be consigned to the cook for her whippings—too repugnant and degrading a humiliation even for her, but Lady Manville was inflexible. The girl bowed herself out shedding warm tears, and moved away to the place where she must undergo her next punishments.

XIV

A Visit

THE following morning Lily commenced her duties, and for the next few days a series of uninterrupted complaints, insults, sarcasms, slaps, whippings and humiliations of all sorts rained down on her. She had not a single moment of leisure.

At six in the morning Lady Manville, who slept little, rang for her. Tearing herself out of her sleep, Lily proceeded rapidly to make herself presentable, so that she had to anticipate the bell by at least a quarter of an hour, which was all the time her mistress allowed her. She had to be properly costumed in the least detail, for Lady Manville examined the girl from head to foot, and she exhibited an extreme rigidity, always ready to punish for the least negligence.

Dressed in a tight-fitting waist of black silk cut low in front, a short black skirt of the same material, bloomers so tight that it was all she could do to crowd her flesh into them, bare arms from her shoulders down, her hair carefully done up to completely uncover the neck, Lily had to report the instant the bell rang, without the loss of a second, in her mistress' room. At her bedside she must fall on her knees, kiss the white hand which hung indolently over the edge of the bed, greet her mistress cheerily and aid her to sit up. Then she had to submit to an examination of her person.

Lady Manville took extreme pleasure in this examination, prolonging it to unnecessary lengths. She invariably found something to criticize, perhaps pulling her hair which she found not arranged to suit her taste, or slapping her for some other paltry reason, provoking tears to her eyes which, considering how much crying they had done, now poured down less frequently.

Her face, breasts, body, arms, legs, were all examined in detail. Lady Manville spared her nothing, being certain to find, without any difficulty whatever, some reason for chastising her maid. Often Lily left her mistress' presence, her head aching, her cheeks on fire, her hands swollen from an application of a highly polished wooden ruler kept handily nearby. Rarely, too, did the examination finish without a solid spanking which, according to her mistress, prepared her seat for more serious corrections to follow later. And for these corrections she was not kept waiting long. Lily, having aided her mistress to rise, attired her carefully in the necessary vestments. This again was the occasion for reproaches on her awkwardness and hard blows rained down on the girl. But the thing she most dreaded was dressing her lady's hair.

While performing this duty Lady Manville kept by her dressing-table a martinet the handle of which was covered in velvet. The thongs of this martinet were frequently plunged in a greasy mixture which toughened them and at the same time conserved their suppleness. But a few minutes would pass in the hair-dressing process before Lily would find herself executing an order to bend over conveniently near, lift her skirt and lower her bloomers, while her mistress lashed her with a dozen or more well directed blows across her buttocks. Then she had to rise and continue with her lady's hair, after humbly thanking her for the correction. And to continue without making any further mistake was now more difficult because the girl could not help writhing inwardly and outwardly from the effect produced by the burning martinet.

After she had managed her bath, rubbed her down and dressed her, Lily had to serve breakfast to her mistress. This breakfast, if it satisfied her appetite, did not satisfy her desire for cruelty. She found no end of pretexts to humiliate and whip her poor suffering maid.

For example, she liked to watch her dejected and heart-sick lady's maid prepare herself for the corporal chastisements she would impose, and frequently, when she saw her pretty servant undressed and ready, she would order her to kneel down in some corner of the room. In this position, her hands at her back, with one clasped over the wrist of the other, the girl had to await the pleasure of her mistress who might leave her for an hour at a time before inflicting the punishment promised. One can imagine the mental agony of the poor girl during this long hour, her lacerated heart gripped with anguish and mortification, fearing her mistress' approach one minute and the next hoping for it that her ordeal might be over. After an hour her knees felt paralyzed, but she dared make no movement, knowing that her mistress watched her unceasingly, although she might be reading or pretending to read some paper. But what was most painful to her was to remain in that position and condition, exposing to other eyes a part of herself which, despite all the whippings she had received this past half-year, she was still unable to think of without blushing.

Two weeks passed thus. The little sleep that she had left her in a state of semi-somnolence, almost dulling her intellectual and physical faculties. She went to bed after eleven o'clock and had to rise before six, which left her certainly little enough time to rest and recuperate from the arduous preceding day, always packed with so many disturbing emotions and fatiguing duties. She leaned more and more to the idea of suicide, convincing herself it would be better if she were dead, and she thought of means she might take to terminate an existence which was fast becoming insufferably beyond hope. Sometimes she stood in contemplation of the angry waves which beat against the shore, the view of which was clear from her lady's chamber; and she would become so absorbed in her thoughts that she would fail to hear her mistress approach, until resounding slaps or a cruel pinch would recall her violently to the realities.

Two weeks passed, we said, when one afternoon the doorbell rang loudly and the boy, William, who sometimes filled in as porter, came rushing breathlessly into Lady Manville's presence to announce that Lord and Lady Clawson accompanied by their maid, Annie, were waiting below. The boy's failure to knock respectfully did not go unnoticed, to be sure.

His mistress was just finishing a thrashing she had been giving to her personal maid, Lily, when the boy burst in. As young William, not forewarned, opened his eyes, he saw the tear-stained face of the girl in the process of robing herself—an added irritation she would have been content to postpone, in these instances, because of her intense pain. Lady Manville beckoned the boy to come near her, after he had made his announcement, and

162

taking hold of him by the shoulder she slapped him violently twice, once across each cheek.

"This is an advance payment, master William, for rushing in like this, you unmannerly little pig! Go down to Mrs. Larkins at once and tell her I want her to give you a sound flogging. Be sure to tell her that I want it thoroughly done and that I wish to inspect the result immediately after she has finished. You will find me with my guests and I shall examine you before them! Remember, if I am not satisfied with the manner in which you have delivered my instructions to Mrs. Larkins, I shall flog you all over again when you report, in such a manner that you will not be able to sit down for two weeks! Get out!" and she descended hastily, leaving Lily alone.

The young girl squirmed uneasily, for she had never forgotten the scene at the inn, and all the witnesses present were vividly graven in her memory. She thought, very justly, that if Lady Marjorie had brought Annie along, it was certainly not with the intention of presenting her with a bag of toasted almonds. Her curiosity, stronger than her fear, caused her to notice that the door of the room she was in was not locked. With infinite precautions she opened it, found herself in the deserted corridor, and proceeded to feel her way stealthily down the heavily carpeted stairs. Her heart beat terrifically against her breast, she could scarcely breathe, still she descended. Once down, she hid behind a heavy tapestry in the folds of which she enveloped herself. After a moment or two, her heart thumping louder than ever, she hazarded a look beyond the tapestry: Lord and Lady Clawson were sitting in comfortable armchairs opposite Lady Manville. Standing in their midst was a graceful young girl, pretty in spite of the plain servant's uniform which indicated that she was Lady Marjorie's maid. She was quite tall and her abundant hair was of a beautiful auburn tint. The girl kept her head lowered, twisting nervously one of the buttons of her waist. No doubt at this moment she would have preferred to find herself leagues from Duncaster House! . . . But she had no choice.

Playing with her rings, Lady Marjorie talked, and what she was saying did not constitute any praise of her maid, judging from the anguished blushing of the latter. Pressing forward a little, Lily managed to hear the conversation.

"Yes, my dear," declared the young lady, "Annie has a stubborn nature and is an unsatisfactory servant. Each day I have to go over the same things with her. I have tried reproaches but they avail nothing, and following your advice I have been whipping her quite frequently. . . ."

Here Annie's blushes became more intense and a light twitching of her hips conveyed more than any other gesture the young girl's embarrassment and confusion.

"Day before yesterday," continued her mistress, "I had her whipped by my cook who handled her just as one would a seven or eight year old child."

"And that was ineffective, too?" questioned Lady Manville softly with a quiet and knowing smile.

"Quite!" answered the pretty visitor.

"Well, it only proves," and her voice took on a still gentler inflection, "that she was not whipped vigorously enough!"

"No doubt about it," concurred Lord Herbert.

"Not everyone is able to judge what constitutes a

164

sufficient amount of correction," responded their hostess. "And there is the question of skill, if I may use that expression, which can only come after a long practice. My suggestion is that you make every effort to develop it as quickly as you can. You have your girl, Annie, right under your hand and she offers a fine field—I use the word in its fullest meaning—for your practice. Her frame is amply padded in the proper places and I think she could undergo with the greatest benefit to you and herself a vigorous routine of corporal chastisement. She should be flogged at least twice a day for the general purpose of being fitted into a methodical whipping routine. And these should be given without prejudice to the other whippings she should receive for the mistakes she makes from day to day. These girls are all dolts, my dear, and if one wishes to arrive anywhere with them their bottoms must be kept in an almost constant state of tenderness. Nothing is so salutary for them as a whipping effectively applied and the only way messages may be communicated to their brains is by lashing them frequently on the fleshiest parts of their body which they used to think was only meant to sit on!"

"How true!" murmured Lady Marjorie. "I am afraid we have been much too lenient."

"I've been telling you that all the time," added Lord Herbert, peevishly.

The subject of this encouraging conversation must have felt herself dying. She fidgeted in every direction, and her hands could scarcely find a place for themselves. So nervous was she indeed that Lady Marjorie noticed it and turned toward her.

"Stop your twisting and fidgeting, you stupid girl!" her mistress exclaimed angrily. "Wait until we get home and you will have good cause for squirming!" With that she rose.

"Thank you, my dear friend," she said to Lady Manville, shaking her hand cordially. "I hope to bring her over here in a month or so, and you must tell me whether you see any improvement in her. We must be going now. Come, Herbert."

They were all about to depart when there was a faint noise at one of the doors leading into the room where the guests had assembled. At the same moment the door at which they were gazing opened softly and young William came walking in, haltingly. His eyes were red from crying and he breathed heavily as he walked painfully forward, his face down on his chest. He had noticed the guests and although he had expected to find them there, he seemed stunned at the realization of the inevitable consequences his entrance was bound to develop.

Lady Manville looked up and smiled sardonically.

"Oh! it is you, William!" she said, cheerily. "I had forgotten that I ordered you to report after your whipping. Has Mrs. Larkins flogged you as I said she should?"

"Yes . . . Milady. . . ."

"Come here, then, and show us what she has accomplished! Take your trousers down! Hurry!"

The young lad, evidently well acquainted with the necessity for immediate obedience, began to execute the order, trying at the same time to restrain his tears which he knew would only irritate his mistress. In less than a minute he stood before this audience, exposing his nudity. The boy, although not yet fifteen, was very tall for his age, typical of the Scotch males. Although grow-

The tawse descended rapidly, leaving an ugly dark and red mark each time to denote its unwelcome visit (page 170)

ing apace he did not exhibit the usual characteristics of adolescents who thin out as a rule in the process of growing. As a matter of fact, he was built staunchly, an attribute which undoubtedly influenced his mistress when she selected him.

Lady Manville ordered him gruffly to lean forward and every one could see that his posterior was covered with freshly made welts. His muscles still quivered indicating that the reverberations of the whipping had not yet entirely sudsided.

"Put your head up and look at me!" his mistress commanded. "What did Larkins whip you with?"

"The tawse . . . Milady. . . ."

"Good! And did you tell her that I wanted you whipped soundly?"

"Yes . . . Milady. . . ."

"We shall see! Marjorie, dear, the cord is right behind you, will you pull it twice, please?"

Lady Marjorie hastened to comply. In a moment Larkins entered. She recognized the visitors at once, bowed low, making her deepest curtsy, and murmured, "Good afternoon, Milady, good afternoon, my Lord."

"Larkins," said Lady Manville, "what did this scamp ask you for when he came to see you?"

"He said that your Ladyship desired me to whip him for intruding in your chamber, and I assumed you were quite angry with him for disturbing you that way, so I whipped him soundly with a tawse, Milady."

"I might have known he wouldn't deliver the whole message! I said you were to give him a perfectly sound flogging for his impudence! Besides, Larkins, I see you have neglected his thighs, they appear to have been only lightly touched! Were you afraid of causing him

169

some pain, by chance?" her mistress asked sarcastically.

Larkins was thoroughly dismayed and flustered.

"I am very sorry, Milady, but I lost track of time and thought I had taken too long with him. I knew your Ladyship wished to inspect him when I was finished. . . . I beg pardon, Milady. Shall I take him back and whip him again?"

"No, Larkins, I shall do it and you may look on and see what you have left unfinished. Fetch me the tawse! Come, William, bend over this stool!"

Larkins bowed her way hastily out, and the poor lad came up trembling to the stool and meekly leaned his upper body over it, making his still livid buttocks jut out prominently. He had no sooner assumed the required position than Larkins was back with the dreaded tawse. Lady Manville at once snapped it vigorously and with a loud report against the boy's thighs. He let out a wild shriek, seemed to have been catapulted away by the shock, but just as quickly recovered and hastened to resume his position. To the onlookers it was an eloquent exhibition of Lady Manville's expert training and Lord Herbert nudged his pretty wife to express his admiration. The tawse descended rapidly, leaving an ugly dark red mark each time to denote its unwelcome visit. The boy shrieked in an unearthly fashion and Lady Manville stopped a moment to exclaim:

"Oh, cease your howling! You shriek like a stuck pig!"

After a few more well-directed lashes, the lady ceased and permitted him to rise. This he did with difficulty for the ordeal had so exhausted him. Lady Manville turned to Larkins.

"When was the last time he was whipped?"

"Day before yesterday, Milady."

"No wonder he carries on so. The usual regimen for a while should do him a great deal of good. For the next week, at any rate, you will whip him twice each day, and you will report to me how he is coming along. Take him away, Larkins, his grimaces annoy me."

"Very well, Milady. I shall see that your orders are carefully carried out."

"Capital, my dear!" exclaimed Lady Marjorie enthusiastically. The lad heard the endorsement of the ill-boding plan as Larkins led him out.

"I am very glad we came," added Lord Herbert. "I do hope Marjorie gathers some profit from our visit." And poor Annie, who had stood by shaking inwardly with astonishment and fearing she might be brought to this soon, started up suddenly at her master's last expression. To add to her discomfiture, Lady Manville put her right hand over the girl's buttocks and gripping them tightly, remarked:

"And don't forget your duty to yourself and to Annie here. She appears very solid and healthy and nothing ought to interfere with her training. I hope you keep steadily after her, and you must keep me informed, won't you?"

"Indeed I shall, dear," responded Marjorie warmly, and the visitors departed.

While they stood at the door saying good-bye, Lily scurried back to the room she left as fast as her legs would carry her. Her nerves were completely unstrung and the blood throbbed in her head. She sank down in a chair and tried to recover her breath. A few minutes later her mistress entered the room. Lily rose at once.

"When I left, did I say you might sit down in my absence, Lily?" demanded Lady Manville.

The poor girl, aghast at her latest lapse, never dreamed she would be taken up on this mistake so suddenly. To be sure, her mistress had impressed on her, over and over again, and with the help of a number of whippings, that none of her slaves dared make a move of any sort, however unimportant in itself, without first obtaining consent. She was left with no alternative.

"No, Milady . . ." she gasped.

"Well, then, I shall sit down and you may come and lie across my lap! But get me the ruler first."

Lily obeyed quickly, and already accustomed to her rôle, she kissed the ruler and extended herself over her mistress' lap. Fortunately, Lady Manville did not make it an extended punishment, but contented herself with twelve or fifteen solid cracks. The girl squirmed but did not cry out and her mistress told her to rise. Lily considered herself mildly paid out, particularly since her curiosity hadn't been discovered.

About an hour later dinner was served. Myra, Ellen and Lily had to be in attendance on their mistress when she dined, and when she was finished they were permitted to have their dinner in a corner of the same dining room under their mistress' supervision; they had to eat their food in perfect silence. Lady Manville then returned to her boudoir, Lily following respectfully behind her. Her mistress was fatigued and required to be made comfortable. She stretched out on a chaise-longue and Lily stood by, ready to obey the first request. Thus she reclined at ease for more than an hour. The clock struck eight and at the same moment the door opened softly. Myra and Ellen were coming in.

They approached and knelt down before their mistress. Myra spoke:

"Milady," she said softly, "do you wish to give us our whipping tonight or shall we ask Mrs. Larkins to give it to us?"

"I am too tired," responded Lady Manville languidly. "Ask Larkins for it."

"Thank you, Milady. Please forgive us for bothering you."

Ellen nudged her kneeling companion as though to remind her of something. Myra added quickly:

"And please, Milady," the girl continued, "shall we come back after we are whipped so you may inspect us and we may bid you good-night?"

"Yes, you may."

"Thank you, Milady."

Myra kissed Lady Manville's hand and foot, then Ellen put her lips gently on the same places, and the girls withdrew silently. Lily breathed hard once more.

XV

Myra's Defense

So the days passed, painfully, laboriously, and crowded with one vexation upon another. Lily knew scarcely an hour of freedom from soreness or tenderness in her buttocks and thighs, nor was any other portion of her body safe from unexpected attack. Even her legs ached and only feebly supported her in the manifold duties she was continually performing. Her mistress did not leave her out of sight for more than a few minutes at a time, permitting her no respite sufficient to allow any relaxation whatever. She noted that the demands made on either Myra or Ellen were not comparable to those made on her, and it seemed that they were permitted some leisure of a sort, at any rate certainly denied to herself. If only she could obtain the same amount of rest allowed to them she might have strength to carry on for awhile, she thought. Her position appeared to be the lowest and most desperate in the household. Perhaps if she found opportunity to talk to the girls they might impart some information which would help her to assuage her misery, if only for an hour. But how was this to be arranged? Arranged!—the word brought a wry smile to her face. As though she were able to arrange anything! She prayed that something, anything, might arise to make such a talk possible. To seek them out and learn their hopes, their aspirations and what their inner hearts would reveal!

174

Then, one early afternoon, her chance came, suddenly!
Lady Manville, sitting in her favorite armchair, was reading some letters. One of them she tore into bits and
threw the scraps carelessly on the floor, this being her
usual way of discarding anything. Lily who was already
accustomed to follow after the things her mistress drop-
ped, stooped promptly to gather up the scraps. A
moment or two later she heard her lady's voice:

"Lily, I shall be going to town in a few moments and
shall not return until dinner. I have to attend a confer-
ence at my solicitor's office, and I cannot take you with
me. You have work to do for still awhile, and the balance of the time you will stay in this room. Remember
not to stir out of it, for if you do and I learn of it, as I
am sure I shall, you will be whipped by myself and by
Larkins until neither of us have an ounce of strength
left! Come to think of it, it would not be a bad thing
to do right now! A little whipping before I leave may
help to keep your mind soberly centered on the importance of perfect obedience, and it may save you from a
much more serious whipping later. Doesn't that seem
good to you, Lily?"

"Yes, Milady, it does. . . . Thank you, Milady . . ."
she winced.

"Well then, come here to me, I have little time to waste
on you, my girl."

Indeed, she gave her what Lily had already come to
consider a mild whipping, although to an unacquainted
onlooker it would have represented something of a formidable one. Ten minutes later, Lady Manville had
departed and Lily was wild with the excitement of the
first few hours she would now have all to herself! Her
breast filled with air and she took a long breath. So

disturbing was her reaction that she felt weak from the surge of her emotions and she slumped down into a chair without thought of the tenderness of her seat, but a few minutes ago set fire to afresh. She rose hastily, dragged her weary feet toward her mistress' chaise-longue, and threw herself face down across its length. Then she broke into a quiet sobbing. After a few minutes she recalled anxiously that there was her work to finish first and if she managed that quickly, she could bestir herself to endeavor to draw Myra and Ellen, or either of them, into conversation for at least two hours that would still be remaining. And she thought, too, she must try and get them to come to her for the risk of leaving the room she was ordered to remain in was very great indeed.

She rose quickly, dried her tears, and began to rearrange the innumerable things which her mistress was always upsetting in her spacious boudoir. She worked feverishly to accomplish the whole task thoroughly, being far from anxious to bring down her mistress' wrath when it was at all possible to put it aside. As she worked she weighed over scheme after scheme for bringing Myra and Ellen to this chamber. Every one she discarded because it did not seem practical. Of course, she could go look for them throughout this enormous house. But the danger of being seen! Not any one of the servants would have dared lie for her if they were questioned and their first interests would be in themselves, not in her. She finished her work sooner than she expected, looked hastily around to see if everything was in perfect order, and then walked to the door and peered down the corridor. Although Lady Manville had gone out her respectfully feared spirit remained behind. There was the stillness of the cemetery about the house. Lily stood at the door, dreading to reconnoitre yet harrassed by the fear that she was letting her long awaited chance slip by. . . .

Suddenly she heard footsteps. She followed the sound with her eyes and noticed at the foot of the staircase that William had come in with some polishing material and was preparing to attack a number of metal ornaments that decorated the foyer. Lily took her courage in her hands and attempted a loud whisper.

"William! William! William!"

The boy heard and looked up with a puzzled expression on his face.

"Will you please come up here for just a minute, William, please?" she asked anxiously. Her whole body quivered in fear he would refuse. But oh, joy of joys, the boy was responding! He had put down his cleaning rags and was running up the steps!

"Oh, William, how can I thank you for coming! Could you find Myra and Ellen and say to them that I beg them to come to me at once? Oh, William, dear, please do this for me! I shall be grateful to you all my life! I must see them, I must," she insisted hysterically, "and I dare not leave this room," she explained, blushing to the back of her ears. "Run, William dear! Bring them back with you!"

"But suppose I am seen, Lily, and get whipped for carrying messages for you?" the boy demurred.

"Oh, William, I promise you, I shall take all the blame on myself," the girl gulped hard as she spoke.

"Very well, Lily, you look so frightened, but I'll go." And off he ran. Lily leaned against the door for support.

The boy was gone but a minute. Before she had time to collect her thoughts he was standing before her.

"Myra is coming to you, Lily," he reported. "Ellen must stay where she is, and Myra says you must go into your room and wait, she will be along in a few minutes." Fearing to loiter a moment longer, the boy ran swiftly down the staircase before Lily could express one word of her profound gratitude. She went into the room and closed the door behind her. Nervously she paced the floor as though the decision of life or death hung on her expected visitor. Her eyes never left the door-knob and suddenly, she saw it turn! Myra had come in!

Unaware of what she was doing, she threw her arms impulsively around Myra's neck and burst into tears. She tried to speak but the words were stifled in her throat. Myra held her tenderly, making no effort to check the emotional outburst, understanding intuitively the girl's urgent need for releasing at least some of her emotions through tears. Presently Lily subsided. Still leaning on Myra's breast, she murmured:

"Forgive me, Myra dear, please forgive me, dear."

Myra dried her tears gently.

"I know, Lily dear, I know. Don't cry . . . let us talk. I am glad to be with you, and if you hadn't sent for me, I would have tried to come to you. Only a little while ago I learned that we would be alone this afternoon."

"Oh, dear Myra! You cannot understand how anxiously I prayed for this moment for weeks! And I hoped we could be friends. . . . We need friends so much, so much!"

Myra kissed her warmly on her cheek and led her gently to a soft chair, then she sat down on the carpet beside her. For the moment, Lily missed the significance of her companion's act.

"I am not allowed to sit on a chair in this room," she

volunteered quietly and simply, "but you must sit where you are, dear, you are weak."

"Oh, Lord!" Lily burst out, "what can I do? How can I escape from this hell? How can you bear it, and Ellen?" she exclaimed.

"It is just what I was seeking to talk to you about, dear," Myra answered. "I wanted to see you alone at the earliest possible moment, I wanted to try and spare you much unnecessary anguish and pain—to spare you so much of what I and Ellen have gone through before we saw our solution. I saw it first and poor Ellen couldn't, now she is seeing it too, but how much she could have avoided if she had not been so stubborn! I thank God I was persuaded and I pray you to listen to me. . . . Lily, dear, you are obeying her ladyship as we did, but you are not yielding! You must submit, dear, submit body and soul! We are not servants, Lily, we are slaves! We are things, like this and like this," pointing to the furniture, "that our superiors buy and sell! We are not even human because we have no will of our own, as we have nothing else of our own. I do not stand up or sit down unless I obtain permission first, nor do I take a drink of water even or respond to the functions of the body until I first obtain consent. We breathe, yes, without permission, but so does a dog or a cat or a fish. And yet I am not terribly unhappy, Lily, certainly not as I was! Do you know why? It is because I have yielded, not only outwardly but inwardly—there is the whole difference! It is the difference between great pains and pains of not so great consequence. Do not make the terrible mistake of thinking you can win! I thought so for a while and you are thinking so now. You are in great danger if you persist. You cannot win . . .

179

you must lose! You must lose—there is no possible
doubt about it! Accept, Lily, as I persuaded Ellen to accept, and you will discover a strange sort of peace. Accept or you will suffer and suffer and suffer. Oh, Lily,
dear, spare yourself these useless agonies! And spare
yourself the awful chagrin that Ellen and I suffered for
our stubborness. Acknowledge your slavery in your
heart and mind and you will see how quickly you will
pacify your mistress."

"Never!" cried Lily. "I prefer to die first. I shall
kill myself! Oh! how could you bring yourself to *that?*"

"I said the same things, dear, and so did Ellen," responded Myra quietly. "But now we are convinced we
are better off, far better off, in our present state, than
we would be if we were dead. Listen to me, dear, and
I shall tell you how our mistress, in her far greater wisdom, after all, convinced me. And learn from it, dear,
from my lesson and not from your own which you are
sure to receive. Rest your shoulders back and relax . . .
this way . . . that's better. Listen carefully because it
may be I don't know how many days before we have
this chance again."

Myra twisted her body about until her back rested
comfortably against the seat of an overstuffed chair opposite Lily. She pulled her legs up until her knees were
almost on a level with her chin, and she began her story.
Except for one minor interruption, Lily sat tensely, fascinated by the girl's amazing story, fearing to stir a
muscle lest she miss the least word. Myra spoke quietly
and evenly, apparently unaware of the effect her words
might have on a person who valued independence, and
whose nature would recoil from her soul-stirring revelation. The girl's voice was soft and musical, and its per-

fectly modulated tones swept caressingly over the enervated fibres of Lily's being, yet so profoundly did her
words impress themselves that for years thereafter Lily
was easily able to imagine that she had heard them but
an hour before. Indeed, the time did come when she
found occasion to recall with exactitude the story she
listened to that memorable day, but that is a matter of
later importance to this tale.

Myra began by suggesting she be permitted to omit
the details of her earlier life, out of consideration for the
time they had and which required to be preciously weighed. It was her service with Lady Manville that she
desired to stress. This dated back not quite two years,
and Ellen had come about two months after she did. For
the first three or four months she went through everything Lily was experiencing now. Her impression was
that she suffered more than Lily did because it took her
very nearly four months to see the light. She ventured
to remark that Lily probably held her in contempt, having
always seen her so abject before their mistress, and that
she must be wondering how anyone could bring herself
so low as to cringe and grovel like a worm before another
woman's feet as she did.

Lily interrupted to protest warmly, assuring her in a
tone of utmost anxiety that such a thought was far from
her mind, but that she shivered, instead, at the prospect
of finding herself in a similar state. An expression of
relief flitted over Myra's beautiful face, and then quickly
she took up the thread of her story.

One day, in the presence of Lady Manville and her
niece, a young lady of about nineteen, who was later
destined to play a most important rôle in her life, she
was ordered to take down her bloomers and prepare for

a whipping. It was in the morning and she had received one whipping but an hour ago. After nearly four months of continuous flogging she was too depressed to think of anything else but prompt obedience, and she proceeded in a mechanical way to execute the order. When she had taken off her bloomers and exposed her still colored flesh, the young lady remarked its appearance and inquired when she had last been whipped. In the same dull manner in which she felt Lily was answering questions now, she responded to those addressed to her by both ladies. At the request of her mistress she took down a tawse, knelt, kissed it, and handed it up. It was in this very room and she stretched across the bench before them now. Mistress Amelia, Lady Manville's niece, expressed a desire to examine her before her mistress began to whip. . . . At no time since that day was she ever able to understand what prompted her to do the crazy, impulsive thing she did. She never intended any rebellion, no such thought was in her poor head. But some stupid recollection of her earlier days must have flashed through her disordered brain, for she had been whipped repeatedly the past few weeks. At any rate, she deliberately jerked her body away as Miss Amelia's cool, white little hand touched one of her still warm buttocks. Never did the thought flash in her brain that she could be guilty of any deliberate disrespect to either her mistress or Miss Amelia. . . . But Lady Manville's fury could not be described! The flogging that followed still curdled her blood at every recollection! So completely did her mistress abandon herself to her temper that Miss Amelia, herself frightened by the sight of what was being done, was stirred to intercede for the hapless girl, and she begged Lady Manville to desist. Several minutes later

182

Myra fainted. But that was far from the end of her punishment for her rash act! Miss Amelia left immediately after lunch, but Lady Manville's anger renewed itself like the flame of a blacksmith's forge, and the poor girl was severely whipped three more times by her mistress before that indefatigable lady retired for the night. Five times in the one day she was whipped, and four of them were possibly the fiercest whippings she received in her life.

Of course, she never closed her eyes all through the night. Even when the pain turned dull she was unable to find a place for herself. It was absolutely impossible to either sit or even lie down in any position and hope to obtain some measure of comparative comfort. Every bone and every bit of flesh on her body ached horribly, and every part of her back from her shoulders to her calves was covered with frightful welts. Her mistress had used every instrument in the house that day, even to a wet towel, the frightfully stinging end of which she knotted when she had dragged her into the bathroom during one of the whippings. In her black misery she decided to kill herself. In the morning she would try to obtain a sharp knife somehow from the kitchen, and she would stab herself through her already bleeding heart at the first opportunity. There was no possibility of doing it at once because she was too weak to attempt to make her way undetected from her room, and Mrs. Larkins slept right near her and was a very light sleeper.

Her sobbing subsided at the thought of the eternal peace she was soon to procure for herself. She began to review her life. She was twenty-two years old. Twenty-two years old! How young to die! It made her shiver! Suddenly, as she mused over her age, a startling idea came into her head. Wasn't there a way to make life easier and to live? Wasn't there something she could do about it? Anything she might experiment with? After all, death was so final, so irrevocable. Why not put it over for a week or two while she planned some program! She could always kill herself when she had resolved every conceivable plan and found them all valueless. What was it then, that Lady Manville sought in her? Or in Ellen? Had she failed to succeed in something she had undertaken with them and was the irritation of that failure falling on their backs? One thing was certain, her mistress was not satisfied with her. She hadn't dominated her subjects sufficiently and that irked her. Perhaps that was it! Complete domination! Was it *that* she was seeking? Well, suppose she achieved it? Suppose it were demonstrated to her satisfaction that she had conquered, indisputably? Would that appease her vanity, maybe? And if it didn't and nothing helped, she could kill herself then, couldn't she? On the other hand, if it did help, perhaps life would be much more endurable, it might solve this enormous problem for her, and perhaps she would want to live on, after all.

What could she do to create a situation less devastating than the present one? One thing was clear, Lady Manville wanted to crush her will, utterly. Very well. She wanted abject slaves around her, living things crawling at her feet. Very well. She was happy only when she most humiliated her slaves. Well, how was one to yield to her there? Evidently, by training oneself not to feel the humiliations so keenly. And how was that to be accomplished? It seemed to her she must start this way: She must determine to consider herself actually a slave, Lady Manville's slave. To be sure, Lady Manville had effectively reduced her to slavery in its fullest sense, but she had never acknowledged herself one in her heart. Now then, a slave and a lady live in worlds apart. One of the things that distinguishes a lady is her sense of modesty. But a slave is rather like a dog or a horse, and animals have no sense of modesty or shame. A dog, for example, has no feeling about clothes, it walks about nude with no concern, following its mistress wherever she goes. It is property, quite simply, like this furniture or these drapes. How can property have a sense of shame, then? If the property be decorative, ornamental, then why should it not be proudly exposed by its owner? Now the circumstances amply demonstrate that there is no question about her being property, too, and property is always subject to its owner's will. The fact that she can go nowhere, possess nothing, has no rights of any sort, the fact that every act, even of the tiniest kind, is executed only at her owner's pleasure—all these things definitely establish her place. And so, since she is property, why should she not be felt, examined, turned around, put down, stood up? Like an attractive vase, her body is well turned too, and has graceful lines also.

Thus she debated all through the night. The more she reasoned in this direction the more practical it appeared to be. What if she took this attitude for a week or two? If she could persuade herself that these things were logical and true, she could show a considerably different quality of service which would be bound to arrest her mistress' attention. And if it made no impression on her, and she still persisted in treating her brutally, as she had this day, she should simply destroy herself and in the quickest possible manner, rather than wait for her mistress to do it by slow and excruciating degrees.

But how should she proceed? First, it was of the utmost importance that for the purpose of this experiment, she must actually think as she acts. For the time being there must be no mental reservations whatever. Every moment that finds her alone must find her thinking of herself as Lady Manville's slave. She must refer to herself as a slave, not only when addressing her mistress, but most especially when she is not in her presence and she can be alone with her thoughts. The words "whip" and "whipping" must become commonplace parts of her speech and her everyday thinking. The more often she would utter them and the more she would think them the less repugnance she would feel toward these words. And the intimate portions of her body should no longer be intimate. It wasn't her body, to be sure; it belonged to her mistress and not to her. She need only detach herself in her mind from the ownership of it, and there would be nothing, then, to conceal, no sense of consciousness about exhibiting it freely to all her superiors. All this seemed quite true to her. Now to manifest it.

She resolved that when her mistress told her to walk a foot she should walk a foot and an inch. That is to say, every ceremony required of her should be faultlessly carried out; every formula should be uttered not like a recitation which degraded her but with a definite ring of sincerity in it; every answer expected should be given not with that reluctant preciseness her mistress had been obtaining, but freely, impulsively almost, and with a few appropriate words even added. If her mistress desired to whip her, she should prepare herself with alacrity and not haltingly, as she had been doing—yes, even with eagerness! And why not with eagerness? She was going to be whipped, that was certain; there wasn't the

remotest chance of avoiding it. Well then, why not prepare herself with a genuine eagerness? Since being
whipped—in the way that Lady Manville whipped, at
any rate—was anything but pleasurable, why not get it
over with as quickly as possible? But to display such
eagerness, one might argue, is dangerous, since it may
encourage more frequent whippings than might otherwise
be imposed. She considered, however, that it might
have the opposite effect, that this alacrity might disarm
her mistress and take some of the sting out of her lashes.
Naturally, she could not hope to escape whippings, that
was out of the question. Slavery would lose much of its
meaning if it were not accompanied by the lash. But if
she should cross her mistress and then show a genuine
eagerness to be corrected, an earnest desire to atone for
her mistake, there couldn't be quite the same urge for increasing the pain of the punishment as there would be
otherwise. Once in that mood, it was inevitable that she
should really feel a sense of gratitude for the correction,
and that she should express this gratitude in words that
were no longer meaningless. Sincerely trying to achieve
perfection in her service, it would follow that she would
experience a deep sense of vexation when she had failed
to execute an order properly, that she should welcome
correction for her error, and be grateful for it when
granted. Reasoning thus, things began to simplify themselves for her.

She noted Lily's horror at the program and that the
thought of swallowing such a pill must be like gall and
wormwood. But for Myra the pill had been laid down;
she had to swallow it whether she liked it or not. She
urged Lily to consider once more the situation she was
in: Her body wracked with ten thousand pains; she had

just been through a series of ordeals which were but the culmination of many other ordeals before and the prelude to many more to come. There was the pill! Either she must swallow it or go on from one hell to another. Bitter indeed it was, but once swallowed and digested the bitterness might vanish like a fast moving cloud, and instead of evil effects there might be good! She would fit herself easily into a niche, then; settle down to a new order of life. The old should pass like a fanciful dream, and she would enjoy a measure of peace. And so it came to pass! She ventured the notion that perhaps it was even a better peace than their mistresses enjoyed! Instead of many concerns, one; instead of a mass of responsibilities, none. For them there was but one thing they needed to remember, obedience!— absolute, unquestioning, perfect obedience! After that, everything settles itself.

There comes the question of the whipping routine. Even that question is resolved smoothly. As Lily well knew, they were being whipped twice each day, either by their mistress or by Mrs. Larkins. These were in addition to those they might naturally incur. But the latter decrease in time, as Lily would see for herself, she hoped, real soon. She doubted that she and Ellen now averaged three a week beside the routine whippings. And as to the two whippings each day, she saw their actual value and the need they had for them. Milady was much wiser than her temper might lead Lily to believe. For as Myra went on with them she found how they kept the muscles toned up, how the skin developed a resistance and recuperative power it did not possess in the beginning. She recalled when she first began to get whipped how her skin would crack in numerous places and how she would

188

bleed after each serious whipping. Another important gain has been in the accommodation of the nerves in that region to a diminishing sensitivity, so that they become less responsive to sudden shock. To be sure, even these routine whippings were painful, but the pain was far from unbearable, more like a temporary discomfort, one might call it. A certain maximum of pain is experienced for the first few minutes and then it begins to subside. Why should she complain, then, about a few minutes pain twice each day? Another genuine profit from the routine whippings lay in this: Occasionally something happens accidently which brings down a complaint followed by rather a severe whipping. If her body was not attuned to them, if some time had elapsed since her last whipping and her skin and nerves had softened in the meantime, one could easily imagine what an old-fashioned ordeal that could develop into. Thanks, however, to the routine whippings, she could face a severe one without going into a million tremors, so that sort of chastisement finally passes with just a great deal more discomfort, but that is all. And if there be witnesses present while she is being whipped, feeling as she does about them now, she doesn't get demoralized any more. What difference, indeed, can it make to her if there be one witness present or five or ten? They all know she is Lady Manville's slave and that her mistress may do as she pleases with her slave's body. Can she hope to conceal her slavery from them? Do not her very clothes, her very deportment and features proclaim that fact, even if not a word were to be said in advance?

And what has been the result of this complete submission? She begged Lily to believe that the benefits have been far from trivial, and that she has learned to cherish them in the light of her revised appreciation of values. There has been a decided let-down and the tenseness which used to pervade the atmosphere has gradually but definitely evaporated. Her mistress is no longer brutal to her. To be sure, she is stern and severe, but that is to be expected. Nothing is forgiven and the slightest ruffling of her mood earns the girl a whipping. And yet, despite this inflexibility, there has been a certain relaxing in her mistress' attitude, which reflects itself in a variety of ways. For example, she and Ellen are given less work to do than formerly, and while they had no time off whatever in the beginning, now at least two hours each day are exclusively theirs for relaxation, with no one around to observe them. There are other little favors bestowed, some delicacies from their mistress' table, perhaps. Another time it may be a ride or a promenade in the country with their mistress. Certainly all these considerate acts were absent before that eventful day.

Throughout this amazing recital Lily sat spellbound. She was unable to utter a word. She thought of herself trying to adjust her mind to conform with Myra's and Ellen's and the blood froze in her veins. Picture upon picture swept before her mind's eye disclosing the sort of life Lady Manville evidently had designed for her, too. She shut her eyes tight, hoping to exclude the vision of herself crushed down to these unspeakable depths if she allowed that tyrant to execute her horrible plan. If she allowed it! Great God! what alternative did she have, what power could she count on to prevent such a catastrophe? Nothing, nothing! Only by killing herself could she escape her inevitable doom! Or escape, flight! But flight to where, and how was it to be accomplished? She had not a farthing, nor did she know how she could obtain any money, even by theft. And to whom could she fly, even if she could hope to escape from a place that was as well guarded as this was. There was the Training School, it was not very far away, to be sure. But how could she get there, and how would Mrs. Wharton feel about it? Surely, she could look for no mercy from that woman, either. There wasn't the slightest question but that she would make her pay dearly for her flight. And would she be able to endure all the punishments Mrs. Wharton would be sure to inflict after all she had had to bear from Lady Manville? Indeed, it was like leaping from the frying-pan into the fire. There was Miss Evelyn. Oh yes, Miss Evelyn, she was human! The only human being left in her world now was Miss Evelyn—and she whipped her continually too. But then . . . but then . . . she didn't know why . . . there was something different about Miss Evelyn! And yet what could that young supervisor do for her, even if she were disposed to do anything? After all, she was only one of the governesses, and whatever Mrs. Wharton would command, Miss Evelyn would faithfully execute. All these and many more thoughts flashed wildly through her brain as Myra moved herself into a more favorable position on the floor. Tucking her legs under her that she might look with less strain at her companion, the girl was continuing with her story. Lily, too, leaned forward with an eagerness that bespoke her fascination.

Several days after the harrowing event which led to her change of heart and mind, Miss Amelia, the young niece of Lady Manville, went traveling on the continent with several friends who were chaperoned by the mothers of two of the young ladies. Myra never forgot how she had intervened between her and her infuriated mistress, and continued to remember her gratefully. But little did she dream that an event was to catch up with her here which would very shortly make, as it promised to do at this time, such an enormous change in her state. About two months ago Miss Amelia returned to Scotland and before going on to her home, arranged to spend a day with her aunt. It appeared that the only real affection Lady Manville had for anyone in the world was expended on this young girl. It is strange, when you stop to think of it, that a person who is at all capable of an affection should narrow it down to embrace but one other person or thing in life; for it would be simpler to understand her nature if it were known that she was incapable of developing an affection of any kind whatever.

To Lady Manville's domestics down below it was revealed suddenly one day that Miss Amelia was coming, because the house took on a bustle of excitement it never ordinarily knew. Lady Manville issued innumerable orders that morning and the duty of supervising their execution fell to Mrs. Larkins who ran around in circles endeavoring to carry them all out. Miss Amelia arrived early in the afternoon but neither Ellen nor Myra saw her. They only knew she was closeted with their mistress and that they were probably engaged in exchanging their experiences these many months.

About three o'clock that afternoon, Ellen and she were at work in the dining-room. Ellen was polishing silverware and Myra was busy setting the immense room in faultless order. The door opened and Mrs. Larkins appeared. She announced brusquely that the

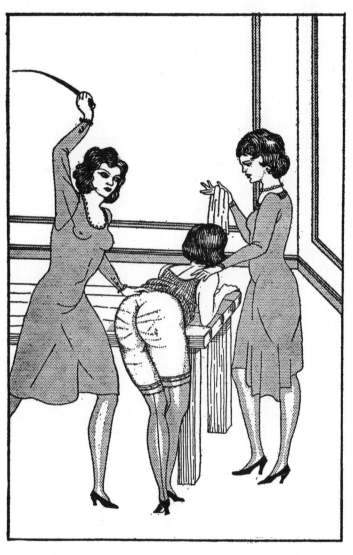

The girl wept, trembled, but kept her eyes carefully posed on the work the governess was showing her (page 227)

two girls were to have their afternoon whippings at once instead of at the usual hour, otherwise she would never get through all the things that remained to be done. She ordered Ellen to come first, telling Myra to continue with her work until Ellen returned, when she was to come in and get her whipping.

The routine whippings took place each day at eleven in the morning and at five in the afternoon. Lady Manville had officiated on both girls in the morning, but the afternoon whippings had been advanced to three o'clock to suit their mistress' convenience for some reason. Ellen, accordingly, followed Mrs. Larkins' directions, but came back sooner than expected. The girl looked relieved, remarking that, luckily for her, Mrs. Larkins had been obliged to cease when she was only half through whipping her, having been called away by William, the page-boy, who ran in to tell her that Lady Manville wished to see her at once. Mrs. Larkins promptly released Ellen, instructing her to notify Myra to present herself to Lady Manville and inquire if her ladyship would consent to administer the afternoon whipping to her instead. Myra, realizing that she would probably be whipped before Miss Amelia, proceeded nevertheless to report promptly.

She walked softly into the room and found Miss Amelia sitting on the edge of a couch, her body bent forward and her hands clasped over her knees, listening attentively to something her aunt was saying. Getting down on her knees, she greeted her mistress and Miss Amelia and, following the usual formula, asked for her whipping. Her mistress extended herself unusually that afternoon, for her niece's benefit, very likely. The girl made the most strenuous efforts not to cry out while she

195

was being whipped, although the martinet her mistress used ignited a scorching fire that she thought would grill her alive. But she was determined not to give way, not only for her own subsequent comfort's sake, but also because she knew her mistress would be pleased if she carried herself off well. That was an added incentive, for she had learned quite thoroughly how it profited her to please her mistress.

When it was finally over and she had completed the ceremony which follows each whipping, she was permitted to stand up. Miss Amelia could not contain her enthusiasm over the remarkable change in the girl since she saw her last, and she praised her aunt in the highest possible terms, saying it had vindicated every conviction the lady had, and which she used to think was the goal undoubtedly wished for but rarely attained. Meanwhile, Myra stood between them while they continued to discuss her at their ease; and Lady Manville recalled to her niece the whipping she last witnessed applied to her, and how she had become so infuriated because the girl had shrunk back from Miss Amelia's examination. What resulted that day, she stated, was something Myra must be eternally grateful for, since it removed, once and for all, every doubt she may have had about her station in life. She felt that Myra understood now how good that experience had been for her soul, and when she intimated that the girl should confirm the truth of it to Miss Amelia, she readily and promptly obeyed. They asked her a number of other questions of the same general nature, and the sincere tone in which she responded must have convinced them that she answered without any reservations. Miss Amelia was delighted with them and appeared reluctant to see the girl go when her mistress ordered her to return to her work.

She withdrew to the dining-room but found herself alone, Ellen having been called away to assist Mrs. Larkins in some other task. She resumed her work, feeling still dreadfully uncomfortable from the sound whipping she had received. Fully an hour later the door opened and young William came in to say that Miss Amelia wanted to see her in her room. She went immediately, wondering what would be required of her. On entering Miss Amelia's room, she saw the young lady pacing somewhat excitedly about. When she saw Myra she paused, and the girl came over to where she stood and knelt at the young lady's feet.

"Myra," she began abruptly, "I have tremendous news and I myself can scarcely believe it is true! After you went down I asked your mistress quite casually if she would consent to sell you to me. I wonder if you can judge my surprise when she practically agreed to do it! Do you realize what that means, my girl? If we settle on the amount and terms, and it appears we shall, you will become my slave, my own personal slave!" she emphasized joyfully.

Myra's heart pumped furiously and her breath completely deserted her. She was stunned. Immediately images began to crowd in on her and she thrilled with excitement. A new mistress! A new home! A new life! A young and extremely beautiful mistress and not a middle-aged woman! A mistress whose lovely young body it would be a joy to attend! She would whip her, to be sure, but there was compassion in her heart, as she had discovered once. There was a certain luster in her eyes, a glimmer of kindliness and warmth

197

which drew her like a magnet, and she felt herself bursting with desire to bury her face between her feet and just keep it there. But her tongue tangled in her mouth and at the moment she could not have spoken even if she had been commanded to. But Miss Amelia was requesting nothing from her, she was speaking again:

"I shall be twenty years old, Myra, in about three months, and on my birthday I come into a certain amount of money my mother left for me in trust. Tomorrow I shall call on my solicitors and ascertain how soon they will be able to forward the sum required to purchase you. I never for a moment expected your mistress would consent to sell you to me, and when I proposed it to her I did it jokingly. But my aunt has always been generous with me, she has never denied me anything. She has consented to accept payment from me for merely the original amount she expended for you, and asks no compensation for the long period it required to make of you what you are; and she is accepting it only because she knows I am coming into a large inheritance and that I shall not be burdened in any way."

She had been talking rapidly, herself excited with the prospect of acquiring the girl, a thought she had clearly never dreamed of when she came that afternoon.

"Well, Myra," she was resuming, "it should be interesting to hear how the prospect pleases you. Not that it matters," she hastened to add with an air of sternness, "but how do you think you shall like being my slave?"

This time Myra let herself go. Still unable to talk and overwhelmed with emotion, her head fell forward; her knees, on which she had remained since she entered, straightened out, and she lay prone on the floor, on her stomach. Her head had fallen between Miss Amelia's feet, her arms moved forward impulsively, folding themselves around the young lady's calves, and all that she could remember was that her lips were kissing whatever of hers they could touch. . . .

This emotional outburst must have affected Miss Amelia too, because she made no effort to insist on the answer to her question. Perhaps it came to her that the girl did not dare express her eagerness to be her slave instead of her aunt's, and this knowledge made her quiver with excitement also, for Myra could feel the young lady's legs vibrating. Presently Miss Amelia spoke:

"You haven't answered me, Myra," she reminded her, but without the slightest trace of annoyance in her voice.

"Oh! Milady!" she found herself able to utter, recalling suddenly she had been spoken to and the duty of answering promptly when addressed. The necessity of being reminded was a new kind of mortification to her.

"Oh! Milady!" she was saying again, "I am very happy! . . ."

Miss Amelia withdrew her feet from her embrace and stepped back to a sofa facing the fireplace. She extended her legs to their fullest length, threw her head back and closed her eyes. For more than a minute she remained like that, saying not a word, but thinking certainly of how pleasant life would be for her with her unexpected acquisition. Then she spoke:

"Get up!" she said. "And come here to me!"

Myra did as she was told. As she stood before Miss Amelia she tried to look at her face but her eyes were dimmed with tears.

"So! The thought of it makes you happy! This is most interesting," she was silent again. Then:

"But why? she asked suddenly. "Do you imagine that I shall not whip you?"

"Oh! No, Milady! It was not for that. . . ."

"For what, then?"

"It was the thought of having you for my mistress. . . . I mean, my actual mistress, Milady."

"You feel you could learn to love me, perhaps?"

"Oh, yes, Milady?"

"Even though I whipped you frequently?"

"That would not affect it, please, Milady."

Miss Amelia pulled her legs in, reached out and took hold of Myra's wrist.

"You understand, Myra, that I shall not relax in your discipline, don't you? I had a demonstration by your mistress and you of its value a little while ago, and I wouldn't permit it to decline for the world. You wouldn't want to see it decline, either, would you?"

"No, Milady. . . . If you please, Milady, I think it would spoil my usefulness."

"That is a very sensible answer, Myra, and I think you may very well be grateful to your mistress for having instilled this good sense into you. And if she hadn't whipped you so well and so often you wouldn't be the desirable slave you are now, and I shouldn't have wanted to buy you. You see that yourself, don't you?"

"Yes, Milady, I hope I shall show myself worthy of your choice."

Miss Amelia lifted her skirt and pulled her in between her legs. She put her hand around the girl's waist and then started to stroke her hips.

"I shall continue the routine whippings, of course,"

200

she said, speaking softly, as though to herself, and then louder:

"Did you hear what I just said?"

"Yes, Milady, I did."

"They accomplish an immense amount of good, and it would be very wrong to relax this routine. Lady Manville speaks very wisely and out of her great experience when she says that whenever you want to teach a slave anything you must turn her over and whip it into her through her bottom, otherwise she will never learn, since that is the only method of learning a slave understands. I shall not attempt to modify that system when I come into possession of you, but that doesn't frighten you, does it?"

"No, Milady, I shall have to learn how to serve you as you require."

"And to impress these things I must whip you often, mustn't I?"

"Yes, Milady."

"And you will be eager to learn?"

"Oh, yes, Milady! If I see that I am pleasing you, I shall be very happy, Milady."

"Good! Your answers gratify me," responded Miss Amelia. "Tomorrow I hope to learn definitely how soon I can take you away. But until then I shall arrange to come here once each week to see how you are conducting yourself, and perhaps I shall whip you at each visit, if you are a good girl. Your mistress has consented to let me take over the routine whenever I come to visit, so it is likely that the early part of the coming week we shall inaugurate our formal relations in the proper manner. Will you be looking forward to your first whipping from me?"

"Oh! Milady! I am so eager to begin!"

"I conclude from your manner," remarked Miss Amelia, dryly, "that you are more eager about a new home and a new mistress than about this first whipping from me. But I shall not ask you to confirm that now," she added. With that she gave her a gentle pat on the side of her face, and brought an end to this momentous interview.

"You may go back now to your work, my girl. I have many more things to discuss with your mistress. Pretty soon we shall see much more of each other, I think. But in the meantime, I hope you will continue to profit from all the instruction and discipline your mistress may be good enough to allot to you. Now get on your knees and kiss me good afternoon."

Once more her arms wound around Miss Amelia's calves, and she kissed the tops of her shoes and the hem of her skirt ardently and with a heart full of gratitude. Who could understand what it all meant to her that day?

For the next five or six days she walked around in a partial trance, not that she was oblivious to her daily obligations, for she carried them out in rather satisfactory form, surprisingly enough, considering the fact that she was tingling with excitement at the prospect of her change. She burned with impatience for the following Thursday to arrive, having heard that her future mistress was to come then. Looking back on those crucial days she recalled that her abstraction and absent-mindedness had gone so unnoticed as to produce only two whippings outside of the routine, and she thought she had been amazingly lucky in having skated so successfully over the thin ice which covered the vast space between that interview and Miss Amelia's next visit. And then Thursday finally arrived.

A few minutes before eleven o'clock she was told that she was to go to Mrs. Larkins for her usual morning whipping. Her vexation and disappointment when she received the order was indescribable. Never except during the first days in Lady Manville's service had she gone more reluctantly to a whipping than she did to this one. Her heart sank at the thought that Miss Amelia might not be coming that day after all. But she breathed a deep sigh of relief when she heard Mrs. Larkins say, as she tucked her closer over her lap and clamped the girl's feet between her legs, that Miss Amelia was expected shortly after lunch, and that if she was a good girl, Mrs. Larkins would recommend her to Madame who, in turn, might recommend her to Miss Amelia, in which case the latter might give her the afternoon whipping. With what good-will she bore Mrs. Larkins' chastisement that morning only her own heart could understand.

It must have been very close to three o'clock that afternoon before she was summoned to Madame's boudoir. Her heart drummed loudly in her breast as she hastened forward to learn whether she was to go into Miss Amelia's service or whether there might not have been some break in their negotiations, and all these longings might turn into a cruel dream. The ladies were facing in the direction of the door as she entered. Both were sitting on the divan, Lady Manville holding Miss Amelia's hand in her lap. She came up and knelt down before them.

"Myra," she heard Lady Manville speak first, "you will be interested to know that I have concluded details with Miss Amelia concerning you. I have consented to sell you to Miss Amelia, and this young lady has agreed to purchase you, under the impression—and I trust she will not be mistaken—that you will make her a faithful, loyal and obedient slave. Are you disposed to accept the change in mistresses submissively?"

"Yes, Milady, I am."

"Very good. You will continue here in my custody for several months until Miss Amelia completes some preliminary arrangements, and when the time arrives she will take you with her to her own home. Until then she intends to spend a day with us each week, and if you are a good girl I shall permit you to stay in her charge each time she comes, and you shall have an opportunity to become acquainted with her methods and her wishes. I hope you will conduct yourself in a manner to give your next mistress complete satisfaction."

After a few more questions and answers pertaining to the change which was about to take place, the girl was dismissed from their presence. Myra started to furnish further details concerning Miss Amelia's subsequent weekly visits and the tremendous differences she perceived between the authority of the young lady and her aunt, and that while Miss Amelia was no less thorough in her manner of whipping, the brutal harshness which characterized the lightest expression of Lady Manville was absent in her niece. She was about to relate one or two specific examples which would serve to illustrate her elation at the forthcoming change, when the sound of a bell downstairs caused them both to start up anxiously. Lily ran to the door and peered out. She heard a bustling commotion below, and the sound of scurrying feet which indicated that Lady Manville must have returned, and that their time was up. Myra read the news in her companion's nervousness, she had barely time to exchange a kiss hurriedly with Lily and she rushed off.

XVI

The Flight

BEFORE a week had passed Lily found herself in what promised to be the most desperate situation of her life. That day her mistress had gone downstairs to inspect the expense account Mrs. Larkins was obliged to keep. Once every month they devoted an hour or more to these details and Lady Manville was always most particular about ascertaining the cause of each expenditure and checking the amounts against the bills of the various tradesmen. Lily assumed she would have at least that hour alone, and she cast about for something she might do for herself during this rare period when she was not likely to be under observation. The thought suddenly flashed through her mind that she would attempt to write a letter to Pauline in London, describe her present plight, and implore the girl to beseech her mistress' aid in extricating her from this infernal predicament. She felt it was very possible to write this letter, but the great problem was what to do with it after it was written. If she could only prevail on William to manage its dispatch! But the boy was as thoroughly intimidated as the rest of the domestics, and he would undoubtedly refuse to assume the dreadful risk. Besides, it was hardly likely that he had access to the outer world, because Lily had seen how steadily he was employed by Mrs. Larkins or Lady Manville, both of whom kept very close watch on the young man. Still, thought Lily, this was an excellent time to write the letter, she could secrete it somewhere, bide her time, and at the first opportunity she could implore William's assistance. Even though it was preposterous to think he would let himself be involved in such a dangerous enterprise, she could not be worse off if she tried to enlist his interest. As a result of these deliberations she decided to write the letter, it was not likely that her mistress would discover her. She tip-toed to Lady Manville's writing desk, snatched the first pencil she saw and some blank writing paper, closed the desk, sat down before a small tabaret and began to compose her plea.

Absorbed in the composition of her story, the poor girl unluckily failed to hear Lady Manville's approach. Suddenly her mistress entered the room and Lily, startled out of her wits, felt her body stiffen with paralysis as the knowledge of her being caught came home. The scene which ensued almost defies description. Enough had been set down on paper to condemn the girl to hanging, drawing and quartering. Lady Manville's fury exceeded all bounds, but when she had delivered herself of one scathing diatribe after the other, she suddenly calmed down. Lily was dumbfounded that she did not immediately begin to whip her. Instead, Lady Manville rang and awaited the response to her summons. For a moment or two there was absolute silence and this ominous silence was more terrifying to the sorry culprit than the searing remarks which preceded it. Mrs. Larkins entered.

"Larkins," Lady Manville said quietly, "I just caught this viper writing a letter to someone pleading for help to escape! We shall teach this miserable slave a lesson that will cause her to remember her ingratitude as long as she lives! Take her down to the cave!"

Mrs. Larkins put her hands on Lily's shoulders and pressed her forward. The girl walked ahead in an absolute daze.................................

No sooner had Larkins departed with her prisoner than William presented himself, made a respectful bow, and announced that Lord Herbert and Lady Marjorie were downstairs. Lady Manville descended and greeted her visitors with her usual warmth. They had brought Annie with them. Their hostess ordered tea to be served and Lord Herbert and the ladies made themselves comfortable. Annie was directed to stand at Lady Marjorie's right, which left her midway between her mistress and her master. After some general exchanges, Lady Marjorie inquired for Lily, and Lady Manville responded that the girl had just been lodged in the cave where she was awaiting punishment.

"Ah!" exclaimed Marjorie. "Is that the celebrated cave I heard about which makes such a charming part of this old castle?"

"Yes, that is correct. We do have such a place here, built in underground, which someone has aptly designated the *Cave of Sighs.*"

"It recalls to my mind the famous *Bridge of Sighs* in Venice."

"Yes, probably both names have the same origin. I do not know just what passed in this *Cave of Sighs,* but I have reason to believe that it was the spot where my ancestor, Peter van Weem, must have chastised or delegated someone to chastise the members of his numerous family as well as his servants, for I found in it an old wooden horse, on which are fixed ankle and wrist bands, as well as iron rings in the stone walls and floor, all of which could have served but one purpose!"

"Oh!" excaimed Lady Marjorie. "What an emotion the first sight of such a room and its equipment must inspire! . . ."

"Yes," remarked Lord Herbert with a melancholy air. "What have become of the good old disciplinarians?"

"Where are the snows of yesterday?" . . . recited Lady Manville, who knew the old authors not only of her own country, but those of France, Germany and Italy as well. "However that may be, I would suggest that we visit the cave later and take Annie along," she added meaningly. "I imagine we shall find my Lily somewhat anxious. I invite you, dear friends, to be present while I introduce Lily to a few punishments and instruments she has not yet become acquainted with, and which she has very warmly invited by her astounding notions that she could escape. When I have finished with her I think I shall have succeeded in dispelling any such fantastic idea, for I intend to whip her as she was never whipped before! Incidentally, I trust your Annie will profit greatly from the spectacle, and when I have finished with Lily we might avail ourselves of the cave's equipment to drive the lesson home on Annie, so that it might crush any similar thoughts your girl may be harboring. At any rate, you may be sure it will help her to understand the obligations she owes her master and mistress, and when you return home you may find her more amenable to proper discipline."

"Thank you, dear, that is a splendid suggestion," replied Lady Marjorie.

The girl's face blanched and her legs shook as she listened to this ill-boding conversation.

It was terribly cold in the cave and Lily trembled in fearful anticipation of the ordeal that awaited her in this torture chamber. It was nothing less than that, she was convinced, because she had heard her mistress speak of the wooden horse on which girls were stretched, and the iron rings and chains to which they were fastened while an infinite variety of punishments were inflicted. The low temperature and the raw state of her nerves set her shivering with such violence that every muscle of her body quivered in an agitation greater than any she ever experienced before. In the corridor she heard the regular paces of a guard. Who was he? Wasn't there any chance of bribing him? . . . She had no means of telling who was there, and although it happened to be William, the page, who was on guard, she could not distinguish him by the sound of his walk. At any rate she shrugged her shoulders at the thought of bribery. For how could she tempt anyone? She had not a single copper and as for counting on a sentiment of pity . . . no. That was folly.

She dared not straighten up nor try walking around in an effort to keep warm, for she feared someone might be spying on her and that she would bring down an additional chastisement for having dared to budge. The position commanded, to remain on her knees, made her limbs terribly stiff . . . and she was weighed down by an infinite distress. All at once the thought came to her that since the cave was so dark it was impossible that any spy could see her budge. She straightened herself with an effort and began making long and hurried paces, swinging her arms about in an attempt to keep warm. Almost a half hour passed thus but the girl's anguish did not diminish. She had no idea of the time she had spent in this cell and she feared every instant that she would see the dreaded silhouette of Lady Manville. She recalled what she had heard her mistress say about this cave and she wondered what cries of despair and suffering must have been flung hopelessly against these four stone walls! Greatly fatigued she approached an old bench and sat down lightly on its edge. If she had matches perhaps she would have risked lighting one of the lamps which Mrs. Larkins had extinguished when she went out, but on the other hand, the least light might bring the attention of her guard, for the door was very likely pierced by a peep-hole or some other contrivance which permitted a secret view of the interior. As she thought about this she noted that the bench on which she was sitting was very old, and that it probably had been there since the castle was built. This bench which stood on four firm legs appeared to be secured to a large stone in the floor under it, and as nearly as she could feel in the dark it was fastened to the stone by two wide bands of iron which ran up each set of legs, under the whole length of the seat, and down the other set of legs where they fastened again to the opposite side of the stone. Lily's hands ran nervously around one of these bands, and her little feet pressed on the stone beneath. Again she thought perhaps someone might be observing her sitting down instead of kneeling, as directed, and she was about

211

to resume her trying position when under the pressure of one of her fingers on the bar, it seemed that the stone underneath moved slightly. The thought that so large and heavy a stone could move startled her and her heart began to thump unaccountably in her breast.

Somewhere before we have said that Lily, like most young girls, was exceedingly curious; when her curiosity was aroused she was unable to resist the temptation to satisfy it, and when the object was particularly intriguing she did not stop to reckon the cost. Consequently her thought about resuming the position on her knees was quickly replaced by an impulse to investigate the meaning of this loose stone. Instead of returning to the designated corner, she did get on her knees again, but before the bench this time, and she pressed with all her might on every inch of the bar's length under the forepart of the bench. Suddenly she felt something giving way under the pressure of her thumb, and to her unbounded amazement both the bench and the stone began to rotate very, very slowly. She looked on fascinated, brusquely reminded of romantic books she had read wherein writers described secret passageways under old castles! This apparently was one of them! Surely Lady Manville could not have known of it or she would never have incarcerated the girl there. She watched the stone turn slowly and her eyes popped out of her head in a wild expectation of what it was about to disclose. Suddenly she felt a gust of cold air across her face, and saw an opening before her wide enough to pass a corpulent person, if need be. She was afraid, at first, to put her hand down the opening lest it might touch a dangerous instrument or some other thing . . . many things . . . she knew not what.

With the utmost precaution she leaned forward and perceived that in what appeared to be the bottom of this hole a faint gleam of light impinged on one spot, indicating that there must be some passageway or other from whence this light, obviously daylight, emanated. There was no doubt whatever that she was in the presence of a secret passageway, constructed by Lady Manville's ancestors for the purpose of furnishing a means of escape from danger when the Scotch barons frequently battled fiercely over the issues of their times.

Lily ventured further on her knees, extending her hands and tapping with her finger-tips the inner recesses of the hole. Presently her hands settled on a cold iron bar. She extended them still further and discovered another bar directly below the first. She understood there must be others and that they evidently constituted a ladder which permitted descent. She settled herself more comfortably in the opening, and then fearfully commenced to descend, counting the bars of iron on which she posed her feet. There were twenty-one. When she reached the bottom rung she noticed a corridor on her right, twenty-five or thirty feet long, which led to the open sky and a series of snow-mantled rocks at least one hundred feet high.

Lily heaved a sigh of despair. How was she going to get past this wall of rocks? What good was her discovery if it only served to drag her down so many more feet underground? However, she noticed that at the terminus of the passageway there was no snow; and on raising her head she saw that the rocks made part of a cliff inclining slightly inward. Proceeding a few feet she distinguished on her right a rusty iron bar part of which was fastened to a rock. This bar served as a lever with which to move

213

the rock thus permitting one to arrive at a narrow path which led to the summit, covered over, here and there, by bushes and shrubs. She doubted no longer that by this path she could effect her escape, and a prodigious elation settled in her disordered being.

Brusquely she recalled that she had failed to cover up the means by which she had made her way from the cave, and she ran back nervously seeking some way of putting the stone back in place. Her movements were now made in the most complete obscurity. Her eyes dazzled by the whiteness of the snow-covered country, prevented her from distinguishing anything, but good fortune favored her. Tapping everything her hands could touch they suddenly settled on a hollow in the passageway, and she came upon a great iron wheel, evidently part of a machine, and she wondered what significance it could have. Then she discovered a crank-handle which she proceeded to turn, still not knowing what its purpose could be. In the stillness she heard from a distance, in the general direction of the iron ladder, a distinct grinding which convinced her that the contrivance she had fortunately stumbled upon was the mechanism which controlled the stone concealing the passageway. Certain that she had set in motion the machinery which restored this stone to its original place, her heart leaped with joy.

From the amount of light coming in at the level where she now found herself, the girl judged it must be about four o'clock in the afternoon. She could not venture out in full daylight without risking discovery, it was most important to wait until evening would come; but she was literally frozen and could scarcely endure the biting cold. To await a propitious hour she sought the innermost part of the passage where she perceived a drain-pipe.

214

This excited her interest and her eyes followed the pipe upward, whereupon she realized that it must have its origin in the floor of the cave in which Larkins had deposited her, for through this pipe she could hear the steady tread of the guard, almost as clearly as when she was in the cave. Looking down again she found that it terminated a few inches above the floor of this corridor in which she stood, and in front of her feet was the beginning of another pipe embedded in the floor, indicating that these pipes must be the ancient system of drainage which carried matter off from the cave to the sea. She was there about a quarter of an hour when the sound of footsteps and the noise of voices were heard overhead. She began to break out in a cold sweat.

"That must be my mistress, learning of my disappearance," she thought. "My God! my God! What will happen . . . I wonder if she has discovered the secret or if she did not know it before! . . ."

All at once she thought:

"If I could only break this mechanism!"

A courage that she never thought she possessed animated her. She crawled along, plunged her hand in the cavity which lodged the wheel and discovered a flat mesh chain at the end of which was a great iron hook, and the chain was wound around a large gear. . . . She lifted the hook, freed the chain and released the wheel, and it seemed possible to her that in this condition the mechanism might no longer function. But her worries were submerged temporarily before a tragi-comic scene which began to take place, the epilogue of which she was about to learn, as we shall soon see.

It appeared that Lady Manville must have changed her program as far as the visitors were concerned, and that she had descended to the *Cave of Sighs* to take Lily back to her boudoir instead, where she intended to execute punishment on the culprit. In the corridor she found William parading back and forth, and Lily realized for the first time that it was no other than the page-boy who was her guard.

"Nothing new?" she asked.

"Nothing, Milady."

"Lily hasn't budged?"

"Oh! No, Milady . . . I have not heard her move. . . ."

"Very good! Open the door."

Master William had the key which had been confided to him by Mrs. Larkins. He opened the door.

"Lily!" ordered the lady. "Come here!"

Profound silence.

"Well! Haven't you heard?"

Same silence.

A disagreeable shiver ran up and down Lady Manville's spine. . . . The girl must have taken desperately sick from the cold! she thought. She struck a match, lit one of the oil lamps, then entered and looked around in the cave. She saw nothing and her shivering recommenced, only more disagreeably this time. The cave was empty. For not a single instant had she dreamed of the stone which supported the bench. She failed to see that when the stone rotated it left traces against the other stones, besides, her footsteps in crossing the floor of the cave had soon effaced all these marks anyway.

Laura—Lily Butler, we should say—was not there! that was incontestable. Now, since she was not pure spirit she could not have dissolved in thin air. She had gone out, and gone out by the door because there existed no other opening.

216

But if she went out by the door William must have seen her! Yet it seemed his affirmation was made in good faith when he said he had not seen her. . . . The result of these reflections was the following conclusion, a conclusion, very logical, but also false, as we know: If Lily Butler went out by the door and William did not see her go, it must follow that master William was absent or asleep.

Convinced of her reasoning, Lady Manville seized master William by the ear.

"Wretch!" she cried. "I understand everything now! You left your post, or still worse, you fell asleep!"

"Oh! No, Milady!" the boy quaked. "I never moved from here except to walk constantly back and forth in front of this door."

"Liar! You dare to tell me anything like that! Confess now! Confess, in your own interest!"

"Milady!" whined the little domestic. "Milady, I have not budged!"

"Very well!" declared his mistress, pale with rage. "Since you will not confess of your own will, you shall be made to confess by force! Prepare your bottom, William!"

The boy fell on his knees, crying and supplicating his mistress, but she had already sat down on the bench and reached for a little whip with which she began to lash his calves. Then she grabbed him by his ear and pulled him out of the cave.

"You are going upstairs with me where I shall be able to handle you more at my ease!"

. . . At this very moment Lily started forth in an attempt to ascend the narrow path leading to the summit of the cliff. Night had fallen, but the reflection of the

snow gave sufficient light so that she could direct herself
with safety. Crawling along over the bushes and bram-
bles which obstructed the path she arrived finally at the
top and noticed several hundred feet away the outline of
the enormous castle which was Lady Manville's domain.
She was surprised at first at seeing the house stretch for
so great a distance. With a thousand precautions she
followed the walls of the old dwelling. The cold was
biting into her and she regretted with all her heart that
she was not better provided against the danger she might
encounter if she were to continue in her flight. What
could she do? What was going to become of her?

. Her first thought was to make her way back to Sloane
House, to Miss Evelyn, but she could not dream of accomplishing that in the middle of the night with all the
snow on the ground, alone, on foot, and hope to prevail
against this awful cold! . . .

A frightful despair invaded her entire being. She had
a momentary temptation to lie right down, to stretch out
in the snow and die, but this thought wrung her heart and
made her weep. All of a sudden she felt the urgent need
of refuge, the association of people, even the wish to
atone through whippings for this last offense, and she
directed herself toward the house. A wall about ten feet
high ran around the castle. From her height she could
see a number of small service buildings within the wall.
Moving forward, toward the side facing the sea, Lily
noticed that the wall had a door which was supposed to
be closed by a latch. As there was nothing to fear at
this time of the year, especially, the latch was down and
Lily had merely to push the door and it opened without
difficulty. At once she noticed on her left a squatty cabin
from which rose an odor of straw, and through the inter-

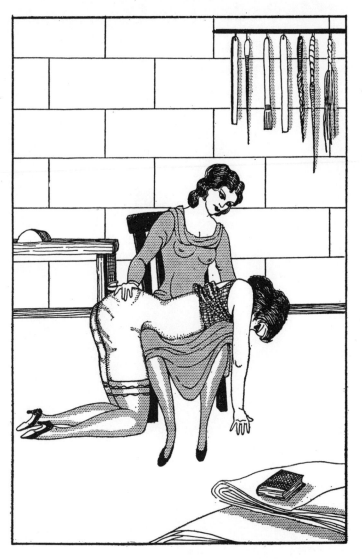

"What did I whip you with yesterday, Lily?" asked Mrs.
Wharton in her most casual tone (page 240)

stices emanated the warm vapor of beasts. She walked toward the cabin, raised the latch and found she was in a stable. There were four horses standing up in their stalls, and on her entrance they turned their smoking noses toward the new arrival but without making the least noise. To her left was a stack of straw, and it seemed as though it would make a warm bed for the night. Lily promptly decided to crouch down on it. She would leave in the morning, at daybreak, and no matter how, attempt to make her way to Sloane.

Near the stack of hay was a saddle and across it lay a heavy woolen blanket. Lily determined to avail herself of it in the morning when she would begin her tramping along the snow-covered road, and having made these various reflections she improvised her bed on the straw. The horses did not appear to be the least bit disconcerted by this intrusion in their domicile. She heard only their regular respiration, and finding herself among such gentle companions the girl felt quite reassured. An old lantern cast a flickering light on the croupes of the good beasts and Lily made, by the aid of this light, a nest for herself in the dry straw. Suddenly she heard a feeble groan and a dull rattling noise which appeared to come from the depths of the ground. A shiver of terror took hold of her and her heart seemed to stop beating. . . .

She listened again, pressing her ear toward the earth; the dull rattle became more precise and with it rose the sound of an irritated voice. These noises came from the direction of the door. Trembling violently Lily walked as noiselessly as possible toward it. She had only to make two steps and at the third she had the impression that it was directly under her feet from whence the sounds came. There, beneath some straw which she parted cautiously, she saw a ray of light filtering through some bars of an iron grill closed over an excavation. Breathlessly Lily knelt and peered down, and that which she saw made her tremble and vibrate to her very marrow. . . .

The grill rested just above a corridor which must have been that leading to the *Cave of Sighs*. There was an indentation in the ceiling of this corridor and an opening which showed that its floor must be not more than fifteen feet below. There, to her complete stupefaction, Lily witnessed a scene of flagellation which our heroine only too well understood, not only from previous observations, but from an intensive, if forced, study of her own.

Lady Manville had convicted master William, found him responsible for the girl's disappearance, and was chastising him. The wooden horse in the *Cave of Sighs* had been dragged out. Stretched over it, the boy had been stripped clean of his lower garments and shackled to this contrivance. By the side of it stood one of the maids, and Lily recognized her as Ellen. She held above her head one of the oil lamps which cast light on the fleshy parts of the boy whom Lady Manville was whipping with all the vigor of which she was capable. William writhed like a serpent whose head has been crushed, he shrieked with all the power of his lungs, and this was quite comprehensible when one understood the severity with which Lady Manville could whip when she was in temper. While inflicting this slashing correction on the unfortunate boy, she did not forget to berate him as she proceeded. But her voice arrived only indistinctly to Lily who, drawn by this spectacle, not at all new to her, to be sure, stretched herself out and pressed her ear to the ground. Now she could hear Lady Manville refer-

222

ring again to the mysterious disappearance of the prisoner.

"I assigned to you the duty of watching this girl!" she cried, while whipping William with the full swing of her arm. "You were in front of her door or at least you should have been there! You can never make me believe that she passed you right under your nose without you seeing her. So much the worse for you! So much the worse for your posterior, you little swine that you are! Here! Here! Here! Here! And I swear to you that when I capture her, she herself will do a dance that she will remember for a long, long time! Give me a better light, Ellen! Or do you want some of this yourself, you also! . . ."

Lily, enormously frightened, felt an impulse to fly at once, to run, cost what it may, through the night toward Sloane House, but a glance through the partly opened door at the exterior made her shiver. She looked once more down below: Lady Manville had finished whipping William. She had straightened herself, tucking back her sleeves first with one hand then the other, and brandishing the strap as if she were preparing to chase after Lily for the purpose of giving her the same treatment just meted out to the page. . . .

Lily experienced such fright that she abandoned her post of observation at once, without even pausing to look with what compassion Ellen nursed William's inflamed flesh, how tenderly her expert hands bathed with soothing cold water the boy's puffed skin, drying it later with the utmost gentleness; and how she finally pulled a veil cautiously over the deeply reddened parts—a veil which was nothing else than the poor young man's shirt.

Lily sank down nervously in her improvised bed and

covered herself with the woolen blanket. It did not take her long to fall asleep, broken as she was by fatigue and emotion; a sleep which left posed on her pink lips the desperate words of prayer she addressed to heaven.

XVII

Return to Sloane House

How did she awaken? She never knew. She only remembered that she jumped up suddenly as though splashed with a pail of icy water, and an awareness of the realities burst squarely, so to speak, on her mind. She rose shivering, shook herself, pulled the wisps of straw from her hair and dress, covered herself with the blanket up to her ears and cheeks, and softly, gently, opened the door.

A vague, indeterminate gleam of light piercing the dark sky announced approaching daylight, but the shadows were still screening the heavens. It snowed. She could not have hoped for a more propitious time to make her departure. The falling snow would efface all traces of her footsteps, and at this early hour no one would be awake in Duncaster House. . . . She took the road to the north, which made it easy since she had only to follow the sound of the sea; for despite the snow which had piled up in drifts, the road was still passable. She quickened her pace, battling against the wind on her right and against the soft flakes in which her feet were continually sinking. Soon she resembled a snow-man, her head and cloak were completely covered, but she felt no anxiety about this. In fact it was a moving refuge in which she felt protected, as it were, against her enemies of the moment, the snow and the wind which beat in her face.

Ten miles under these atrocious conditions the poor girl had to trudge, and she tramped in the snow for more than five hours to make it. Again and again she battled against the desire to lie down in the narrow road, to envelop herself in her shawl and sleep right there. . . . Instinctively she understood that to do this meant death.

A strong wind came up, the snow ceased falling, and from a distance she heard the faint sound of clocks from the church steeples. They were the bells of Thurso which were ringing the hour. She counted eleven strokes and her heart began to beat precipitately. She must be approaching Sloane, and only the uniformly white blanket of snow prevented distinguishing the hard school she was returning to of her own accord.

What sort of reception was she likely to receive? What new miseries were ahead? Had she not made a great mistake in running away from Lady Manville? No! That was much worse! At Duncaster House she had not a single friend who could be of use to her. At Sloane at least, she could look to Miss Evelyn, who under an antagonistic appearance was actually kind-hearted. She hastened her walk.

Soon the high wall about Sloane House appeared, all covered with snow. The main entrance gate was open and Lily took the path in. Timidly she rang the bell, after having taken care to conceal her face in the folds of her shawl. The door opened and she entered the vestibule. Hannah, who served as porter, half opened a peep-hole to prevent the cold from rushing into the comfortably heated room.

"What do you want?" she grumbled, munching on a piece of buttered toast.

"I want to see Miss Evelyn!" responded Lily, lowering

226

her voice which, in fact, required no effort to disguise because of a cold she had contracted en route.

Hannah did not insist and let the peep-hole snap back. She was used to seeing women laundresses come to Thurso bringing things back to Miss Evelyn, and it was very fortunate for Lily who was thus able to proceed toward the laundry without further questioning. The moment she entered her ear caught sounds which gripped her heart. They were the sounds of groans and sobs, accompanying the characteristic noises of a correction applied on the bare skin. Making a strong effort, Lily turned the knob of the door and entered, and this is what she saw:

With her elbows on the laundry table, a young girl was looking at a length of material which a governess was holding before her. The latter was reproaching the girl for her clumsy work, pointing out the imperfections, while on the other side Miss Evelyn, with a strap in her hand, was methodically striking the young girl's posterior from which the skirts had been turned back. She was evidently a "novice" who was being "lectured" about her faulty sewing, and in the usual Scotch fashion, as anyone could see. . . .

The girl wept, trembled, but kept her eyes carefully posed on the work which the governess was showing her. . . .

Lily's entrance marked the end of her punishment.

Miss Evelyn stood still, her mouth wide open and her arm lifted; the other governess had let the piece of cloth fall to the floor, and the burning tears of the punished girl seemed to have halted in their course down her cheeks.

Lily, trembling and apprehensive, began to remove her

227

shawl. She had taken care to shake the snow off it before she entered.

"Good Lord!" exclaimed Miss Evelyn. "Is that Lily Butler I see there? . . ."

"It actually is!" confirmed the governess.

Lily fell at the knees of Miss Evelyn and kissed her hands passionately.

"Miss Evelyn!" she sobbed. "Save me! Have pity on me! . . ."

"She is soaking wet, the poor creature!" exclaimed Miss Evelyn, passing her hand over Lily's hair, while the governess sat down and began to adjust the skirts of the chastised pupil. She turned to this colleague:

"Listen, dear, leave me alone with Lily for a while. I am going to thaw her out and make her dry. Please take that fool along with you and show her how to sew. I shall join you as soon as I've put this one in some shape."

The governess rose, took her pupil by the hand and withdrew without saying a word. Then Miss Evelyn took Lily in her arms, drew near the stove, gave her a chair and reached behind a pile of linen for a bottle of wine, some of which she poured into a glass.

"There!" she said. "That feels better, does it not? But how in heaven's name do you come to be here? And in what an outfit, good Lord! Come! Tell me everything, quickly! What are you going to say to Mrs. Wharton?"

Thanks to Miss Evelyn's solicitude Lily was already feeling much more comfortable. She reached once again for the young woman's hand and kissed it many times, then she commenced her story, taking particular care to leave a good many pertinent details in the shadows. She hadn't talked for more than five minutes when the door opened noisily and Mrs. Wharton appeared. Lily sensed herself fainting.

"What do they tell me?" exclaimed the mistress of the house. "That Lily Butler has arrived? From where? How? Why? What does this mean? . . ."

"Madame!" said Miss Evelyn. "She was frozen wet from the snow . . . I have just made her warm. . . ."

"A good whipping would have warmed her much better!" snapped Mrs. Wharton. "Besides she shall not escape it if I am not completely satisfied with her explanation. Change her quickly! I am going to take her upstairs with me!"

Miss Evelyn did not say a word. She took Lily, disrobed her rapidly, making the buttons snap in her haste, and in the flash of an eye she had put the girl in the costume of our first mother.

"Oh! exclaimed Mrs. Wharton, as she examined Lily from all directions, "I suppose this young person didn't find everything to her complete satisfaction at Duncaster House! And so you believe that things will be more comfortable for you at Sloane, do you? . . . Don't deceive yourself! I shall teach you what it costs to desert a post!"

"Madame!" groaned Lily. "I implore you, take me back! She would have *killed* me! Take me! Take care of me here! . . . Please! . . ."

Mrs. Wharton appeared to reflect for a second, then her face brightened.

"Indeed! . . ." she commenced.

But she did not finish expressing the thought which had come to her. She walked over to Evelyn who, in silence, was aiding Lily to dress in fresh clothes, and she whispered, very low, in the young woman's ear:

"Not a word whatever to anyone of Lily's return. If Lady Manville comes here to inquire, we must respond that no one here has seen the girl. Do you understand that quite clearly?"

"I understand very well, Madame," responded Evelyn promptly, very happy at what she interpreted as an unexpected wave of humanity.

"Finish dressing her, I shall give you orders later. . . ."

The directress disappeared and Miss Evelyn permitted the girl whom everyone persisted in calling Lily Butler, to nestle in her breast.

"Lily Butler," she said, "I am glad to have you back again. There isn't any doubt that you shall receive a good many whippings here, but I shall be at hand to look after you, I hope. Good heavens! I don't know why it is, but for some reason or another I like you and I am glad to have you around!"

Lily, moved beyond all power of expression, threw her arms impulsively about the young woman's neck and embraced her with a rapturous heart. It was not such a dismal prospect now, to be whipped! She would never quit Miss Evelyn and with her aid, perhaps, she might some day get out of this Training School in which she had been plunged originally in so outrageous a fashion. . . . In the meantime Mrs. Wharton gave orders throughout the establishment and, wisely enough, she lost no time about it, for scarcely had she completed her rounds than the doorbell rang in an agitated manner.

Hannah opened it and saw, standing out in the snow, the old Manville carriage on the bench of which Joe sat coughing and spitting. Lady Manville herself penetrated like a shot, followed by Ellen who seemed to move with difficulty. Without a doubt the noble lady, exacerbated

230

by Lily's disappearance, had visited a portion of her rage
on the fleshiest part of her unfortunate servant's body.

She precipitated herself toward Mrs. Wharton.

"Lily!" she cried. "Lily Butler! Have you not seen
her? . . ."

"How should I have seen her?" responded Mrs.
Wharton with the most astonished air in the world.
"How could I see her when she is at your place?"

"But that is precisely where she isn't," Lady Manville
responded desolately. "She disappeared last night and
every effort I've made to find her has been unavailing;
hence I thought she might have sought refuge here."

"Lord!" exclaimed Mrs. Wharton. "What a strange
thing that is! . . . But we haven't seen her, have we,
Hannah? If you do not succeed in finding her I should
like to wager that she drowned, perhaps deliberately—
she had such an odd character—or accidently perhaps,
which would not surprise me if she tried to run away
during the night."

"She must have had the Devil's wings!" muttered
Lady Manville, after a moment's reflection. "I shall wait
a few days and, if I do not find her, I shall have to ask
you to furnish me with another girl."

"With the greatest of pleasure. But here it is noon,
couldn't I offer you some lunch?"

"Thanks, we are going on to the village where I have
some purchases to make. See you soon."

The two respectable ladies exchanged an affectionate
handshake, one of them enchanted in having tricked the
other, and Mrs. Wharton returned to the laundry.

Lily had put her absence to profit to resume her story
to Miss Evelyn down to the least details this time, but the
good young woman made very certain to betray no indig-

nation, lest her disciplinary position be impaired; yet in
the course of Lily's recital she endeavored to calm the
girl, whose nerves were greatly wrought up at the recollection of her experiences. Suddenly Mrs. Wharton
entered and Lily's narration stopped right there.

"You are ready, I suppose," said the directress. "It
is time for lunch. Go take it with your companions . . .
or rather no. Follow me. You shall have your lunch
in my room."

She was actually relieved, in fact, at this change of
order because she did not want her companions to learn
too soon of her return, lest they begin to chatter, and dis-
torted portions of her story might come to Mrs.
Wharton's ear. But she was greatly grieved at having
to leave Miss Evelyn, and she followed the directress into
the latter's chamber. On Mrs. Wharton's order she stood
in a corner next to a small round table and a few minutes
later an appetizing slice of roast beef and vegetables were
placed before her which she ate with good appetite, notwithstanding the disquieting presence of Mrs. Wharton
who had already dined. The latter never withdrew her
gaze from the girl.

When she had finished her repast, she heard the voice
of the directress calling her. Mrs. Wharton was sitting
near a window, in a deep and comfortable armchair.

"Come here, on your knees before me, and tell me
everything that happened," she ordered.

Lily obeyed, her nerves twittering violently. She was
enormously agitated, for it was necessary to tell a good
many lies, to fabricate a whole story, and she feared that
Mrs. Wharton would muddle her up with insidious interrogations. She related that Lady Manville had put her
for three days on bread and water in a room which

had no fire, that she had dared to protest, and that the lady's fury, which her remark had stirred up, knew no limits. She had stripped her of her clothes, pinched her in the most sensitive parts of her body until she bled and, finally, had whipped her and then had her whipped by other servants for more than two hours without pause. . .

Mrs. Wharton, who took a lively interest in this recital, frowned. "Oh! oh!" she said. "What a batch of lies! Come up here on my lap so that I can examine you. . . ."

Lily, more dead than alive, extended herself across the lady's knees.

"It is not" . . . she began.

"Keep quiet! You will talk when I ask you to."

Mrs. Wharton pulled back the girl's skirts and proceeded to examine those parts which, having been whipped for so long a period and so often, should have shown many welts or bruises, but except for a general sluggishness, and a few insignificant abrasions the flesh did not display any impressive excoriation.

"How does it happen," asked Mrs. Wharton at last, putting the young girl back on her feet and looking at her severely, "that your bottom looks almost as well as if you had never received a whipping?"

"Madame!" stammered Lily, pale with fright, "that is because Lady Manville and the servants whipped me with their hands only. . . ."

"Hum! . . ." said Mrs. Wharton. "Continue I pray you."

Lily resumed her story. She invented a flight which, according to her, was effected in the most natural way in the world and she terminated by imploring the directress to pardon her. Greatly worried by the fear that Mrs. Wharton might not take her back, she blurted out impulsively, in an effort to give greater force to her plea, that even if she had to submit to exemplary corrections each day she would prefer a hundred times over to receive them at Sloane rather than at Duncaster House.

"You are not returning to Duncaster," said Mrs. Wharton, "but you can understand yourself that the interests of discipline require that I inflict a severe chastisement on you at once, and you are quite ready to receive it, aren't you?"

This statement and question obviously forced the girl's hand.

"Yes, Madame . . ." groaned Lily.

Mrs. Wharton rose and pointed out her armchair to the girl.

"Get on your knees here on this chair and prepare your clothes," she said.

For a moment Lily was tempted to supplicate, to crawl at the directress' knees, if only to retard for a minute the infamous and dolorous chastisement, but she reminded herself in time that any sign of hesitation always brought down a terrible aggravation of the punishment. She knelt down and pulled up her skirts. Her chin rested on the back of the armchair and she sobbed quietly. Her skirt tucked under her armpits, she buried her face, congested with shame and anguish, in her hands, and she waited, contracting her shivering flesh. Without any haste Mrs. Wharton made herself ready. She went to a drawer of her secretary and pulled out a long, thin, brown leather strap. Returning to Lily, she pinned back the girl's shirt and skirts to the shoulders in order to securely retain all the turned-up clothes, then she tucked back her sleeves to the elbow in order to be more free in her movements and to be able to chastise with greater force. That

234

done, she brought the tip of the strap around to Lily's mouth.

"Kiss it!" she said. "Humble yourself. Repent. Whatever be the reasons you can invoke to excuse your actions, they can in no way attenuate the offense you have committed. I am going to whip you now. After that I shall put you in a cell and twice each day, for a period of two weeks, I shall come in to whip you. After that I shall begin to think about another mistress for you. The best thing you can do is to accept your punishment with the most absolute submission, otherwise it will cost you dear, and you know just how I shall pay you out! Is all this understood?"

"Yes . . . Madame . . ." sobbed Lily.

Mrs. Wharton then passed behind her and, for a preliminary, struck alternately with the flat of her hand each of the fleshy hemispheres which shivered with every contact. It was a burning and smarting chastisement, prolonged for nearly five minutes, the lady concentrating, one might say, on the business of seeing that every part of the girl's posterior attained the same degree of heat and the same somber reddish color. As this lengthy correction proceeded, Mrs. Wharton changed hands from time to time to avoid becoming fatigued, and the severity of each slap never diminished, on the contrary. Finally she took the strap and Lily, who had stoically supported the first part of her correction, began to kick her legs frantically up and down while her heretofore subdued moans changed to cries.

"Will you keep quiet!" grumbled Mrs. Wharton, cracking away harder. "Do you want me to tie your hands and feet and whip you with a cat-o'nine-tails? Answer me? Answer me? Answer me? Do you want that?

Otherwise you must bear your smarting without complaint! Ah! You may wriggle! You may fidget! But spare me your shrieks! Someone might think you were being scorched alive! . . ."

Lily tried to shove her little fists in her mouth in a desperate effort to support the horrible biting of the strap without weakening, and she succeeded tolerably well. Incontestibly, this docile attitude which the girl not very long ago would never have believed she could ever bring herself to, must have impressed itself on Mrs. Wharton who was never the woman to content herself with a few lashes, once she began to whip. She was, however, not too unreasonable and Lily was spared enduring any additional ordeals at this session.

"Now," said Mrs. Wharton, when she had carefully put the strap back in the drawer and pulled down her sleeves, "now, Lily, you will sit down here, on this chair, and you will read these passages in the Bible in a low voice. Let us hope that this pious task will help advance you in the road to moral progress where we are trying to lead you."

Having pronounced these words without the faintest smile to betray her profound dignity, Mrs. Wharton stalked out of the room.

Lily was left alone. The letters in the book danced before her eyes and the text took on the most bizarre appearance. A most uncomfortable tingling irritated that part of her body on which the severity of Mrs. Wharton had exercised itself, with such a result that she could scarcely distinguish a thought in the pious meditations which that lady had commanded.

Evelyn! She longed for Miss Evelyn! Her anxiety to be back under her supervision mounted with every moment; instead, she was to be put in a cell where she would be obliged to submit to the frightfully annoying regimen of two whippings a day for two full weeks. . . . Mrs. Wharton talked of a new post for her. . . . God! Anything, even death, rather than to fall back into the hands of another Lady Manville!

Dreaming thus, two hours passed. The door opened and Mrs. Wharton entered.

"Lily!" said the directress, "come with me, your cell is ready. Take your Bible along. You can do nothing better than to occupy yourself with its reading when you will be alone, except for the two intervals each morning and evening when you shall pay the installments of the punishment for your flight."

She took her by the hand and conducted her to one of the cells we have already penetrated formerly, and where the furniture was most summary. There the girl was locked in.

XVIII

The Shackles Become Glamourous

Each morning when she began to make her toilette in the cell she was obliged to gaze with frightened eyes upon the different instruments of correction which hung over the door. Then the hour would swiftly approach for Mrs. Wharton's regular visit, and for two days already, morning and evening, the girl had passed through atrocious moments each time her mistress arrived.

All at once she shivered. In the corridor she heard footsteps which she knew only too well. The door opened and Mrs. Wharton appeared. She was dressed in a long black peignoir, gathered tightly at the waist by a silken cord. This gown gave the lady an air which fitted well with her pale complexion and austere features. She closed the door carefully and came over to Lily whose trembling hands she took.

"Good morning, Madame!" quaked the girl.

"Good morning, Lily. How do you feel this morning?"

"Very well . . . Madame . . ." sputtered Lily, her anguish increasing.

"And your state of mind? How is that disposed? Do you begin to feel yourself arriving at true submission, do you sense your entire being abandoning itself with full will, and with even a certain pleasure, to my wishes? To the will of your superiors, no matter what it may be? And, finally, the present regimen and coercive training which I have prescribed for you, is it beginning to be effective?"

"Yes, Madame. . . ."

"We shall see. I trust you appreciate how good I am to you: I could augment your humiliations by chastising you in public, or at least before a certain number of persons. I am not doing this. I come to you all alone, I close myself in with you so that just the two of us only can remain in the most complete intimacy . . . I trust you are grateful for this attention. Now prepare your clothes, Lily. . . ."

The girl, turning livid and crimson, suffered more from these unctuously pronounced words than she would have suffered from a furious tirade, but already the crushing regime of the whip had effectively humbled her. She raised her skirts without saying a word, repressing her tears, and since girls confined to the cells certainly wore no bloomers or drawers, she found herself quickly exposed and in a state of readiness to receive the routine whipping.

"Extend yourself on this bench, Lily," requested Mrs. Wharton. "It is much more practical."

Lily obeyed. Mrs. Wharton leaned over on the bench and began, without any other formalities, the infliction of a vigorous spanking, applied methodically and with a dignified preciseness. Lily was already so well accustomed to these proceedings that she uttered no complaint about this usual hors d'oeuvre. Only the leather tawse or the cat-o'nine-tails had the power of making her cry now. The hand-spanking terminated, the girl rose from her place, knelt down and kissed Mrs. Wharton's warm hand, as well as the hem of her dress, in proof of her gratitude and humility. Then she extended herself once more on the bench and presented her reddened flesh for the rest of her chastisement.

"What did I whip you with yesterday, Lily?" asked Mrs. Wharton in her most casual tone. "Good Lord, what a terrible memory I have! . . . Was it the riding-whip or the tawse?"

"The riding-whip, Madame," groaned Lily. She would gladly have said the tawse instead, but she dreaded the possibility of a trap on the part of her pitiless disciplinarian. And although she cringed in fear of the tawse with its dull, brutal power for crushing the muscles under the skin—a power less acute in the riding-whip because its lashes were lighter, she dared not lie. Mrs. Wharton smiled knowingly and went to lift the tawse from its hook on the door. She pulled up her own skirts, sat herself down astride over Lily's waist, brandished the leather band. . . .

Smack! . . . Smack! . . . Smack! . . . Smack! . . .

The sonorous and characteristic blows resounded in the small room and with its sounds were mingled the dolorous groans of Lily who, incapable of supporting the severe whipping without budging, began to twitch and writhe on her bench of pain. Twenty-five times the tawse cracked solidly against the fleshy globes, marking them with wide red-colored stripes, and when Mrs. Wharton, quite pale and nostrils throbbing, stopped, Lily's cries had died down to moans of agony. Mrs. Wharton hung up the tawse and came back to the girl who had remained prostrate on the bench. The whipped flesh was still agitated by tumultuous quivering. The skin resembled a somber red on a field of blue and violet. The directress knelt down and began to massage the region in a manner that showed expert knowledge. Little by little, under her accustomed hands, the flesh resumed a uniform tone, the welts became less prominent, and ten minutes had scarcely passed before the color of the skin was greatly modified. The congested posterior resumed the lively red color which the manual spanking had first produced, and even the smarting lessened somewhat. Only an intense and fiery heat now pervaded the region, a heat which kept recalling incessantly to Lily the severe chastisement to which she had just submitted. Finally, Mrs. Wharton drew from her corsage a little perfumed handkerchief and wiped the perspiration which ran in small beads along the girl's temples and cheeks.

"Stand up, Lily!" she said at last.

Lily stood up and with trembling fingers let her skirt down. A red almost as deep as that which colored the other side of her person was spread over her face, and the tears still ran softly along her cheeks.

"Give me the kiss of peace," said Mrs. Wharton.

Lily approached and embraced her mistress on the mouth.

"Now that you have received this correction, I am going to withdraw and leave you to your meditations. Take your Bible, read it earnestly, and let us hope it will drive out some of your wicked thoughts before long. . . ."

Mrs. Wharton withdrew.

Just as she did after each of her visits, Lily burst into tears, threw herself on the blankets and indulged in the luxury of a little crisis of nerves, then, after a while, a calmness returned and to pass the time rather than out of any zealousness she opened her Bible and plunged into the reading of passages which were quite obscure to her. For more than an hour she remained at comparative ease, when she detected distant footsteps once more in

the corridor, and a fresh trembling seized her. Was it
Mrs. Wharton again? Why? What new humiliations
was she going to inflict now? . . .

It was not Mrs. Wharton. It was Evelyn. Lily
breathed a deep sigh of relief. The very sight of her
favorite supervisor soothed her nerves beyond expression,
and in an impulsive gesture of gratitude for the visit, she
ran toward Miss Evelyn, fell on her knees and pressed
warm kisses on that young lady's hand. For a moment
she was unable to utter a word, but through her mind
ran the reassuring thought that Miss Evelyn could not
have been sent in to whip her, for that appeared to be
Mrs. Wharton's prerogative for the ensuing two weeks.
Miss Evelyn was the first to speak.

"Well, Lily, how are you coming along with your
punishment? I understand Madame has already been in
to see you this morning."

"Oh yes, Miss! Oh yes . . . she has been in. . . ."

"And are you settling down to the routine of your
whippings?"

"Oh, Miss, it is so hard! . . . so hard. . . ."

"Of course it's hard! It has to be, if it wasn't it
could scarcely be called punishment. After all, you didn't
expect to receive anything less after running away from
your post, did you?"

"No, Miss, I expected to be punished . . . but please,
Miss. . . ."

"But what, Lily?"

"Madame's ways . . . and her words, Miss, are so . . .
harsh . . . Oh, please forgive me, Miss."

"You don't expect her to be silent while she whips you?
I think that much of what she says is good for you to
hear, my girl, for your future's sake. And if you have

the good sense I think you have, Lily, it would be well for you to buckle down as cheerfully as possible to what is ahead for you for the next twelve or thirteen days, any-way. You know you have to go through with it, why don't you try to take what is coming to you without all this mental straining. You know already you can't get out of preparing your bottom, and to that you are becom-ing resigned, but you still think you can get out of pre-paring your mind, and to accomplish that end Madame talks to you as she does. The longer you fight against it the harder it will be for you, and I am going to tell you this while I am about it; if you show an honest effort to get rid of this stubborness, I shall like you much better and help you whenever I can, but if you persist in re-maining obdurate and stupidly continue to make your lot worse for yourself, I shall lose all interest in you. Do you care or don't you?"

"Oh, Miss, I do care, I do! . . . If you didn't love—I mean like me, I would be so much more unhappy, Miss!"

"Then you will have to justify my opinion of your intelligence," Miss Evelyn insisted. "Will you promise me to make a sincere effort?"

"Yes, Miss, I promise to do anything you ask," she responded earnestly.

"Very well. First you must resolve to answer Mad-ame's questions promptly and respectfully; and when she is ready to whip you, show as much eagerness as possible to atone for your flight from Lady Manville. During these two weeks, if you keep your promise, I shall try to see you whenever I can manage."

"Oh, thank you, Miss, thank you. Please Miss, do you think there is any chance of my being put back in your charge . . . afterward?"

"I don't know, Lily. I should like to have you, but I could have no great say in the matter. However, I shall try to suggest it if I can find a favorable occasion. A great deal would depend on how you conduct yourself in the cell for the balance of your imprisonment. Before I go now, I want to hear you promise again that you will devote yourself to your obligations, and that when Madame comes in this evening you will make every effort to show your goodwill to make the discipline profitable to yourself."

Lily fell on her knees once more, kissed Miss Evelyn's hand fervently and promised with a full heart that she would do her utmost to meet all the requirements. Evelyn helped her up, pressed her arm in a friendly manner and went out, Lily missed her enormously. Here was the only person in authority, since the first day of this strange existence, who was human and considerate; the only person who was not continually harsh, whose store of the milk of human kindness had not been utterly drained by the rigorous disciplinary tactics of which she made a part. Whatever the sacrifice, whatever the cost, Lily thought, she must not alienate Miss Evelyn's friendly interest; and in this frame of mind, and in obedience to that young lady's latest admonitions, she resolved that henceforth she would try with all her might to measure up to the supervisor's expectations.

A certain composure came over her as these reflections took root, and in the new mood she almost looked forward to Mrs. Wharton's next visit, so eager was she to present evidence of it. As she pondered over it all and recalled the whippings she had received from Miss Evelyn, particularly, an old subconscious thought began to make itself articulate, and the knowledge of it startled

244

Her object was to wedge her slave's waistline in the special harness as tautly as the hands would allow (page 267)

her. She remembered a vague sense of contentment she would feel while Miss Evelyn was whipping her, and not only that contentment but a subtle blending of the pain into a bewildering snugness and well-being. And when the whipping was over and her mind was not so distracted by the smarting, she could discern through the intense heat pervading her an indistinct felicity which never fully delineated itself because of her mental agonizing over the nature of her new existence. But why did she not feel these sensations when Mrs. Wharton or anyone else whipped her? The pain was pretty much alike generally, therefore, the difference between pain exclusively and pain blending into a bitter-sweet and ticklish attraction must be in the frame of mind, the attitude brought to this potentially two-edged discipline. More than that, if the power to extract joy from pain was real, that power could only derive and must be predicated on an unequivocal affection for the one who inflicted the pain. Therein lay the secret, then. Miss Evelyn, wittingly or unwittingly, had quickened the girl's admiration and affection by her humane character, and it was this feeling which had endowed Miss Evelyn's good right palm with its double force, the force to create terrific pain and the force to galvanize it into ineffable joy.

Lily spent the best part of that long day exploring the labyrinth of these strange emotions, not forgetting to prepare herself against the expected visit of her mistress after her own frugal evening meal. This would be her sixth whipping with twenty-two more whipping-payments to be made before she could stand cleared of her offense. Shortly after seven she heard noises in the corridor and she steeled herself against Mrs. Wharton's entry. She prayed fervently that signs of her changed

247

behavior would earn her some amelioration of the amount of punishment she would have to endure at each session thereafter. Mrs. Wharton entered.

"Have you spent the day making good resolutions, Lily?" she immediately asked.

"Yes, Madame," the girl was prompt to answer, while she fingered her skirt nervously.

"Well, we shall see how you manifest these resolutions as we go along. Are you over the effects of this morning's whipping and are you ready for the present one?"

"Yes, Madame, I am ready."

"Come over here on my lap and show me your bottom. I want to see how it looks after this morning's punishment."

The girl obeyed immediately. She picked up her skirt, tucked it under her arms, extended herself face down on her mistress' lap, and waited. Mrs. Wharton tapped around roughly, taking up portions of the girl's flesh between her fingers until she had examined both sides of the large area. Then she ordered her to stand up.

"You recover quickly," she asserted. "Your skin looks very well, a sign of good health, and I think we need have no fear of proceeding with your training. Since I put you in this cell, Lily," the lady continued, "I have been thinking a good deal about the causes of your flight and about your future. As to what actually prompted you to run away, I am inclined to believe, the more I think of it, that the fault is largely our own for having failed to complete your training before binding you out. This time we shall remedy that neglect. Despite the fact that we whipped you regularly, we did not whip you often enough. The result was that we didn't fully attune your bottom to endure severe whippings. Consequently, when we bound you out into formal service you found the new regimen too uncomfortable, and you decided, since the whippings you received here were more bearable, you would make your way back to us at the first opportunity. Escaping as you did, you cast an ugly reflection on our institution and our system of training. For that you must be soundly punished, because we cannot permit you to ever do that again, and we shall take the necessary safeguards this time. You must know, Lily, that our Home enjoys the enviable reputation of turning out the best disciplined maids in the country, and under no circumstances will we allow anyone to jeopardize the fame which is ours. Obviously, we are not going to take any chances next time, and when we find another post for you, we shall make sure you will never think of flight again. Thanks to our reputation, the class of ladies attracted to us come here for their maids because they are accustomed to deal severely with them, and they very naturally look to us first to supply them with girls that meet their rigid requirements.

"Accordingly, I have decided that after you have received your present punishment in full, you will be reassigned to some task where you will be granted the same favors we bestow on all the girls in satisfactory standing. But while you have completed your punishment for the offense which brings you here, your training will be far from complete. I shall, consequently, issue orders that for at least a full month, after your two weeks here are up, and until I see reasons for rescinding my order, you will be whipped twice each day just the same. The object of this regimen will be to bring the skin on your bottom and the muscles and nerves in that region up to a satisfactory state of endurance, so that when the time comes that I can bind you out to another mistress, you will be sure to fulfill faithfully all the promises I make respecting your eligibility for her service. Will you help us to bring you to that desirable state or are you going to try and resist it?"

Lily listened to this ambitious program with a sinking heart. She had to call on the last resources of her feeble strength to make prompt reply and her voice reached no higher than a hoarse whisper. Across her harried brain flashed the figures of Myra and Ellen, the similarity in the reasoning of these ladies, like Mrs. Wharton and Lady Manville, as to methods of procedure in "breaking in" their girls; the extreme likelihood that despite her determination they would ultimately make of her the same sort of "thing" they had made of Myra, and her eyes swam in hot tears.

"No, Madame, I won't resist . . ." she managed to pronounce in a dying voice.

"A very sensible answer, Lily. It encourages me to proceed along the precise lines I have indicated, and I am hoping we shall have gratifying results from you yet. Make yourself ready now for this whipping."

In the space of two minutes Lily was lying stretched out on the bench, her nervous posterior exposed to the forthcoming trial. Mrs. Wharton used the tawse again and the powerful instrument bit mercilessly into her flesh. Through the first dozen lashes the girl vibrated like one afflicted with the ague, then a sort of torpor settled into the flagellated area and for the balance of the chastisement she lay comparatively quiet, quivering slightly and moaning in a low tone. Aside from an ominous statement that hereafter she would gradually add to each dose for the balance of the two weeks, Mrs. Wharton refrained from the usual diatribes she delivered as she whipped. In her grim way she thus expressed, negatively, her satisfaction at the change in attitude. After the usual ceremonies which followed the conclusion of each whipping, Mrs. Wharton left the cell with the promise that she would be back in the morning.

For the next few hours Lily endeavored cautiously to reduce the turgidity of her aching posterior by massaging it gently with her hands. Slowly the discomfort lessened, and as she lay flat on her stomach across the blankets she had wearily spread on the floor, her mind dwelt on the whippings she had to look forward to now. Instead of the twenty-two still ahead, she could add at least sixty more to them. Eighty-two whippings to be endured in continuous order, not counting a few extra for ordinary derelictions! . . . She cried herself softly to sleep.

So it went on for eleven more painful and monotonous days. Miss Evelyn came to see her several times, and the young lady's visits were like balm to her anguished heart. Notwithstanding the admonitions Miss Evelyn would be sure to deliver before going out, Lily construed the supervisor's visits as those of a warm friend who came to the bedside of a lonely hospital patient. When she left the pangs of her solitude returned to plague her misery. At last her two weeks' incarceration came to an end, and her joy was unbounded when she learned from Mrs. Wharton that because of her satisfactory behavior during her imprisonment she would be allowed to resume her old tasks under the supervision of Miss Evelyn. Her spirits rose with each tick of the clock, and it was with a singing heart and an elation she hadn't known in many black months that she reported for work as directed. But her crowning pleasure still remained to be revealed. When she learned that Miss Evelyn had been instructed to impose the twice-daily routine whippings, the plan previously designed by Mrs. Wharton for her further education in submissiveness and endurance, Lily's transports of joy carried her on wings, and were it not for her wise reflection that Mrs. Wharton's suspicions of her feelings would be aroused, she would gladly have cast herself down before the lady and kissed her feet in expression of her immense gratitude.

Hence, it was with an alacrity of a never-ending amazement to herself that she made herself ready twice each day for Miss Evelyn's whippings. That young lady performed these tasks with a new and astonishing vigor, and lest Lily marvel at this extraordinary thoroughness, she was considerate enough to explain that this was no time to soften the quality of her whippings, for if the girl was to be bound out again it was to her best interest to make her attain that degree of endurance which she would be sure to require under the sovereignty of a new mistress. Notwithstanding, then, the terrific smarting and consuming heat with which she emerged from each of these sessions. Lily's eagerness to continue with her assigned disciplinarian did not abate in the slightest degree. Moreover, her fondness for the young woman who chastised her so soundly and so continually increased with the coming of each day, and when she went to bed at night she would find herself praying ardently that no evil would descend to tear her from her strangely passionate longing to remain under the dominion of Miss Evelyn.

Several weeks went by when Lily awoke one morning to learn that her supervisor had suddenly been called away by a telegram and would be absent for two days. It caused her great distress when she found that Miss Brenton was to substitute until Miss Evelyn's return. She was unable to expel the disquiet which seized her, and she wondered what the cause could be which called her favorite supervisor away. She did not dare ask, nor did anyone volunteer any information, and she tried to content herself in the meantime with the consoling knowledge that in two days she would be back. The whippings received from Miss Brenton were exceedingly trying, and she emerged from each of them with the sensation that her posterior was puffed out to double its size and that an enormous weight seemed to bear it down. And when she resumed her work she could only painfully and wearily drag one leg after the other.

Before noon of the third day Miss Evelyn returned. When she came into the laundry Lily could not restrain herself from falling at the young lady's feet and kissing her hands passionately. Miss Evelyn, although visibly gratified, seemed absorbed, and several times that day she went to see Mrs. Wharton in her chambers. Toward evening Lily noticed a sudden lighting-up of Miss Evelyn's features which had appeared to be faintly downcast during the day. Her curiosity gave her no rest but she knew better than to interrogate her superiors about anything. And when after supper she received her final whipping for the day from Miss Evelyn she thought she detected a slight slackening in the severity with which it was imposed. The young lady was annoyingly uncommunicative and sent her to bed later without vouchsafing the least information.

Shortly after ten o'clock the next morning Lily received the first whipping of the day, and after she had expressed thanks in the required formula and had adjusted her clothes, she began to walk back to her table where her work lay. But Miss Evelyn halted her.

"Lily," she said, "I want you to go to my bedroom and wait for me. I shall be up in a few minutes."

The girl did as she was told, puzzled as she went up about this mysterious and unusual order. She had scarcely time to make a conjecture when Miss Evelyn appeared. She sat down in one of the chairs and called Lily to her. The girl came and stood at her side.

"Lily," she began, "I don't think you will be pleased to hear what I choose to tell you, although there is no reason why I should mention it especially to anyone of my girls. I have come into a small inheritance and I have indicated to Mrs. Wharton that I should like to leave at once, because I shall have a sufficient income to live modestly but independently. It is my desire to take up a freer life elsewhere, and Mrs. Wharton has consented to let me go this next Sunday, which means that we shall be together only three days more. Do you think you will miss me?"

Lily was stunned. Her face blanched and her body swayed; she tried to answer but the words stuck in her mouth. Miss Evelyn appeared not to notice her emotion, nor her failure to respond.

"Before I leave, I think you might appreciate some advice from me which will be useful to you in case there is a sudden change in your life, as there is likely to be very soon. When a new mistress is found for you. . . ."

The girl's knees were no longer able to sustain her, her body sank to the floor and she swooned away. Miss Evelyn bathed her temples, slapped her wrists and quickly restored her only to see the girl slump once more to the floor where she lay moaning. She helped Lily to her feet, dragged her to the corridor, called for assistance and together with one of the girls they carried her to her own bed in the dormitory where Miss Evelyn made her comfortable.

About an hour later Miss Evelyn came up to see her. The girl had succeeded in composing herself somewhat, but her face was still very pale and her eyes looked haggard, like those of a person who hadn't slept for nights. Miss Evelyn sat down on the edge of her bed.

"You're a foolish child," she said kindly. "I didn't realize that this would be such a tragedy for you," she smiled. "I am also sorry to leave you, Lily," she continued, "but I must consider myself, not you. After all, I am young and free, and now that it has been my good fortune to obtain the means with which to arrange my life, I would be foolish to stay on here and grow old in this establishment."

"Oh, Miss," the girl cried softly, but her eyes revealed her panic, "you are the only one that liked me a little bit. Oh, how miserable I will be without you!"

"But you wouldn't have me very long anyway," Miss Evelyn replied. "Have you forgotten that in a month or two some visiting lady might decide to purchase you and take you away for her service?"

"Couldn't you . . . buy me, please Miss, wouldn't you care to . . . buy me?" she asked wistfully.

"Oh no! I couldn't afford to pay the price Mrs. Wharton would demand for you."

"Oh, oh! What will become of me!" she cried.

"Cheer up, Lily, don't be such a little coward!" Miss Evelyn admonished her with a trace of sternness. "Who knows what your luck may be? You may be selected by a lady who will prove to be kind to you, even if she does whip you often. Now you stay in bed for another hour and pull yourself together, then you must come down and return to your work. If Mrs. Wharton should find you being pampered like this she would tan your bottom beautifully for you." She rose, tapped the girl's tear-stained cheek gently with her hand, and went out.

That night Lily couldn't sleep. She tossed silently in her little bed, innumerable and conflicting pictures flashed across her brain and gave her no rest. Over and over again she would see the outlines of various women grinding their heels into her neck, her nude body prone on the ground, the women lashing her brutally from morning till night, with long heavy horsewhips continually between their hands. She would shake off each one of these terrifying visions with a start, only to find another and still more terrifying in its place. . . . It seemed she had just closed her eyes when the morning bell rang through the dormitory.

At ten o'clock, following the customary routine, Lily reported to Miss Evelyn for her scheduled whipping. Instead of taking off her skirt, as she should have done at once, she fell on her knees before the supervisor.

"Oh dear Miss," she implored, "may I have these last few whippings from you in your bedroom? Please Miss! . . . It is only for these days. . . . I may never see you again!"

"You are a strange girl, indeed! It is very wrong to humor you, and you know you are forbidden to make any special requests, don't you? It is my duty to punish you for this, and I shall probably do so, but I shall let you have your wish anyway. Go to my room," she added, smiling imperceptibly.

256

It was in Miss Evelyn's bedroom that Lily received her whipping that morning, and it was an exceptionally sound one, her chastiser omitting no portion of the girl's anatomy from the small of her back to the inside of her knees, each bit of skin received a vigorous allotment. Though she felt she had been baked in a hot oven, Lily tried to show her gratitude in the warm kisses she left on Miss Evelyn's hand, on the hem of her skirt and on her shoetops. Then the plea which had been ruminating in her head and which had been behind her wish to be whipped privately broke forth.

"Miss, dear, dear Miss, I implore you! Please, please, buy me and take me along with you. I'll be your most faithful slave, all my life, as long as you will keep me! Don't let them sell me to anyone else! You will see how grateful I will be. I will obey you in everything, no matter what you may want me to do. Oh, dear Miss Evelyn, I shall try so hard to please you! And I will learn how to take my whippings better than I do," she added eagerly and in a frantic effort to persuade the young lady. "I don't want to serve anybody else but you, Miss, only you." She subsided into fitful sobbing, crawling closer to Miss Evelyn's feet and holding them tight lest they move away.

"Get up," said Miss Evelyn finally. "I want you to compose yourself and return to your work. What you ask is absurd! I haven't enough money to treat myself to the luxury of your service. I can promise you nothing, except that I shall talk to Mrs. Wharton about you, but I haven't as yet any idea of what I can say to her. Come! I want you to go back to work." She took her by the hand, helped her up, then motioned her to walk ahead to the sewing-room. Once back, she assigned Lily to some task, cautioning her in a loud voice to work industriously if she did not want another whipping, and turned to inspect the work of her other charges.

In the evening she told Lily she could have her final whipping for the day in her bedroom again, and instructed the girl to go up and make herself ready. When Miss Evelyn came up, she found Lily in the proper state of nudity and, as soon as the young lady sat down, Lily put herself in the required position across her lap. This time she was treated no more indulgently than she had been in the morning, and when Miss Evelyn was through Lily knew from the state of her posterior that she had received as sound a whipping as Miss Evelyn had ever administered under similar circumstances, although she had often been whipped much more ruthlessly with some of the instruments designed for these operations.

It has been stated before that Lily was not without a good share of wisdom. Although she was dying with anxiety to know if Miss Evelyn had spoken to Mrs. Wharton, she suppressed every impulse to inquire, trusting to Miss Evelyn to inform her in her own good time; and she contented herself with reciting the usual formula of thanks, only putting all the fervor of which she was capable in her expression. The reward for her wisdom and patience was forthcoming immediately.

"Lily," began Miss Evelyn, "I have talked with Mrs. Wharton. I broached the question of purchasing you for myself, but as I thought, she asks much more than I can afford to pay. However, I made her my own proposal, and I pointed out some things to her which caused her to promise to take my offer under advisement, and we shall discuss it again tomorrow. Until then the matter rests, but in the meantime I have a few things to say to you. Should we come to an agreement and I consent to take you, my consent would be conditioned on my previous understanding with you. Now, these are my conditions and unless you accept them with a full heart and unmistakeable proofs of your sincerity, I am content to leave you alone and Mrs. Wharton can arrange to bind you out whenever it suits her will to whatever lady she likes: If you come into my service, you must come as my absolute slave, in the same unconditional manner that Lady Manville acquired you, with the exception, of course, that I am not Lady Manville. I shall require you to sign a bond in which you signify your complete understanding of that status. And when I say slave I mean it in the fullest sense of the word. It will mean that you pass over and henceforth belong to me body and soul, and that if I ever want to sell you to someone else I may do so without the slightest hindrance from anyone. You will give up every right and privilege and become subject to my will and mine alone, to do with as I please, to chastise when I like, and to move only at my direction and pleasure. I shall lay out new routines, new ceremonies, a strictly defined relationship, and your obedience to all these will have to be most scrupulously observed. Now, do you still want to become my slave, in fact as well as in name?"

Lily trembled as she listened to these words, but not with fear! Instead, she trembled with an indescribable eagerness of anticipation! The blood pounded in her veins and throbbed in her temples, her face flushed hot with desire—the prospect of leaving Sloane House, the nightmares of Mrs. Wharton, Lady Manville and all the others behind. To be with Miss Evelyn, forever—that was her newly conceived understanding of bliss. . . . She

answered, and her answer was as simple as it was eloquent.

"If you could show me the paper, Miss, with these
things written down and tell me where to sign, I could
show you what I now understand about obedience. . . ."

Miss Evelyn's breath stopped short before this spontaneous and significant avowal, but the only visible expression she gave of her profound emotional disturbance
was in the deep inhalation which lifted her beautiful
breasts to their greatest expansion.

"The fog is lifting for you, Lily," she said softly.
"Now, more than ever before, you need a superior hand
to lead you out of your former element, so alien to your
real nature, and deposit you in your proper place. Once
there all your doubts will cease to exist and you will be
content and happy. I should like to direct you to it, to
bring you where you really belong. . . . You must lie
down now and rest. Does your bottom still hurt?"

"Yes, Miss, it burns . . . but . . . but it doesn't matter . . ." she smiled bravely.

"I want you to go to your bed at once. Good night."

"Good night, Miss," she responded obediently, and
walked out.

*   *   *   *   *

The following day brought success to Evelyn's negotiations. Mrs. Wharton, who at first appeared adamant in
her determination to exact the price she had demanded,
was led to reconsider her position by a few adroitly and
tactfully placed observations from Miss Evelyn. The
latter had suggested the thought that should it ever leak

out how Lily was granted refuge, of a sort, at Sloane House, and it should reach Lady Manville's ears how very close she had come to recovering her rightful property, that the last-named lady might fly into a dreadful rage prompting her to the almost irresponsible acts she would inevitably commit. Miss Evelyn further observed that Lily was content to become her personal maid, but if she was bound to another mistress and found herself discontented and unhappy, one could never be sure what the girl might be goaded into doing or saying in retaliation, if she found her misery prodding her into so rash an act. These thoughts left a deep impress on the guilty conscience of Mrs. Wharton, and after a good night's reflection she concluded that Evelyn ought to be rewarded for her faithful services by the virtual presentation—to be sure, the small sum she was accepting made it practically that—of one of the girl's she had helped train, in this case, Lily Butler.

XIX

The Strange Music of Chains

Miss Evelyn Douglas, young—only a few months past her twenty-fifth year—pretty, in perfect health, and endowed with an attractive figure whose splendid curves were revealed in every move, lay on her bed in Sloane House. She had stretched her full length on her back, her beautiful arms folded behind her head, fingers clasped; and she looked up at the almost invisible ceiling, for there was no moon this night. Except for the ticking of her clock, and perhaps the beat of her heart, not a sound came from the house; everyone was fast asleep for hours. Indeed, the only break in the deep stillness had been the chiming of a clock in the corridor but a few minutes ago, announcing the hour of twelve. She was not trying to fight herself into sleep, far from it; too many delicious thoughts were tickling her fancy. The Fates had been more than kind: Mrs. Wharton had yielded after a brief struggle; Lily had yielded after a different sort of struggle and a longer, but she had yielded. And now for her, the curtain was about to rise on a new and wondrous life.

Her mind paused to muse upon the remarkable potency of the Whip, and the amazing changes she had seen wrought with its aid these last four years that she had been an assistant at Sloane House. Judiciously applied, she could foresee the comforts it would bring her in the days to come, under her own roof, when she could be the absolute and exclusive master of every situation. A host of plans ranged across her mind: out of the development of them she would fashion the most perfect slave-girl of all times. Contrary to the views of Lady Manville and all the Lady Manvilles, she would demonstrate that there was no need to resort to the essential cruelty which seemed such an important concomitant in their scheme of things. She abhorred cruelty and she abhorred their wanton practices. It was brutal and barbarous to pinch a helpless girl's tongue with your nails or nearly flay the skin off her back, or to put her on a lengthy diet of bread and water and thrust her in a cold, dark, underground cell. There were no end of humane punishments which could be imposed instead. She had demonstrated that it was possible to whip a girl frequently and soundly and yet have the gratification of the girl's love and unbounded devotion.

The same Whip which had so completely transformed Laura Blake free into Lily Butler slave, had many more powers not yet drawn upon. Thus far it had brought this girl to a frame of mind where, confronted with the picture of her ultimate state, she stood by comprehending it placidly and in a spirit of submission. The Whip had broken, then pulverized her inferior will. Become clay, she had been deposited fortuitously on the workbench of Miss Evelyn, her indisputable master; and the living evidence of how plastic she made the material which came to her hands was now before the eyes of this proud young lady. She was fascinated by the sight of the unrestrained eagerness with which her living figure awaited the step that must lead to the total obliteration of her past, and her rebirth into an absolute chattel-slave, exactly like those of Antiquity. A free soul hovering in unfamiliar space had been crystallized and molded into an animate piece of property, directed to its place, thenceforth and forevermore bound to an owner, and subject to the unlimited and despotic will of that owner, whoever it may be.

But another day or two and she would take possession of this body, solely hers by right of purchase and contract. She would teach this living, breathing, piece of property new duties, new obligations, new ceremonies. Particularly the latter she intended to develop to their utmost magnificence. Soon she would begin to expand the secret luxuries her inner nature craved, to revel in the invention of fanciful apparel, address, formulae, the precise method of bowing and bending she would require from her slave. The commonplace rituals which preceded, accompanied and followed the girl's past whippings should be made much more elaborate, as befits her real status of slave, than was ever conceived at Sloane House. And all these plans would be crowned with the laurel of her slave's unfaltering devotion, the quality of which would be further enriched by the girl's ecstatic happiness in her lot. For she would be intensely happy in her bondage, she was certain.

Equally certain was she, from the number of transformations she had witnessed in her four years' experience. that it was foreordained by nature that some should find contentment and peace only when their wills were blotted out by those who were similarly foreordained to be the superior sons of Adam and daughters of Eve. And when those widely divergent natures met it was inevitable that the inferior wills must succumb. Time and again she had seen the breaking down and utter destruction of those inadequate wills at Sloane. A strange destiny seemed to direct the footsteps of girls belonging in that category to this establishment. At Sloane House they passed through the fires which stripped their natures bare. They came in still dreaming of what they conceived their rightful place in the sun, with the superior races of the earth whose peers they felt they were; they went out shorn of their ill-fitting patrician notions which cloaked their latent slave mentalities, and in their nakedness they stood revealed for the inferiors they were. These were their true natures, unmasked. If they were ever to feel the sweet solace of peace and contentment, they could only realize it when they had been forcibly brought to a just appreciation of their *true* selves. . . .

Lily was the living personification of this thesis. Here in this low and humble state she belonged; her inner nature craved a master. Once divested of her unfortunate illusion, it only required patience and direction for the realities to penetrate, then her eyes opened on her real self and her ears caught the imperious sound of her true master's voice. But before these truths could unfold in their fullness, her senses must naturally stagger before the revelation, and her eyes could only hazily register the picture of her actual nature. At this crucial point it required the magnetic touch and the firm hand of a superior to remove the film and scatter the haze. For the girl, happiness now lay only a little while ahead, and she was moving instinctively toward it. If it had been only the brutal power of the Whip that bent helpless girls to the wills of those that wielded it, Lily would never have trembled with eagerness to pass forever under the rule of one who used it constantly. She would have passed under the compulsion of its stinging prodding, yes, but only rebelliously and with a never-ceasing inner recal-citrance. . . .

These were the Eternal Verities, thought Evelyn, and thanks to their opportune, providential manifestation she would soon bask in the gorgeous radiance of her power, the power to mold her slave to her perfect pattern! How the prospect enchanted! . . . Her arms slid gently to her side . . . she was asleep.

* * * * *

Sunday morning Miss Evelyn Douglas and her slave, Lily, made their adieus to the ladies of Sloane House. Their baggage was ready and they were waiting for the cab which was to convey them to the railroad station. Miss Evelyn had gone back to her old room for some letters she had forgotten in her dressing-table. Down-stairs the cab was announced, there was not too much time. Lily ran to Miss Evelyn's room and knocked gently on the door.

"Who is it?" Miss Evelyn called.

"It is Lily, Milady. If you please, the cab has come."

The name Lily came naturally from the girl's lips now, as though she had had it all her life; and in obedience to one of the first orders from her new mistress she had changed the style of addressing her from Miss to Milady. . . .

In a few minutes they had left Sloane House behind them forever. By easy stages they were proceeding to Margate, the watering-place in Kent where some of the property bequeathed to Miss Evelyn was situated. She had visited Margate in her schooldays and it was with pleasant recollections of the town that she looked forward to making her home there.

And so it came to pass that she selected a charming cottage within sound of the sea she loved, and she and her slave settled down to their new lives. For her it was a delicious enchantment, and for Lily a bittersweet but fascinating adjustment. During the weeks that passed, while they fitted their home out, Miss Evelyn would frequently take Lily along to the shops where she made her purchases. For the street the girl was provided with several black silk dresses, trimmed with white silk edging around the neck and sleeves. These dresses fitted very tightly, molding in bold outline every inch of the girl's flesh, and their strictly severe design and short length— barely covering the knees—made the girl look, indeed, a thing apart. An additional emphasis was added to the costume by her specially created headgear. The bonnet, if it may be called that, was affixed to the back of her head and was in the shape of an inverted open can, about two inches high and less than four inches in diameter. It was covered in lustrous black satin, with a tiny white satin stripe at its base. At its back a sort of pompon of the same material was attached, and from its end hung two wide, black satin streamer-ribbons, gathered into a great bow in front of her neck.

Underneath her tight dress she was obliged to wear a wide girdle which descended to her upper thighs. It had been made to Miss Evelyn's order, and instead of elastic or hooks, it was equipped with strong wide laces which her mistress always adjusted herself. These she would pull as tight as she possibly could; her object was to wedge her slave's waistline in the special harness as tautly as the bands would allow. It was highly uncom-

fortable and even painful, but the pain was far from unbearable, and once saddled, she would experience an in-
definable tumult in her blood which subsided presently
into a soothing simmer. Ordinarily, this tight strapping
of the waist would have given much greater prominence
to the loins and buttocks, but the girdle was swathed as
closely as possible over them also. Miss Evelyn had no
wish to accentuate them unnecessarily in public, for their
proportions had increased conspicuously since the girl's
training first began. But at home she put no hindrance
about the abundant flesh at any time, and she let the
hips sway unconstrained to their widest expanse.

* * * * *

They are driving to town to visit a draper's shop. Lily
sits gingerly forward by the side of her mistress, for the
painfully tight girdle and a soreness in her posterior, still
tender from a whipping several hours before, prompts
her to arrange herself cautiously.

"I think I shall buy another footstool for the other
side of my bed, also," reflects Miss Evelyn aloud, breaking a bewitching reverie.

"If you please, Milady," her slave ventures, "I could
always keep the one we have ready for either side."

"Or I could use your back for that purpose, couldn't
I?" her mistress laughs heartily.

"Oh yes, Milady!" the slave answers earnestly, with
spontaneous concurrence. . . .

It is a far cry from another carriage ride taken in the
long, long ago with another mistress whose name was
Lady Manville. . . .

* * * * *

Who could dream that the humble and meticulously dressed girl, wearing only high-heeled slippers, very long stockings, girdle, dress and funny-looking cap, walking in small and measured steps, because of her discomfort, beside the proud and beautiful young lady, is not the commonplace servant-maid her uniform denotes but the absolute slave, the living property of her mistress? A mistress who owns her exclusively, in whose shadow she breathes and by whose complaisance she lives! Who could dream that but a few hours ago this slave-girl stripped off her clothes with her own hands, stretched over a designated bench and maintained, without assistance, a position so favorable that her buttocks and thighs could jut out most prominently, that her mistress might lash them more effectively with one of a variety of leather whips? That she went on her knees when her whipping was terminated, kissed the hand that wielded the whip, the leather strap which lashed her quivering posterior, kissed likewise her owner's toes and the soles of her feet; that she expressed her deepest gratitude and thanks for the whipping her dear mistress had deigned to inflict on her unworthy slave; that she begged her Lady not to forget another whipping due her later in the day, and craved permission to remind her when the time arrived? . . .

Who could read or hear of such a relationship without laughing it down derisively as incredible and fantastic in our day and age? In the meek yet serene expression of the girl who stands respectfully back of her who sits absorbed before mundane drapes, curtains and the chatter of a salesperson, what eye can penetrate the mystery of the psychic bridge which spans their stations as it buckles their interests? . . . For how much, indeed, do we know of the world about us beyond what our primal five senses perceive? And that which is locked deep in the hearts of the men and women who rub our elbows in life, may go down with them to their tombs and be reckoned with the dust.

THE END

DELECTUS BOOKS

"The world's premiere publisher of classic erotica." *Bizarre*.

A GUIDE TO THE CORRECTION OF YOUNG GENTLEMEN
By A Lady

The ultimate guide to Victorian domestic discipline, lost since all previously known copies were destroyed by court order nearly seventy years ago.

"Her careful arrangement of subordinate clauses is truly masterful." *The Daily Telegraph*. "I rate this book as near biblical in stature" *The Naughty Victorian*. "The lady guides us through the corporal stages with uncommon relish and an experienced eye to detail...An absolute gem of a book." *Zeitgeist*. "An exhaustive guide to female domination." *Divinity*. "Essential reading for the modern enthusiast with taste." *Skin Two*.

> Delectus 1994 hbk with a superb cover by Sardax 140p with over 30 illustrations. £19.95

THE ROMANCE OF CHASTISEMENT; OR, REVELATIONS OF SCHOOL AND BEDROOM
By an Expert

The Romance is filled with saucy tales comprising headmistresses taking a birch to the bare backsides of schoolgirls, women whipping each other, men spanking women, an aunt whipping her nephew and further painful pleasures.
A renowned rare and elegant collection of verse, prose and anecdotes on the subject of the Victorian gentleman's favourite vice: Flagellation! We have produced a complete facsimile of the rare 1888 edition.

"One of the all time flagellation classics." *The Literary Review*, "In an entirely different class...A chronicle of punishment, pain and pleasure." *Time Out*. "A classic of Victorian vice." *Forum*, "A very intense volume...a potent, single-minded ode to flagellation." *Divinity*, "A delightful book of awesome contemporary significance...the book is beautifully written." *Daily Telegraph*. "Stylishly reproduced and lovingly illuminated with elegant graphics and pictures...written in a style which is charming, archaic and packed with fine detail." *The Redeemer*.

> Delectus 1993 hbk 160p. £19.95

THE PETTICOAT DOMINANT OR, WOMAN'S REVENGE.

An insolent aristocratic youth, Charles makes an unwelcome, though not initially discouraged pass at his voluptuous tutoress Laura. In disgust at this transgression she sends Charles to stay with her cousin Diane d'Erebe, in a large country house inhabited by a coterie of governesses. They put him through a strict regime of corrective training, involving urolagnia, and enforced cross-dressing in corsets and petticoats to rectify his unruly character. First published in 1898 by Leonard Smithers' "Erotica Biblion Society", Delectus have reset the original into a new edition.

"Frantic...breathless...spicy...restating the publisher's place at the top of the erotic heap." *Divinity*. "A great classic of fetish erotica...A marvellous period piece." *Bizarre*.

Delectus 1994 hbk 120p. £19.95

120 DAYS OF SODOM

Adapted for the stage by Nick Hedges from the novel by the Marquis de Sade.

Four libertines take a group of young adults and four old whore's to a deserted castle, there they engage in a four month marathon of cruelty, debasement, and debauchery. The award winning play now available from Delectus, featuring stills from the London production and a revealing interview with the director.

"A bizarre pantomime of depravity that makes the Kama Sutra read like a guide to personal hygiene." *What's On.*, "If you missed the play, you definitely need to get the book." *Rouge*. "Unforgettable...their most talked about publication so far." *Risque*.

Delectus 1991 pbk 112p. £6.95

PAINFUL PLEASURES

A fascinating miscellany of relentless spankomania comprising letters, short stories etc. Originally published in New York in 1931, Delectus have produced a complete facsimile complemented by the beautiful line illustrations depicting punishment scenes from the book.

Both genders end up with smarting backsides in such stories as "The Adventures of Miss Flossie Evans," and, probably the best spanking story ever written, "Discipline at Parame" in which a stern and uncompromising disciplinarian brings her two cousins Elsie & Peter to meek and prompt obedience. An earlier section contains genuine letters and an essay discussing the various merits of discipline and corporal punishment.

The writing is of the highest quality putting many of the current mass market publishers to shame, and Delectus into a class of its own.

"An extraordinary collection...as fresh and appealing now as in its days of shady celebrity...especailly brilliant...another masterpiece...a collectors treasure." *Paddles*. "An American S&M classic". *The Bookseller*, "Sophisticated...handsomely printed...classy illustrations...beautifully bound." *Desire*. "For anyone who delights in the roguish elegance of Victorian erotica...this book is highly recommended." *Lust Magazine*. "A cracking good read." *Mayfair*.
Delectus Books 1995 hbk in imperial purple d/j 272p. £19.95.

THE MISTRESS & THE SLAVE
A Parisian gentleman of position & wealth begins a romantic liaison with a poor but voluptuous young woman and falls wholly under her spell. The perversity of her nature, with its absolute domination over him, eventually culminates in a tragic ending.

"But, my child, you don't seem to understand what a Mistress is. For instance: your child, your favourite daughter, might be dying and I should send you to the Bastille to get me a twopenny trinket. You would go, you would obey! Do you understand?" - "Yes!" he murmured, so pale and troubled that he could scarcely breathe. "And you will do everything I wish?" - "Everything, darling Mistress! Everything! I swear it to you!"
Delectus 1995 hbk in d/j 160p. £19.95

WHITE STAINS - ANAIS NIN & FRIENDS
Lost classic of 1940s erotica first published by Sam Roth in New York. This collection of six sensual yet explicit short stories is thought to have been written for an Oklahoma oil millionaire, Roy M. Johnson, who is said to have paid a dollar per page. This facsimile reproduction also contains an explicit sex manual, "Love's Cyclopaedia", originally published with the stories, and an introduction by C.J.Scheiner MD PhD, examining all the evidence for the Anais Nin attribution.
Delectus 1995 hbk in d/j 220p. £19.95

FREDERIQUE: THE STORY OF A YOUTH TRANSFORMED INTO A YOUNG GIRL
Don Brennus Alera

A young orphan is left in the charge of his widowed aristocratic aunt, Baroness Saint-Genest. This elegant and wealthy lady teaches Frederique poise & manners and with eager assistance from her maid Rose transforms him into a young woman, while at the same time keeping him as her personal slave and sissy maid using discipline to ensure complete obedience. Originally published by The Select Bibliotheque, Paris in 1921, this marvellous transvestite tale has been translated for the first time into florid English by Valerie Opren and includes all of the 14 line drawings from the French edition.

Delectus Books 1995 hbk in d/j 180p. £19.95

MEMOIRS OF A DOMINATRICE
Jean Clacqueret & Liane Laure

An elegant and aristocratic Governess recalls her life and the experiences with the young men in her charge. Translated from the French by Clair Auclair from the French edition first published The Collection des Orties Blanches in Paris during the 1920s. Illustrated with reproductions of the 10 "Jim Black" drawings from the original French edition.

Delectus Books 1995 hbk 140p. £19.95

THERE'S A WHIP IN MY VALISE
Greta X

Launching the new Delectus paperback series, bringing you the best erotica from the 50s & 60s, is this superb novel first published in 1961.

A businessman picks up two Swedish hikers and discovers a taste for unusual sex. He is soon searching Europe for the perfect dominant mistress, and finds the voluptuous Marlene. Together with her beautiful assistant, who has an accute rubber fetish and lesbian leanings! Marlene travels Europe to satisfy the strange desires of masochistic men. The plot reaches its climax when five sadistic women, including Marlene and her assistant, descend on the home of Mr. Petersen to give him the time of his life.

Delectus Books 1995 pbk 200p. £9.99

MASOCHISM IN AMERICA, OR MEMOIRS OF A VICTIM OF FEMINISM
Pierre Mac Orlan

A French erotic classic, first published in the 1920s, by surrealist, war hero and renowned thriller writer, Pierre Mac Orlan, translated for the first time into English by Alexis Lykiard.
This novel recounts the story of one man's masochist odyssey through America and includes all the illustrations from the French original.

     Delectus 1995 hbk 200p. £19.95

THE STRAP RETURNS: NEW NOTES ON FLAGELLATION
Anon

A superb and attractive anthology from 1933, originally issued by the same publishers of two other Delectus titles, *Painful Pleasures* and *Modern Slaves*.
The book contains letters, authentic episodes and short stories including " A Governess Lectures on the art of Spanking ", "A Woman's Revenge" and "The Price of a Silk Handkerchief or, How a Guilty Valet was Rewarded. " along with decorations and six full page line drawings by Vladimir Alaxandre Karenin.

     Delectus 1995 hbk 220p. £19.95

EROTICA, SEXOLOGY & CURIOSA - THE CATALOGUE
"For the true connoisseur, there is no better source." *Bizarre*

Delectus are the only global specialists in selling quality rare, antiquarian, and second hand erotica by mail order. Our unique catalogues are dispatched quarterly to almost 5500 customers in over 50 countries worldwide. Prices range from £5.00 to several thousand pounds representing the finest erotic literature from the last three hundred years in English, French, German and Italian including large selections from Olympia, Luxor & Grove Press.

"Mouthwatering lists for serious collectors...decidedly decadent." *Risque*, "The leading source for hard to find erotica" *Screw*. "I have never seen a catalogue so complete and so detailed. A must" *Secret Magazine*. "One of the largest ranges of old and new erotic literature I have ever seen." *Fatal Visions.*
For our current catalogue send: £2.50/$5.00 Payment accepted by cheque, cash, postal order, Visa, Mastercard, J.C.B. and Switch.

Send to:

Delectus Books, Dept. MS
27 Old Gloucester Street,
London, WC1N 3XX, England.
Tel: 0181.963.0979.
Fax: 0181.963.0502.
Mail order business only.
Trade enquiries welcome.

**NOTE: Postage is extra at £1.30 per book U.K.,
£2.00 EEC & Europe, £5.00 U.S.A., £6.00 Elsewhere.**

COMING SOON: Happy Tears, Lustful Lucy, Sacher-Masoch's Venus
& Adonis, The Amorous Widow, Pageant of Lust, With Rod and Bum
& many more.

Further publications due in the next few months see our full catalogue
for further details.

"Certain publishing houses have consistently merited exceptional praise
and recommendations for their offerings. Delectus Books is one such."
Paddles